I AM *NOT* THE MESSIAH!

Mr Zootherapy tells all

James Sinclaire

I am *not* the Messiah!

Ver.2.1

Published in 2021

IamnottheMessiah.com

That which we call fact may well be a veil spun by language to shroud the mind from reality. George Steiner, *Language and Silence*

Man is a fraction of the animal world. Our history is an afterthought, no more, tacked to an infinite calendar. We are not as unique as we should like to believe. And if man in a time of need seeks deeper knowledge concerning himself, then he must explore those animal horizons from which we have made our quick little march. Robert Ardrey, *African Genesis*

It is not, for example, the province of the reasoning faculty to decide how a baby ought to be treated. We have had exquisitely precise instincts, expert in every detail of child care, since long before we became anything resembling *Homo sapiens*. But we have conspired to baffle this long-standing knowledge so utterly that we now employ researchers full time to puzzle out how we should behave toward children, one another, and ourselves. Jean Liedloff, *The Continuum Concept*

[B]ald eagles fly as high as they possibly can, up into the thinnest air, making the elegant flight patterns of intended mating all the way up, then cleave to each other and fall, fall, fall, mating as they fall fluttering, plummeting down toward the great rock mountains. …[E]agles, geese, wolves, and many other creatures of land and sea and air are stuck with all this obsolete magic and mystery because they can't read and they can't listen to lectures. All they have is instinct. John D MacDonald, *A Tan and Sandy Silence*

FROM THE OXFORD ENGLISH DICTIONARY, 2030 EDITION

zoo-

(ˈzəʊəʊ, zəʊ ˈʊ)

before a vowel properly zo-, repr. Gr. ζῳο-, combining form of ζ ov animal, occurring in numerous scientific and technical terms, of which the more important will be found in their alphabetical places. (The second element is usually and properly from Greek, but in a few recent words from Latin or English.)

In biological and botanical terms the prefix sometimes denotes the power of spontaneous movement (formerly supposed to be a distinctive characteristic of animals): see zoogamete, zoogonidium, zoosperm, zoozygosphere; zoospore.

Additions 2027

Add: Zootherapy

(ˈzuːθɛrəpɪ)

psychological therapy encompassing the imaginative assumption of animal characteristics, especially outlook.

2001 *Encyclopædia Britannica* Originating in New Zealand, Zootherapy is spreading like wildfire across the Anglophone world. **2013** *Economist* 22 July Pastoral production has taken second place to Zootherapy as [New Zealand's] principal export earner. **2028** P. CARRUTHERS, *Our Humanity* 264 Largely thanks to Zootherapy, violent political conflict is a thing of the past.

Prologue: New Zealand bush, 2022

The year 2022. Somewhere in the bush country in New Zealand's north island. Gorse-covered hills enclose a clearing, sheltering a patch of meadow from the soft, warm, sweetly-scented breeze. A bell bird calls plaintively from a distant tree. At one end of the clearing, at the bottom of a gentle slope, there's an easel upon which is a cardboard target: a silhouette of the top half of a man, to the chest of which has been pinned a plastic bag filled with water. At the other end of the clearing stand two men a few metres apart from each other, both facing the target. They pick up their rifles and aim. After a second, there's an electronic beep coming from a loudspeaker near the target. There's a sharp, spluttering sound from the rifles and at the same moment the water spurts out of the plastic bag. The taller of the two men, heavyset, with short black hair, greying temples, picks up a pair of binoculars, and gives a thumbs-up sign.

'Gotcha' he says. 'The old belt and braces approach', says the other man; a compact, muscled, stocky figure, with short closely cropped blonde hair, and a pallor rarely seen in these parts. They both walk toward the target. Nearby, wedged under a garish red plastic hamper are discarded cardboard targets and burst plastic bags. There are no bullets nor bullet holes; just tiny darts, with transparent flights, almost invisible, sticking out of a small circle on the target boards.

'Yeah; I reckon we've earned our alcohol-free.' Their accents are English. The taller man grabs a couple of bottles of zero-percent beer from the hamper. They sit down on a blanket on the grass, twist off the tops and begin drinking.

'Can't get used to the sun going in a different direction' says the shorter man.

'I know; I did a job in Melbourne once, did surveillance dawn to dusk. Saw the whole thing; I knew something weird was going on, couldn't work it out at first.'

'Yeah, and it's summer – in November!'

They finish drinking, and gather up the targets, darts, beer bottles, bottle tops, packing everything into boxes and black plastic bin-liners.

'Mickey Mouse bullets, Mickey Mouse beer, Mickey Mouse car;' he sighs, 'I guess it fits; a Mickey Mouse op.'

'But one you can actually talk about. While sipping wine with some luscious chick on the Riviera...'

The men put their boxes, bags and loudspeaker and all their other bits and pieces into the boot of the car: a white rental. Then they scan the grass looking for anything they might have missed. Finding nothing, they get into the car, and the tall man looks just a little comical as he gets into the driver's seat, extended as far back as it will go.

They belt up. Before starting the car, the compact man consults his smartphone.

'Figure on three hours to...' he stumbles over the word 'Rot-or-ua.'

'It's Rotorua,' says the tall man, pronouncing it correctly, with a long initial 'o'. 'Also known as Stinktown.'

'Why's that?'

'You'll find out.'

'You've been before?'

'After that little business across the water I needed to hunker down for a while. Spent a few days there. Lots of visitors, always busy. And far enough away from our upcoming gig, which is probably why he wants to see us there.'

The compact man continues. 'OK, Rotorua. Meet up with the big chief. There's hot pools there?' The other man nods, 'Splash around in hot pools. Our last days of freedom before going down to the big city.'

'It's the capital but it's not that big.'

'Wellington. What do the locals call that?'

'I dunno. Gumboot City, I guess.'

The compact guy starts the car. They give each other a high-five: 'To Gumboot City!' the tall man says. 'To Gumboot City!' echoes the compact man. They move off slowly, bumping over the grass. Everything is exactly as if they'd never been there. Nothing, not a scrap of cardboard, burst plastic bag, nor a bottle top, nor any of the darts – nothing – remains of their presence. The sun slowly continues its clockwise descent, falling below the tops of the trees; the bell bird resumes its plaintive call.

INTRODUCTION, 2031

Zootherapy itself is as simple as this statement: see the world through animal eyes. But we're human and our overwhelming preoccupation is to make the simple, complicated and the short, long. So much so that anything too simple and short, we discredit on sight. That perennial standby question posed in music exams comes to mind: what makes the old song *Frere Jacques* less compelling than that of Beethoven's setting of Ode to Joy in his Ninth Symphony? It's not the words or the melodies, but what's made of them. Simplicity has its merits, but spinning a long tale out of a single insight need not always be cynical. In that spirit, I present the unexpurgated, complete and utterly truthful story of the genesis of Zootherapy. Let it deepen, but not substitute for, Zootherapy's simple, subtle, insight. A warning: if you are new to Zootherapy and are aware only of its laudatory reputation, try to forget what you know. And don't read this book with the expectation that your problems will go away, that you will be any happier after practising Zootherapy; or, indeed with any expectation at all. As well, you must be clear that:

I AM *NOT* THE MESSIAH

I am not, nor have I ever been, The Messiah. I have no divine nor supernatural powers. Let me ask, upfront and clearly that, if there's nothing else you take from this tome, you take on board this: I am not, nor have I ever been, The Messiah.

True, there is world peace, which is to say, the absence of deadly, large-scale, political violence. True, too, that I had something to do with it. We don't, any more, threaten each other with nuclear weapons. States don't fight. Terrorism has ended. Civil wars are passé. Even quarrels between individuals rarely turn deadly these days. And maybe we do need reminding that it wasn't always like this and that, relative to humanity's brutal past, we are living in an enlightened age.

'Thank God', some say. More say 'Thank God for James Sinclaire', and still more – too many - say 'Thank James Sinclaire'.

But I am not the Messiah, nor even *a* messiah, nor a prophet, nor one of God's top emissaries - all of which titles I've been granted by certain people in the recent past. If war is unthinkable now it's got nothing to do with any spark of divinity that I might or might not possess. It's because of a sequence of events that began in the benighted year of 1986, not in the parched, shimmering landscape of an ancient Middle Eastern desert, but in a rambling old rented house within easy walking distance of the bus routes along the busy main road heading south from the centre of New Zealand's capital city.

GORILLAGRAM, 1986

The year is 1986 and humanity, in every sense except the narrowly technical, might as well still be in the dark ages. War and the threat of war are accepted as ways of resolving conflict. There's the shadow of nuclear catastrophe, with weapons proliferating everywhere. Like the ancient Greeks we thought then that war was an inescapable part of human destiny; a curse on humanity to be sure, with its arbitrary killing of innocents, its refugees and destruction, its endless suffering - but an inexorable part of being human. So how did world peace come about? The actuality, not the dream?

It's some time between 10 and 11am one weekday in the early summer in a damp, drafty house in Newtown, then a downmarket inner-city suburb of Wellington, New Zealand, not far from the General Hospital. I'm a post-graduate, part-time student, doing a Master's degree in Sociology and Economics at Victoria University of Wellington, and I'm typing my thesis on one of the first mass market word processors (an Amstrad PCW 8256 I'd had sent from the UK and of which I am very proud). Four of us share the house; there's me, Angela and Steve, the professional couple who are away at work. And then there's Tom. From down the hallway I hear dry, strangled retching from the bathroom. It's Tom, a final-year postgraduate student, presumably after another heavy night out. The toilet flushes. Then the phone rings on the wall outside my bedroom door. It's Tom, ringing from the bathroom on his new mobile phone – all of ten metres down the narrow hallway. He wants to ask me something. Sighing, I make my way to the bathroom. Tom's kneeling beside the toilet, in his dressing gown, his mobile phone beside him. It's the size of a man's shoe, heavy as a bag of sugar, expensive to buy and to use, and it's the only one I've ever seen.

I glance at the toilet bowl, and pull the chain again. I try shallow breathing. Tom sees me wince.

'It's OK James, I've finished.' Vomiting, he means. 'I need a favour', he says, as I help him get up and lead him back to his room. We step through the haze and thin, pungent smell of stale cigarette smoke, around the clothes scattered on the carpet and the beat-up armchair. Lurid purple curtains, closed against the daylight; this is the biggest, best room in the house, befitting Tom's status as an ambitious but not very diligent final-year law student and eldest son of a big-shot corporate lawyer in Auckland (and something of a tyrant, we've gathered from hearing Tom's end of their weekly phone conversations). Tom flops onto his bed. There's a humming sound from the computer on his desk, around which are strewn floppy disks, a couple of yellow legal pads with writing and doodles, and a fancy new dot-matrix printer. There's a heavy, Victorian wardrobe, its doors wide open.

I sigh: 'What sort of favour?'

'It's a birthday, for some bureaucrat or other.' Tom points to the cluttered dusty surface of the dresser. I can't see much, so open the curtains; there's a memo addressed to Tom, in a catchpenny font, headed *From Dave, Ministry of Fun, To Tom Wilkins*. (I should say, especially for those unfamiliar with Anglophone irony, that the Ministry of Fun is not an official government department. It's a smallish, private, Wellington-based business that organises office functions; things like farewell dos and Christmas parties and book launches.) Tom does some work for them on a part-time, temporary basis during vacations.

The memo is a request for Tom to do a Gorillagram at 3pm that day at the Ministry of Agriculture and Fisheries. The street address of the MAF building is given, and so is the location of the cafeteria (on the twelfth floor) within it. There'd been a family row a couple of weeks before, apparently, when Tom had failed to show up in similar circumstances and word had reached his father. I think I know what Tom wants me to do.

'You want me to call and say you're sick; you can't make it?'

'James...'

A pained expression. He looks directly at me. It dawns on me. He wants me to do the Gorillagram.

'Oh no. Oh no. No way. Sorry Tom.'

'James,' That look in his eyes! I almost feel sorry for him.

'Tom, I can't do it man. I can't sing. I never - I've got my assignment due in. I've-'

'It's $25, for less than an hour of your time. I'll pay for a taxi there. Ten minutes to get there, ten minutes there, and ten minutes to get back. Thirty minutes, that's all I'm asking.' He must have seen the expression on my face. 'Taxis there and back. Five dollars each way; you keep the change. Just to dress up as a gorilla and sing 'Happy Birthday'. You know the words.'

'I can't sing.'

'Are you kidding? What about at Angela's birthday party?'

'That's different Tom; we were in a group, singing together. We'd all been drinking.'

'This will be the same; they'll all join in after a couple of seconds – I promise you. Here.' Tom was peeling off ten-dollar bills. 'Forty dollars; they only pay me fifteen; here's forty. You keep anything left after the taxi.'

Forty dollars, of which I'll get to keep at least thirty; very useful. So I agree and, with a touch of trepidation, accept the money. Tom points to the wardrobe. 'It's hung up in there', he says, 'the head's on the top shelf.'

I experience the mild disorientation arising from car-lag as I approach the MAF building on Lambton Quay: and a journey to town that would normally be at least half an hour by bus takes just a few minutes in the taxi, slicing through the sparse, working-hours traffic. It adds to the unreality of my situation. Now I'm on the twelfth floor, facing the mirror above the wash basin in the gents' lavatory. I'm alone, I've taken my shoes off and am contorting myself in the confined space as I step into the gorilla costume. Almost done. Now I pack my shoes and jeans into Tom's battered old suitcase that held the costume. I'm sweating and flustered, probably because I've given myself too much time to worry. Anxious to get it right, I clutch the Ministry of Fun's instructions to Tom.

I repeat to myself the name of the recipient of the Gorillagram and his work group: 'Don Keenan, Biometrics; Don Keenan, Biometrics; Don Keenan....' And I take the gorilla head out of its plastic bag and put it on. I have to twist it a fraction so that the cutouts for its eyes align with mine. Ah, I can see now, though with limited peripheral vision. The head's a bit of a weight, and it's hot and stuffy in there, with a sweet and pungent smell of rubber. No problem, I think: it's only for a few minutes.

I glance up at the mirror, and I'm astonished - nothing could have prepared me for what I see: a hairy black gorilla stands there, facing me with muscular arms and a smooth glossy plastic eight-pack abdomen. A moment's disorientation and, tentatively at first, then more forcefully, I beat my hands against my chest. I grunt, more and more vigorously and then there's a moment of high comedy, when as my grunts turn into howls and reach their peak volume, I see behind me in the mirror the door to the lavatory opening and a man about to come in. He's a pale, mild-looking, MAF employee, with rolled-up shirt sleeves, and gold-framed glasses. He's not expecting to see a costume gorilla in the washroom. I smile, trying to reassure; but of course he can't see that. He reacts quite calmly, and backs out; not so much startled, but more resigned; presumably to having to use the washroom on another floor. I'm alone again; in my normal voice I re-start my mantra of the day: 'Don Keenan, Biometrics'.

It's a short distance from the washroom to the MAF cafeteria, and I stride across it boldly and through the doors. First impression: it seems like a happy shop: relaxed chatter, little ceremony, nothing pompous, grounded. These are people who work in the city, for the government, but they have some connection to farming and fishing. Few jackets, some ties; the men sport rolled up shirt-sleeves. There's no hierarchy apparent in the cafeteria; I suppose I'm comparing it with the Ministry of Welfare. I hear – slightly muffled by the gorilla head - the chatter dying away as a result of my entrance. For a fraction of a second I wonder why everyone's staring in my direction.

I surprise myself by proclaiming, in a loud, confident voice:

'It's someone's birthday today!'

Murmurings from the MAF employees.

'Come on! Don't be shy!' I continue, 'Is there a Don Keenan here today? Don Keenan, from Biometrics: Mr Donald Keenan, where are you? Stand up, stand up wherever you are!'

Looking around, it becomes obvious who my victim is, as his neighbours point exaggeratedly at his head; then very quickly everyone else looks at the embarrassed Mr Keenan. His co-workers jeer at him, good-naturedly.

I hear my own voice: 'Well I don't know where Don Keenan is but here's a special song for the man over there with the glasses and the red face!'

Everybody laughs. I begin singing 'Happy Birthday'; several others join in before I've finished the first line – as Tom had promised. At the end, applause and cheers break out. There is great hilarity in the cafeteria as I go up to Don and hug and kiss him extravagantly.

I don't forget my lines: 'And that's from all your friends and colleagues in the Biometrics Group!'

I wave jauntily to everybody and, before making my exit, turn to face everyone and beat my chest, whooping loudly. I leave the canteen to applause and laughter.

I did it! I hear the laughs and applause as I exit through the fire door to the stairwell, pick up my things from lavatory, descend the stairs, and yank off the gorilla head. Outside the back entrance of the MAF building, still in my gorilla costume, in my elation, I hail a taxi to take me home. I get into the front seat, the gorilla head on my lap.

No trumpets sounding, no heavenly portents; still the same scrubbed blue sky and intense sun; it's just a normal working day out there! At least, there are no visible differences, but I feel a vividness in the air, a clarity to the city scene outside the car. I'm buzzing with adrenalin but the taxi-driver, a Fijian Indian by his looks, shows no reaction to my costume. I guess he's seen this and more before. There's no wild acclaim either from the Wellingtonians in their business outfits earnestly striding to and from meetings as we drive down The Terrace, nor any reaction from the bus passengers looking out of the windows or car drivers as we drive along Adelaide Road, and wait to turn off into my street.

But I am changed. I pay off the taxi (rounding up the fare!) and go back to the house and my room. Car-lag again, adding to the unreality: it's been less than two hours since I set out. Who would have thought it? I've sung 'Happy Birthday' to a crowd of people. I've saved Tom grief with the Ministry of Fun and his father. I've also earned myself some very useful dollars. From such small beginnings....

THIS IS WHAT I LEARNED: LESSON 1

- *Putting on a gorilla costume can give you confidence.*

This is the first, irreducible, inescapable core discovery of my single Gorillagram experience. Until that day I'd never felt comfortable standing up in front of an audience and performing. This marked me out from my kiwi-raised colleagues: they might not be very proficient at writing long screeds in correct English (something that I can do, having been educated in England), but they are enviably adept at speaking off the cuff at meetings, farewell functions, funerals and any other sort of public occasion.

There was a broader lesson:

- *Instantaneous change is possible! It can take just as long as putting on an animal costume. It can last as long as you want it to last. Don't prejudge what will happen when you put on the costume. Believe this and that's 50 percent of the battle.*

The gorilla costume had been hot, cumbersome and uncomfortable; too big in places, too pinched in others. Its hair was a spiky polyester. The head was heavy, had a sweet, chemical smell, and the eye-holes blocked some of my peripheral vision. None of this had mattered. So:

- *The costume doesn't have to be an exact fit.*

Not exactly earth-shattering; just the boring, literal truth. But it gets me thinking about animals in general. How comfortable are real animals in their own skin anyway? Surely they can't be in perfect health all the time, and there's not much they can do about it. If I have a toothache I make sure all my friends and colleagues know about it. But animals function despite not being 100 percent fit. They have to, I guess; they're almost always hungry and always under threat. They have to survive even when they're not feeling great.

Thursday night, and we four housemates have our weekly dinner together. This week we're joined by Tom's latest conquest: an attractive young real estate agent called Zoe. It's Tom's turn to organise the food; mine to bring along a bottle of wine. Unlike the rest of us, who make an effort with groceries and our ancient kitchen, Tom takes the relaxed approach: this time he's ordered a delivery of pizzas and garlic bread. After our customary mock-congratulatory remarks to Tom about how he's got the balance between the various ingredients just right, I talk about how I feel having done the Gorillagram. There's a ferment around the table; they all catch my mood, echo it, and even amplify it. By some dim instinct, or just plain luck, I emigrated to a country that's receptive to new ideas, that's small and young enough to encourage original thinking, however simplistic it might seem. A country where it doesn't matter what you look like, or how you speak. The country of the Fair Go. And so, over dinner and a bottle of Italian Red, I'm inspired by my pals' New World optimism. So bracing after all those years in 'What's-the-point? Why rock the boat?' England. I start to believe that something – I've no idea what - will come of it.

JENNY, 1986

A bright, warm and windy Wellington November day. It's not a long trip from Newtown to the Ministry's barn-like offices in the city centre but today my bus gets stuck behind a trolley bus, one of whose long, whippy poles has detached from the overhead power lines. It's a common occurrence; the buses are old and costly to maintain, but we like them for their quietness and their sentimental value, even when they seem to spend half their time like beached whales, blocking the rest of the traffic. Plastic bags scud along the pavement, whitecaps show in the harbour. It's a relief to escape the wind and get into the office building.

After years of government intervention in the economy, wage and price freezes, and a currency crisis, New Zealand, until recently known as Poland-on-the-Pacific, is undergoing a backlash taking the form of deregulation, getting rid of import licensing, freeing up of capital and labour markets and privatisation. So, against the spirit of the times, and with some reluctance, I have to admit the unfashionable truth that - well, there's no easy way of saying it: I work for the government. Specifically, I work four nine-hour days a week for a full-time salary at the Ministry for Social Welfare, which allows me the time to study for my Master's.

Getting off the bus, I make my way up the gentle slope of a windswept Bowen Street, and take the crowded lift up to the fifth floor, overlooking the car park. Wellington's a company town, and the company is the New Zealand Government, but this is a small country and the bureaucracy is of commensurate (and diminishing) size. From the windows to the south of my floor you can see gorse-covered hills and, from the other side, the harbour. My job title is

Assistant Researcher and my work entails interviewing a representative sample of welfare beneficiaries and seeing how well they are served by the payments system, then undergoing some drastic changes along with the rest of the economy. The writing-up and number-crunching are as boring as they sound, but the office is warm and quiet, my colleagues mostly friendly, and I get to meet people – clients - I'd otherwise never encounter. I'm not really supposed to engage with my interviewees' problems but, because I see them every fortnight for about three months, I sometimes do.

A few minutes before 11am this morning there's a tentative knock on the side of my cubicle. Jenny. Poor Jenny. I know quite a bit about her: she's in a relationship with a violent (male) partner who doesn't seem to have a regular job and binge drinks at least every weekend; She's shown me pictures of her two bright-faced daughters, one from another guy, who was also abusive. Jenny: watery grey eyes in a blotchy, pale, but potentially handsome, face, long light brown, straggly hair; perpetually apologetic and deferential. As happens in Wellington, the wind has blown the morning gloom clean away. The bright sun throws hard shadows on my desk. Jenny's wearing the same old tatty denim jeans and bottle-green cardigan that I've seen many times; she brings with her a faint odour of defeat, stale cigarette smoke and cheap talcum powder. Her whole demeanour is submissive. She stands just outside my cubicle. As ever, her size comes as a surprise: between interviews I have this image of her as a small, bird-like creature, when she actually has a large, sturdy, frame. I feel pity, sadness, overlaid with what's called professionalism; an attempt at distance, emotional detachment, telling myself that it's not my job to sort out her problems. But surely I can try?

As usual, we go to one of the windowless meeting rooms for privacy. After several meetings and with my repeatedly having given my absolute assurance of no intervention on the part of any

19

government or police body ('It's illegal; I'd be sacked', I've assured Jenny, not wholly accurately), we have been talking about her male partner and the beatings. I had to force myself, in the early stages, not to show the slightest feeling of judgementalism – the Ministry is militant about that. My sole remit is to find out what she knows about government benefits in cash or kind, for her family. I am allowed to find out facts behind the data and to make interviewees aware of sources of information and assistance. But I am not supposed to advise or suggest anything. Not during office hours anyway.

We begin to discuss her latest tribulations. Glide time means I can take from 30 minutes to two hours for lunch any time between noon and 2pm. What I do during lunch would be in my own time, I've told myself. Nothing to do with my status as a Ministry employee.

Me: 'But this has been going on for months now. He's unlikely to change. Don't you think?'

'It's only when he's had a drink.' (Read: many drinks.) 'And he never hits me like he hits a bloke. And he never hits the kids. Hardly ever.'

'But he keeps doing it. Do you really think it's going to stop?'

'I'm not leaving Duncan. I know what you're thinking, but I have to do right by my kids.'

'Sure. Okay. It's your decision. It just doesn't seem to get better. You say it's not getting worse. But, you know, the children might be better off in a more relaxed environment.'

That is further than I really should go, in my official position. There's no such thing as mandatory reporting for lowly researchers like me and, even if I told the police, they probably wouldn't do anything. There are one or two Women's Refuges in Wellington, run on a shoestring by tireless, dedicated volunteers. They gave our team a slide show a couple of months ago. But that's all. New Zealand's not the clean green easy-going pastoral paradise of your imagination – or mine, before I migrated here. The casual, non-hierarchical approach works wonderfully sometimes, making it easy to forgive the holes and trenches in the pavement crudely filled in with old oil cans. But once you get out of Wellington city centre, with its comparatively well-educated white-collar bureaucrats and secure career paths, you're in a surprisingly raw culture, featuring serious drinking, males with a big chip on their shoulder, bitterness, aggressive (and incompetent) driving and appalling levels of domestic violence. Glue-sniffers on the bus. A world leader in youth suicides. Roots are shallow here. To me, coming from England with its layers and layers of history, its clubs and societies for everyone from pigeon fanciers to Anglo-Mongolian musicologists, New Zealand culture, with its obsessional emphasis on sport, can seem thin and soulless and shallow. The flip side of being in the New World.

Jenny sighs. 'I have feelings for him, you know.' On the government-issue wall clock, the minute hand clicks into the vertical position. I glance at my watch: yes, it is definitely 12 o'clock. The opening of our designated two-hour lunch window.

I've brought my suitcase with the gorilla costume and, next to it, the head, in a plastic supermarket bag.

'Jenny – I want to try something different today. It's just a bit of role play. I want you to put this on.' It's poignant how she automatically assents, so used is she to taking orders from a man.

'It's just a bit of play acting.' Fortunately, the way she's dressed, all she has to do is slip off her shoes and step into the costume. (The pathos... I try not to notice her cracked heels.) If she's wondering what's going on, she's not saying anything. I pass her the gorilla's

21

head. It's something of a shock when she puts on, rotating it a fraction so that her eyes coincide with the holes in the plastic.

Policy is always to keep the meeting room door open when conducting one-on-one interviews with clients, so I leave it ajar, then fiddle with the internal window blinds to make sure that no-one can see us from the corridor.

'Now I just want to pretend. We're at your home.' For the first time I feel nervous. What seemed like a brilliant idea a couple of evenings ago now looks to be juvenile and – much worse - manipulative. But I am committed now. 'I'm Duncan, right? And you're a gorilla. And I've been drinking and I'm about to hit you.'

I'm well over the line now. But this is New Zealand: a place that has grown up around bending or ignoring the rules. The same, let's call it 'flexibility,' that lets just about anybody loose on the road with a massive chunk of metal and rubber has its benefits. I wouldn't of course actually hit Jenny but I begin teasing her, approaching her from the front; I'm about to poke the plasticised gorilla stomach muscles with my forefinger. But my finger doesn't reach it. She fights back! She strikes out at me with her gorilla hands. I jump with alarm as one of the gorilla's fingernails grazes my cheek. There must be some sharp plastic shard on it, as it leaves a tiny scratch. Jenny removes the gorilla head. I dab my cheek with a tissue; there are tiny beads of blood.

'I'm sorry; Mr Sinclaire. I'm truly-'

'It's fine; it's perfectly all right.' I say. I'm actually grinning. 'This is what we want to see'. Jenny's no fool. She senses my elation. I think we're both high on adrenalin. I keep reassuring her, as she steps out of the costume. Is it my imagination, or is there a spring in her step as she leaves? And I'm almost sure she wants to hug me. I demur, trying to maintain some semblance of professionalism.

I leave the Ministry building a few minutes after Jenny, and nip down Lambton Quay. Too buzzed to sit down or buy a sandwich I wander up and down, mingling with the lunchtime crowds; I pop into a bookshop, then quickly out again; it's not a time for contemplation. Before I know it, I'm back in my cubicle. Everything feels mundane now.

At home that evening I ask Tom about borrowing the gorilla costume next week: he says I can hang on to it; he's finished with the Ministry of Fun ('let's just say acrimony was involved'), has no intention of returning the costume, and is instead going to work as a summer intern for a National Party Member of Parliament; one of his father's golf club buddies.

A fortnight later we do it again. I bait Jenny; she reacts aggressively, then apologises. And again the fortnight after that: this time she smiles as she apologises. She doesn't draw blood, but she clouts me a couple of times on my arms as I parry her blows. It's still our secret. I imagine that I see subtle signs of an increasing assertiveness; there's definitely a spring in her step as we go into the meeting room, and afterwards, as she leaves the building.

But she fails to turn up for our last scheduled interview in mid-December, just before the great New Zealand Christmas summer shutdown. I'm disappointed but not too surprised, given the minefield of Jenny's domestic life, when she doesn't appear that day. Inevitably, I catastrophise. Has Duncan threatened her, put her on lockdown? Maybe she's in hospital. Or maybe she's reported me to my Director or the police or some Ombudsperson? What had I been thinking of, carrying out my crazy experiment with a vulnerable person? And now the never-ending pageant of all my screw-ups, big and small, strides across my mind. I left the UK to escape my past, to start afresh in New Zealand. Where next: the Chatham Islands? The space shuttle? The suitcase with the gorilla costume sits unopened on top of the metal filing cabinet in my cubicle; the head in its plastic bag, in the empty drawer at the bottom.

A few weeks pass and now, in early January, when most of my colleagues are still on holiday, and the office is pleasantly quiet, a rare, handwritten letter, addressed to me and postmarked Manurewa, shows up in my in-tray.

> *Dear Mr Sinclair I just want to thank you for giving me the courage to leave Duncan. I really think it was you when you made me pretend to be a gerilla when something snapped in me. When Duncan came back late that night and started hitting me I hit him back for the first time then I called the womans refuge, then they came to collect me and the kids and we have gone to my sisters house 20 minutes from Manuwera. I want to thank you for your help with talking to me and with the gerilla suit. I am looking for work and no way will we return to Wellington so this is also to say goodbye. Yours sincerely ....*

Relief first, then delight! The gorilla costume has worked its magic on Jenny. Belatedly I think I really should find out more about gorillas, whereupon a book in an unfamiliar aisle at Wellington Library tells me that they are, most of the time, quite docile animals. Unless they're disturbed, they're not aggressive. They are even quite shy. No matter, it's what people think they know about gorillas that really matters; not what gorillas are actually like. And our collective image of gorillas is that they beat their chests and attack if provoked even slightly.

I'm lucky with time as well as location: these are good days for out-of-the-box ideas. Something called the New Age began recently with a trickle, now a torrent of books, courses, and cassettes, featuring smiling happy people bathed in white light, with unnervingly regular features, impeccable hair and preternaturally perfect teeth; the looks, the charisma, the confidence, the self-assurance all saying the same thing. 'You too can be like me! Read this, study that, buy this, sign here: just do what I do and you can be as happy and successful as me!' Serenity for fun and profit! Thursday dinnertime again, and the enthusiasm is catching: 'Go for it!' sums up the reaction from the flatmates plus Tom's current girlfriend.

I try the gorilla costume on a couple of my other female interviewees, one also suffering from 'battered wife' syndrome, the other enmeshed in an emotionally abusive relationship. As with Jenny, I schedule them into my pre-lunchtime slots so that I could carry out my unorthodox role-play unofficially and in my own time. The results, I'm happy to say, are as heart-warming. One gains enough courage, as Jenny had, to leave her abusive partner (this took four gorilla sessions). The other, having rehearsed with me, fights her abuser back, shocking him into contrition. It took some weeks but, while they attended couples-counselling at a church-supported guidance centre, the arguments and fighting were gradually to become ritualised; still physical, but without the infliction of bodily harm; a harmless but energetic outlet for their pent-up emotions that would take place on a weekly schedule.

I take stock: without the gorilla costume there would have been no MAF cafeteria performance and three women still being abused. Seeing the world through a gorilla's eyes has worked for them as it worked for me. Moreover: my newly liberated interviewees had (presumably) decided to do something about their parlous state while dressed in a normal civilian outfit. Obviously, then:

LESSON 2
- *The few minutes during which you behave as a gorilla can have effects that last beyond the time allocated for role play.*

Questions flare up in my mind: could gorilla role-play solve other problems? Was it just the gorilla costume or could other animals work? How exactly does it work? I suspect I am onto something big, but I am wary of extrapolating from my sample size of four. And yet – I tell myself – this is four times as big as Samuel Hahnemann's sample size when he laid down the foundations of homeopathy. And look where homeopathy is today! Clinics, hospitals, royal patronage even; a multibillion-dollar business, and one that does some good, even if only through the placebo effect. Is that so wrong?

But I want more than that: the possibilities are immense! Helping a few people: not bad. But not enough. I want to solve the world's problems. Why not? There's nothing stopping me. It's Friday afternoon. I've got the weekend and the rest of my life ahead of me.

DIALOGUE WITH JASON 1, YOU CANNOT BE SERIOUS!
'Tell me, James...have you ever visited Planet Earth?'

That's Jason talking, on Friday evening, when we and our colleagues are having our weekly TGIF drinking session at Quay Point in Lambton Quay. Jason's a policy analyst with the Ministry and is another migrant from England, but he had come to New Zealand with his family when he was 11. Tonight he's not playing in his band, so we'd go on after the beer to a movie and a meal.

'I'm serious Jason, there's something about being an animal that really fired them up to shake up their lives.'

'Animals?', he says, putting his pint glass down. We're half way through our second beers and have to raise our voices now: the exuberance of the Friday crowd. 'What do you know about animals? You're the most urban person I've ever met. You were brought up in Manchester, for God's sake.' I can't dispute that. We'd had pets in the family, in those far away days when I had been part of a family. And I'd worked on a dairy farm in North Yorkshire for a few months between school and college. But I have a city boy's knowledge of animals. A tortoise when I was very young, various dogs over the years, one cat, and I used to keep tropical fish. I've read a few newspaper articles, watched animals when they did something sufficiently bizarre to appear on TV news, and I've seen some TV documentaries. But Jason is right. I am no authority on animals. So what am I trying to prove? I *might* have helped a few women escape their abusers. That's about all. Jason's scepticism is necessary. Others can and do encourage me as they'll encourage anything new and not obviously destructive. But what I need now is to be grounded.

As we head toward dinner at our usual Chinese on Courtenay Place, I tell Jason about the time I put on the gorilla costume at home for the first time. I'd waited until one quiet, late Sunday morning the flatmates were all out doing their own thing. I stepped into the costume then put the gorilla head on. Glancing in my wall mirror I had two distinct, reactions. First, I saw myself as others would see me: a guy in a gorilla costume. In that sombre Sunday setting, alone in the house, an ambulance siren wailing in the background, it all seemed a bit silly. My second reaction was different. I stopped looking at myself and turned away from the mirror. Instantly my senses were heightened. It was as if I had not so much added a hairy rubbery plastic layer to my body, but more that I'd stripped off my humanness: my past, my fears, my anxieties. I was alert, vibrant and in the moment. I was seeing the world as an animal sees it: raw, undistorted. Reaching Courtenay Place I tell Jason about the roar given out by used water spiralling down the plughole of the old bathtub in our house. Like reverse thrust on landing somewhere new. That Sunday, with the gorilla outfit on, the rest of the house empty, that's what I'd felt, rather than heard: a thrilling sound; that of my past draining away. Normally I'd be more reticent about such a subjective experience, but it's Friday evening and we've had a couple of beers and it's easier to talk about matters of the soul when you're both walking, rather than face to face.

'You understand? I don't actually have to know about animals...or put it this way: we *are* animals, even guys like me who don't know anything about them.'

'Well, I don't know. Maybe you're just projecting your own ideals onto them. Easy enough with the animals we know most about: cows, sheep, cats and dogs.' Then, while we're waiting to cross Taranaki St: 'Are you serious about all this James? I mean, it's a bit simplistic; you put on a costume and you change personality. It's not so earth-shattering.'

'Like a uniform, Jason, or a masonic apron, or putting on your Sunday best and going to church or, I don't know, clerical vestments, or wearing a suit when you go to the Minister's office.' But is Jason right? I feel deflated. In my defensiveness, I try to deflect: 'You become someone different. I mean: you play bass guitar in the band: is that rational? Is music rational?'

And so the conversation meanders away from gorillas and animals and then we find that our usual stand-by is closed. 'Campylobacter in the chicken,' explains the proprietor of the second-hand book store next door, as he locks up for the night.

Or 'Your animal pals getting their revenge', as Jason puts it. So we cross over Courtenay Place and go into a (relatively) upmarket trattoria on one of the side streets.

Our usual convivial Friday evening, but something has unsettled me. At home late that night it comes to the surface. If putting on an animal costume is the same as putting on a uniform, then, well, what's so special about that? It's just the same as any other costume. But ...why do I have to be special?

Well, it had been special for me. Can't I be happy with that? But then it *seems* to have liberated my abused interviewees. And what about my brief experience last Sunday? I need a word for it. I settle on 'gorillatising'. I don't know how long I gorillatised that first time. Probably a matter of seconds rather than minutes. But it did something for me. It opened up moments of clarity in the way I look at things. Specifically, solipsistically, my life so far. You might almost define thinking as spinning a narrative that, because it is not actually life and purports only to comment on it, cannot keep up, cannot be accurate. Gorillatising, for a few fleeting moments, paused the spinning. It put distance between myself and my narratives. I could see them, instead of live them. And I see two of them:

Narrative One: I'm the unluckiest person in the world. The victim of victims. An upbringing bordering on the abusive; physical beatings (admittedly rare), emotional cruelty and bullying (continuous). I was born to one of the millions of mothers who had no choice as to whether to marry and have children. Material benefits – yes! And precious minutes when, especially in the early years, we could sit together round the table, or in front of the TV, *as a family*. But all that does is make me realise just what an ideal family life could be, and what I am missing out on. On balance, when I think about settling down, I'm terrified.

Narrative Two: I'm the luckiest person in the world. I hit the jackpot. Born in England. Never cold, never hungry, and holidays in Europe. I was protected from the harsher realities of life. No wars, no conscription, no physical disabilities. Never had to work very hard to survive. Sure, I did some hard work in vacations, like Marie Antoinette at the Trianon, enjoyable (mostly) because they were temporary. Born in England, yes, I'd won the lottery of life. Better, actually, than winning big on the pools or the Premium Bonds: no false friends, no hangers-on and no constraints on my behaviour. My parents are gone but they gave me material security and freedom.

They don't compete, these narratives, because at any one moment, I am fully invested in one or the other. Most times I am predisposed to burrow deeply into Narrative Two. Not because of any great wisdom on my part; more because of the instinctive distrust I have for prevailing currents; the therapeutic culture and the sanctification of victimhood. A puckish need to be contrarian. If the dominant ethos were one of stiff upper lips and starched collars, maybe I'd go the other way. Whatever, gorillatising puts a stop to it; to the endless replaying of either narrative; fleetingly, to be sure, but enough to see them as the phantoms they are.

Cows 1, 1975

Actually I'm not totally ignorant of animals. It's 1975, and I was spending part of my gap year on a farm in North Yorkshire, England. Academically competent but devoid of practical experience, I was taken by the *idea* of agriculture. Of course, I knew nothing about actual farming. The guys who ran the farm had broad accents, which meant they had to repeat every instruction, and there were many. It also didn't help also that the farm manager was, as the village gossip had it, a 'cheap man'; not particularly sympathetic, mean-spirited. The other guy was more amenable, more experienced, but both had an irrational hatred and fear of cows – fully reciprocated by the poor beasts. Unfortunate, as it was a dairy farm. After I'd graduated from feeding the calves and cleaning the milking parlour, and proved my incompetence with tractors and mud, they were happy to leave me alone to milk the cows, twice a day. A herd of 80. I remember the cows to this day: number 57, nervous, wiry, would try to kick the farm manager with her back leg, as he stood in the pit in the milking parlour. I was more patient with her. Then there was number 45 who would always linger meditatively by the slurry lagoon after being milked. Number eight, with udders disproportionately big. Number 13, svelte, placid and docile enough to be milked by hand. And I remember most clearly of all one of the older ones, big with a dirty grey and white coat, whose calf was born in one of the little barns by the milking parlour. She was allowed to nurse it for just two days before he was taken away. She was inconsolable and succeeded in escaping from the barn, bellowing and running along the path that the lorry taking her son away had driven up the day before. Her cries seared your soul. She was beaten for the trouble she caused. No, farm life was not for me. Within a couple of years or so all the cows except for a few high-yielders would be condemned, trucked away, slaughtered and their corpses converted into some meat product. The routine cruelty was heartbreaking.

Which is to say... I have form. It was the cows and me against the farmers. It was the animal kingdom and me against the system.

THE HUMAN CONDITION
Yet there were times when I actually envied the cows; enslaved and exploited as they were. What was that about? I don't mean simply that they had no worries about credit card debt, or getting the boiler fixed or drought in the Sahel. It went deeper. They didn't worry about human things, but they had other reasons to be anxious and afraid. There were the casual brutalities, the occasional beatings, the shocks from the electric fences, the indignities. But the worst barbarities inflicted on the cows were intermittent. The cows didn't carry the memory of them such that they became sources of anxiety – at least not to the point of wishing to put an end to it all. Any animal, however brutalised and tortured, will cling to life; never do you see a self-destructive animal. There must be something to their worldview.

Actually the cows had their comforts, even on my farm. True, they were closed up in a barn over the four or five winter months. Not much in the way of entertainment or intellectual stimulation, but they had each other and were warm and well fed, with plenty of straw on which to lie. Then one day in early spring, we released them into a paddock. With utter delight in their expanded universe - the space and the green grass - they charged up and down as a group. Their needs are simple and, that day at least, completely satisfied. Within a few hours, the field is churned up, the grass trodden into the mud, but the farmers anticipate this and wait a day or two till they've calmed down before leading them to prime grazing land. For the next seven or eight months they'll be outside in pasture. And all year round there is the social life of the herd, with its hierarchy, its togetherness-in-adversity and its opportunities for bovine social events and gossip. Sure, the cows have their fears, but they are fears of immediate threats. They can be alert to those threats. So alert that they have no space to worry about past traumas, or things that might never happen. And they don't bother spitting out formulas, such as 'I'm a victim' or 'the world owes me a living', which are rarely accurate and always unhelpful.

Well that's what I think. We humans create anxiety from nothing. Even great material wealth doesn't alleviate it. We play status games just as avidly as the cows, but more joylessly. Look at me: I'm even anxious about this great gift, this gorilla suit thing I've discovered. Does it really signify anything or am I kidding myself? Am I subconsciously doing what Jason suggested, taking the Mickey? Or idealising the life of animals? Extrapolating from the life of the few animals I've ever met – our (not-particularly-pampered) pets and the (not-at-all pampered) dairy cows? No, that won't do. Animals suffer, and not only because of humans. Their offspring die, they get diseases. What they don't do is add to the suffering, encasing it in an ideology. Maybe, just possibly, my sample size of gorilla-costume beneficiaries is too small, too unrepresentative. Maybe I'm just compensating for failures in other areas of my life by trying to comfort myself with my own personal belief system. Maybe there's nothing more to my gorilla antics than simple role-play.

'ZOOTHERAPY'

The Ministry of Social Welfare, unlike MAF, doesn't have a canteen. A trolley comes round at 10am and 3pm and we'll gather round it and chat for a few minutes. One morning:

'Climate change – don't talk to me about climate change.'

Rob's old school. A classic organisation subversive; in his sixties, an ex-milkman who'd done statistics at night school; an avid, eclectic reader. The proverbial thorn in the threat of management. I don't think he's ever been promoted from his Junior Analyst position in the Policy Services section.

'Rising sea levels. Got nothing to do with us changing the climate. Look out there,' he gestures to the harbour outside the window, whitecaps showing on the turquoise surface of the sea. Then he pats his not inconsiderable paunch. 'We're all getting fatter, and we're all spending more time on the beach in the sea, swimming, or on boats sailing. Or cruising – you've seen how fat those Americans are when they come off the cruise ships. Archimedes: the bigger we are, the more water we displace. Melting ice caps? Pull the other one.'

Returning to our cubicles, Sue, a wise old bird whose cubicle is adjacent to mine says 'Sometimes it's difficult to tell when Rob's serious. But not this time. At least, I don't think so.'

It's Sue with whom I've talked most about my gorilla sessions with Jenny and the other abused wives. Her entire working life has been spent as a public servant. She once saw me leaving the meeting room with the suitcase and bag containing the gorilla costume and head, returning from a session with one of the ladies. A quizzical look, and I explained about the gorilla outfit and reassured her that I'm doing it unofficially and (technically) outside office hours. 'I call it Gorillatising', I say. A seasoned and meticulous office administrator, Sue has become my confidante. And vice versa: we each overhear our private phone conversations and never once allude to them. After tea that afternoon the two of us are chatting and I describe my own experiences with the gorilla costume.

'I find it sort of focuses my mind whenever I wear it. Sometimes even just the head.'

'Interesting. But what happens if you try a different animal? You'd need to find another name for it.'

'Yeah, well I don't really like Gorillatising...'

Heading back to our cubicles, we brainstorm. 'Sinclairotherapy', she suggests. I prefer 'Animalisation'. She suggests 'Animo-therapy'.

Sounds good, but a few minutes later, when we're back in our own workspaces, she looks over the cubicle divider and says:

'Zootherapy'.

I like it. I like the 'Z', with its vague suggestion of Zen (trendy) and its quirky location at the unexplored outlying end of the alphabet.

Most evenings now I put on the gorilla head, sometime also stepping into the gorilla suit. Or, as I now say: I practise Zootherapy. And a funny thing happens; I have vivid dreams, or perhaps I just remember them more clearly. Either way, I become more aware of my past. It is as if Zootherapy were allowing me to access those sad and disturbing memories because my mind knows that it can now deal with them.

A SCHOOL PLAYGROUND IN ENGLAND, 1971
I'm nine years old it's my first day wearing glasses at school. I've done my best to avoid them, but it became inevitable: I am very short-sighted. I'm apprehensive about how my peers will react, but I'm also enjoying the novelty of seeing more than a few feet ahead of me and the chance to read the blackboard and make friends with

human beings rather than books and – don't laugh – my fingers. I know I'll attract some attention, but as it happens my schoolmates aren't too merciless. Lunch break and I'm playing in a scrappy game of playground football. I can see, which improves my game a little, but doesn't turn me into one of the lads. I miskick and the ball goes straight to one of the other team, who duly scores.

'Hey James, get some new specs!'

'Speccy four-eyes, speccy four-eyes!'

'You need some new specs, Professor!'

The ribbing isn't pleasant, but it's bearable, and no worse than that inflicted on the other kids who've turned up with new glasses in recent months. My team is several goals ahead anyway. Then with relief, I see Sally Dempster came out of the school building, shrinking as she does so. She's a bit pudgy, but not grossly so. She just has the ill luck to have been chosen as the boys' lightning conductor for our insecurities. We all mock her.

'Eugh look, here's fatty Dempster!'

'Eugh, Dempster's dress is so big. It's a tent.'

'Or a parachute!'

How we laughed!

'Look at the way the ground cracks up when Dempster walks on it!'

The lad with the football shouts 'See if I can hit fatty Dempster!'

'You can't miss; she's so fat.'

Poor Sally flinches as the dirty blue plastic ball hits her body.

'Look at that; Dempster's stopped the ball with her flab!'

They start chanting. Correction: *we* start chanting. I'm not the first, but not through any sense of compassion on my part; I never do take the initiative outside the classroom. But once it starts, and to my shame - it grieves me even now - I join in. How thrilling it is to be a member of a crowd, united in our contempt for someone else. Anyone else. Anyone except me!

'Fatty Dempster! Fatty Dempster!'

It ends when another girl comes along and comforts Sally, who is close to tears. They walk together to a remote corner of the playground. We continue chanting half-heartedly then resume our football game.

I will be honest: I'm still, at times, overwhelmed by what I did to poor Sally. Sure, I didn't actually instigate it. Sure, if Sally had stood up for herself, or if I had felt more secure in myself.... No, none of this will wash. Fact is that I have the propensity for doing evil.

I guess I've done worse things than that, and more recently too. Things that I can't blame on an immature prefrontal cortex. They say the unexamined life isn't worth living. But if you do examine all the terrible things you did, all the other lives you screwed up, temporarily or permanently, intentionally or not, what then? You're hobbled by guilt.

Or perhaps Zootherapy is trying to tell me something. It gives me a way of looking at the world that enables me to face the truth about myself, without the hobbling. Only in dreams, to be sure, but it's a start.

And maybe it's not just me. Another old memory from the old country: wily old British Labour Prime Minister Harold Wilson campaigning in the 1975 referendum for Britain to stay in the European Economic Community. Taunted by opponents, who said his party was full of people who disagree with him, he retorts that, just as the people of Britain aren't unanimous in their thinking about the EEC, neither is his Labour Party. Therefore, the Labour Party truly represents Britain. So: in embodying the potential for evil, as my dreams remind me, do I represent the human race? Not quite. It's more like: I am an ordinary human being. I suspect it's only Zootherapy that lets me see this, as an animal would, without flinching. Just the facts. While I'm asleep, anyway.

And it's not just shame or guilt. What about those times I behaved stupidly, whose recollection is enough to raise my body temperature with embarrassment years later? And then there are the traumas that we all suffer. The time somebody (you see the horror of it? I can't even say who...) threw a shoe, smashing the panes of my glasses into my eyes, resulting in a trip to the Eye Hospital, a made-up story about my falling down, and a deft bit of surgery. Then the constant reminders by the shoe-thrower that, if I misbehave again, the next time she'd do the job properly and it would be permanent blindness for me.

All that leads to a certain narrative: like 'I'm a victim'. But when I tell a cousin about the shoe-throwing, glass in eye incident, he just laughs and laughs. He knew the person involved, you see, and it was quite in character: absurd, bizarre, hilarious. So outlandish, so outrageous for a mother (there, I said it) to do that to her son, as to be high, transgressive comedy. So one single event can be seen as tragedy or comedy. Within reason, I guess. I mean, it didn't kill me, nor even blind me, so why not laugh it off? It was only one eye anyway. And while it required a hospital visit, it was only as an outpatient: we were in and out in couple of hours. It's what happens. And would I want to be judged by the worst thing I've done? And did the perpetrator come to feel about it, in later life, how I feel now about Sally D? And, and, and.... It's only humans, with our memory, that make a big deal of it. Which view do you go for – victimhood or hilarity, and what criteria do we use to choose one or the other? The mood you're in? The prevailing social view? The incentives on offer? It was just one event! What about the time she rang the home of the guy who'd been bullying me, had his mother round, and dramatised my daily discomfiture, with me whimpering on her knee? All for my benefit. You never get 100 percent yin or 100 percent yang. Moses struck the rock; Jesus blasted the fig tree.

But in this respect animals are wiser than us: they don't bother with narratives or judgment, still less with choosing one amongst multiple interpretations of the same event. They don't waste their energy on personal tales, nor on the more generic things: fear of death, fear of being alone, growing old, losing their health. Losing their mind. Nor is there the free-floating anxiety that permeates much of our lives, that's assuaged only by alcohol or medication. The dread of something unspecified. Then there's the pain one feels when seeing injustice. As far as we can tell, no animal has these baroque memories and fears. They have some basic ones, the ones useful to them right now. But it's only humans who distort reality by wanting to rewrite the past and determine the future. We want the world to be different. We imagine alternatives and compare. We do it all the time. Animals don't.

THIS IS WHAT I LEARNED: LESSON 3

- *The gorilla suit allows you to look at your past and so deal with it. How? Because when you look at it as a gorilla would, you don't try to do anything about it. You know that, as a gorilla, you cannot rewrite the past. So you look without flinching. This can free you from the guilt that impedes your fulfilment. It can free you from your narrative. Zootherapy makes you see your narrative, your entire past, all the hurts you've inflicted on others or experienced yourself, as a distraction from the living present. See life through the eyes of a gorilla. It's more efficient.*

Sounds preposterous doesn't it? Until you look at wars and mass killings or turn on the TV news and then you see that Zootherapy maybe does have something going for it. Nobody with any sense of history can say that animals are demonstrably worse than us. Whatever gorillas do, it can't be worse than man's inhumanity to man. Well, that at least is what the small sample of humanity in Wellington who are flatmates of mine, or colleagues, think. Or say they think - are they just being polite?

DIALOGUE WITH JASON, 1987
'I don't know James. Look at the numbers. Most humans aren't killers and most animals are; they have to be.'

It's a warm Friday evening in late February 1987. We're having beers on the sunny terrace of a bar overlooking the bus terminal on Courtenay Place.

Jason goes on: 'Sure, there have been mass murderers but most of us aren't as bad as that. You haven't killed anyone. Well, I'm pretty sure you haven't. I certainly haven't. Everybody does things they regret.'

Jason would never know the whole story; I certainly hadn't killed anybody but that was probably for want of weapons. Feelings ran high in the family into which I'd been born. But firearms were almost impossible to buy in 1970s England, even for adults. Ach! I've come to New Zealand to get away from all of that, or as much of it as I can.

'And what's stopping gorillas killing everything is just that they don't have the technology. He gestures upward and around, taking in Mount Victoria and, a few streets back, the harbour, 'You know this whole country was devastated by rats and cats. The flightless birds....'

'Hang on, it was humans who killed all the moas.'

'Sure, but you can't really say animals are more peace-loving and compassionate than humans.'

I have to agree. Just the other morning I'd heard a guy from the Department of Conservation on National Radio talking about how a dog can sniff the gamey scent of kiwis from miles away and kill dozens of them in a few hours – and, given any opportunity, they do. And they don't need the kiwis for food. They just leave the bodies strewn around the bush.

I concede: 'Okay; let's say that, at their worst, some animals, some of the time, are as bad as us. But you've got to admit there are times and circumstances where animals do better than humans. Their killing is instinctive; they don't train for it, or study it, or do it in cold blood.'

'Yeah, well, they haven't got the technology. They just haven't advanced as far as us in that direction. They'd be just as bad as us if they had the means.'

We eschew the Chinese this week, even though it's reopened, and return to the pizzeria. Seems apt, this time, for me to order the vegetarian option. We share a carafe of the house red.

I try to explain the freshness of mind, the vitality and clarity, that Zootherapy gives me. I do a poor job, and Jason remains unconvinced:

'I'm not sure I want to forget the past. This narrative you want me to throw away: it is me. Even the awful bits. We developed memories and fears for a reason.' He pauses. He gestures in the direction of Courtenay Place, well-known haunt of inebriated 14-year old girls late at night. 'Look, you see a stunning young woman in the street; you can't just go up to her and have sex with her. You could get in a lot of trouble for that: it's a licence to take advantage of any woman you see around. We don't do that any more.'

'They do in some countries.'

'Well, not here. We've evolved. It's a licence for coercive sex. You'd get arrested. Anyway, it's not exactly joyful.'

Inexperienced as I am (relatively), and having seen how it affects others, I think I know how joyless sex, even the human variety, can be.

I argue anyway. 'Let's just say there are times when we'd be happier if we were a gorilla or any animal. Can't we take that as a minimum? We don't need all the guilt. It's not about throwing our morals and knowledge away; it's about using them when it helps, and forgetting about it when it doesn't.'

But I'm glad of Jason's scepticism. I never really expected Jason to put on the gorilla head or to be taken with the idea. He has the healthy English disdain for any new ideology or philosophy. But he is as accepting of my excursions into Zootherapy as I am of his band music. I've seen his band perform just once (at the Bodega), and he's given me a CD they'd produced, which I've listened to, once. I have no ear for rock music. If he were to take to Zootherapy with any enthusiasm it would be well out of character. And I recognise his point: Zootherapy originates in a mind that has accumulated a load of assumptions about ethics, morals and empathy, all of which come from the background we share in a benign, post-war, baby booming, Great Britain and in its former dominion.

Outside, the evening's grown cool, but the TGIF drinkers, neckties loosened, are spilling out onto the pavement. After our climb up to The Terrace, and just before we head our separate ways, Jason asks 'What do they think of all this gorilla stuff in the office?'

It's a good question.

Of course, my colleagues got to know about it. Most likely not from Sue, but from my ducking into the meeting room with abused women, the tatty suitcase, and the plastic bag with tufts of hair sticking out. One morning, just after tea, my Section Head, Mike, appears over the top of my cubicle and beckons me into his sweaty, smoky office.

For reasons that it would serve no useful purpose to describe, my adrenaline levels shoot up. The primeval part of my brain expects arbitrary, harsh, physical punishment. I'm a little boy again! It could be anything. It could be the gorilla costume; it could simply be the fact of my existence.

I don't have to wait long. Mike gestures at me to pull up chair and we both sit at his desk. He lights up. He turns toward me and leaning back, asks:

'How's the data gathering going?'

'Fine'

'And what's all this I hear about the gorilla costume thing?' He waves his hand reassuringly.

'It's just a sort of role play I do at lunchtime with some of the ladies.'

'That's what I've heard. I just need to be sure that you're being discreet about it. You're sure it's all in your lunch hour, right?'

'Absolutely.'

'That's fine. What you do in your own time is no real concern of ours.'

I begin to respond, but he waves his hand again. 'It's fine, and I don't need to know. Just make sure nobody from outside can see you. You don't want people getting the wrong idea.'

I guess that someone must have caught a glimpse of one of the ladies in the costume, either through the blinds, or via the door that I'd been careful to leave an inch or two ajar.

I say nothing. He blows smoke towards the open window. 'You can carry on with it. Just be discreet, that's all. What you do in your own time – it's entirely your business.' He sighs, and inhales deeply from his cigarette. And now the conversation takes a bizarre turn. 'Do you know what naturism is?'

'Well, I think most kiwis are into nature,' I say. 'One of the great things about this country. It's all around. It's never very far away.' I gesture to the hills beyond the windows.

'I don't mean that. That's naturalism; I'm talking about naturism. You know, enjoying life without clothes? There's a sun club we go to, up Foxton way whenever we can. Don't look like that! I'm not trying to convert you.' He chuckles. I look blank. 'Well, we're naturists.' He nods at the framed photo of he and his wife on the desk. I recall having chatted to her briefly at our team's Christmas lunch.

'What I'm saying is, it's a perfectly normal thing for perfectly normal people. And it's fine! We wear nothing; you or your interviewees or whoever, role play as gorillas. Just - you know what people are like – keep it quiet.'

'Sure.' I say, though of course I'm imagining his wife, a pretty, petite lady with curly brown hair, naked.

'Everyone has their own way of finding freedom and feeling good about themselves. And it's all fine. Getting rid of all our inhibitions. For me and Raewyn it's being naked and enjoying the sun and the outdoors in the company of other like-minded people. For you it might be putting on a gorilla costume and pretending to be a gorilla or whatever. For some,' he gestures toward our section's cubicles 'it's music; for others it's acting or doing the haka or rugby or beer or fishing. You know what I'm saying? Dancing, beer, church; my dentist goes kayaking on the South Island every weekend. It's all the same. It's all fine.

'Oh and... I haven't made any of this a feature of my conversations with our colleagues. Discretion, right?'

To my relief, Mike goes on to talk about my prospects with the Ministry. 'Once you've got all these statistics, you'll get some more interesting work. You're still on track for your Master's, right?' I nod. 'Then you'll be doing even better'.

He stubs out his cigarette, and stands up. He pats me on the shoulder. 'Discretion, right?'

I understand. Having worked in England, it still surprises - and cheers - me how freely management and employee can talk to each other in New Zealand.

FRIENDS ALL GETTING HITCHED

At that point I am wearing the gorilla head most evenings, and putting on the full suit at least once every weekend. I have more time now, as my social life is eroding. Angela and Steve's relationship is going well; Tom always has some striking-looking female company, so I'm on my own at home. As well, the drinking sessions after work on Fridays at Quay Point, and later The Oxford, are shrinking, as one-by-one, and perfectly understandably, my colleagues opt to spend their time with girlfriends and boyfriends. Jason has been one of the holdouts. But, after a succession of good-looking-and-very-much-aware-of-it girlfriends, he is now living with a quiet, assured church-going Malaysian-Chinese lady. At first our regular Fridays were transferred to Thursdays when, rather than take in drinks, a meal, and a movie, we'd go home after a couple of beers. Now, pressure of work and a more enticing home life mean that we meet up only occasionally.

There's no need to share the painful consequences of being alone, or the even more painful explanations for it, except insofar as they determine my hopes for, and expectations of Zootherapy. Everyone needs family, or a god, or an ideology, or some grand organising principle, and I can see myself elevating Zootherapy into mine. A happy family life would be ideal, but if that's not going to happen, then Zootherapy might be the answer. I still hope that there exists someone, somewhere, who will share her life with mine. But I have to be realistic. I'm thirty years old, New Zealand's a small country and let's just say that I am, on a good day, only averagely attractive to women. And there's something else. Whenever I detect some interest the first thought that comes to mind is 'You like me? What's wrong with you?' No reason to go into why that is. Sufficient to say it's one instance of a psychological trope that isn't dissolved just by being aware of it. The hatred (I'm talking of family members) went on for too long, too intensely. If I have a world role, I would tell myself, it's similar to that of the sarcophagus being built over the Chernobyl reactor: to absorb the malevolence and protect the rest of the world. And to remind others that there is a class of person, or a human pathology, that will set about destroying something like family harmony simply because others value it.

This self-image was baggage on my migration to New Zealand; the airline didn't lose it, nor could I just abandon it on the luggage carousel at Auckland International Arrivals. And again, because a proper relationship would mean everything to me, then it's just too unlikely or too life-changing to contemplate. I'm not happy being single, but it does have its advantages. One is that people find it easier to confide in someone who won't discuss them with an intimate partner. So being alone doesn't prevent friendships with females. Maybe it even encourages them: they know and I know that I'm not relationship material, so there's no tension, no game-playing, and conversation and confidences flow freely. The ladies in my circle – colleagues, colleagues' girlfriends, or friends of flatmates – share that healthy New World enthusiasm for life. They've never been told not to have ideas above their station. Unencumbered by the notions of class and status of the old world, they don't have to prove anything to anyone.

There's a paradox here: when I put on the gorilla suit I do so without any expectation about what will or should happen. So while I have - must have – high hopes for Zootherapy, when actually practising Zootherapy all my hopes are suspended. In Zootherapy itself, hopes, expectations, fears and anxieties; all fall away. The gorilla suit frees my mind of all that human stuff, but it doesn't do any more than set the scene for something that might or might not happen. A blessing really: it's never contaminated by our thoughts about what it should be.

But, in the spirit of total honesty, I am pretty sure I wouldn't be devoting so much time and energy into Zootherapy if there were a lady in my life.

KARL, 1988
Of course, some people would be more amenable to dressing up as an animal than others. So far, I've tried it only on women prone to act submissively to men. Time to do something different. Gorillas don't seem the ideal animal for everyone. Karl, for instance; another of my interviewees whose progress I am charting. After school he did some casual labouring jobs on building sites and a dairy plant, but has had problems staying in gainful, legal employment. He's been registered as unemployed for almost four years. He keeps losing his temper or, as my briefing notes have it 'repeatedly and aggressively questions management decisions.' I find him flinty, unresponsive; a lean, wiry pole of a man with thinning hair and pale face. There's something new on the New Zealand scene: anger management courses, which I've tried subtly to suggest as an option

for Karl. But no dice. It's hard enough getting the statistical information I need. A challenging candidate for Zootherapy, I think. His most recent employment was a few weeks' picking fruit on the east coast. I think the gorilla costume wouldn't help attenuate his aggressive tendencies and I can't anyway imagine him meekly stepping into the gorilla suit. Well no, the truth is that I'm afraid of how he'll react if I insist. So I take the convenient option....

I've already gathered the data I need from Karl, who's sitting across from me in the meeting room. It's just gone 12 o'clock. I've opaqued the blinds to the corridor, and the door's almost closed. I'm showing Karl a picture of cows grazing in sight of Mount Egmont in the Taranaki region of the North Island, from an old wall calendar of New Zealand panoramas.

'So the next time you get those feelings, I just want you to imagine that you're a cow. Think like a cow, grazing in a paddock. Lots of lush green pasture. OK?'

No reaction. Surely he knows about cows? Even the most urban kiwi will have seen them placidly grazing by the roadside. This is New Zealand after all, not Manhattan, Tokyo or Sao Paulo. Even if only from a truck's driving seat, Karl will know that cows are friendly animals. Walk into a mob of cows and some of them will come up to you and lick your hand. I feel a bit stupid now, but I persist. There's a lot riding on this. I press on, drawing on my not entirely negligible stock of rural experience.

'Lots of grass. Now someone comes along and disturbs you. Let's say it's a farmer come to check your ear tag, OK? You look up for a minute. He's carrying a notebook. Now you just carry on chewing. It's a nice warm sunny day.'

Karl blinks. Well, it's a reaction or sorts. Is it a flutter of acquiescence? Bemusement?

'Look, I'll show you. Now I'm just play-acting OK? You're in a paddock, OK? You're with all the other cows. You're comfortable, being part of the mob. Now here I come, just checking your ear tag. But that's OK. You react like a cow right? In fact, you are a cow. Just stare at me first, then carry on eating the grass.'

I get up from my seat and sidle up to him. 'Now just take it easy; relax. I'm just the farmer. See me through cow eyes. You see me every day. It's happened before; you're just going to feel a tickling sensation behind your left ear, and you just carry on being a cow, grazing the grass, chewing the cud.'

As I touch his ear, Karl lashes out.

WELLINGTON HOSPITAL, 1988

I emerge from sleep into a world of antiseptic smells, dull, aching pain, and brightness behind my closed eyelids. 'You're in Wellington Public Hospital! You're going to be all right!' the female voice penetrates the murk, shrill, insistent. I want no part of that, and go back to sleep. A few moments, or a few minutes or maybe hours later, I hear the voice again, quieter: 'He's waking up'. My ribs ache. And now I realise my left eye is taped over. I roll over just enough to see two nurses peering at me as I open my right eye again.

'This is Mr James Sinclaire, minor concussion, abdominal bruising, contusion around left eye.' says one voice. 'Suspected fractured rib. We're waiting on the X-rays. How are you feeling Mr Sinclaire?' I can only groan.

I think I drift off again. It can't be much later though, as I hear the nurse asking,

'Any pain?' A dull ache in my abdomen and a slight headache; nothing much really.

'Just groggy', I croak, and go back to sleep.

When I wake up again it's dark. I can hear coughing, various dull electronic beeps and subdued activity. Night-time hospital sounds.

Nothing to do but think. Memories swirl up and around. The old familiar hurts, resentments, regrets, shame and anxieties. Maybe it's the accumulated effects of Zootherapy, or the drugs I'm on, that make me see these memories differently, as if they're actors on a distant stage. In the limelight, to be sure, but far away. I observe with disinterest and detachment. It's like the effect of beer on an empty stomach, or laughing gas at the dentist.

I start to question Zootherapy. Is it just a way of unleashing aggression? Beginning with Jenny, and ending with Karl, that's all it's really done, at least when practised by others. And then I recall one fresh, cold, morning at the farm. One of the cows had given birth in the field with the other dry cows, and she and her calf had to be brought up to the farm. The farmer's son was back home on vacation from agricultural college. He explained why there needed to be two of us.

'The other beasts can turn on you.' I'd never have believed it and it didn't happen to us that day, nor have I ever seen any cow show aggression. We separated the proud mother and her baby from the rest of the herd and walked them up the wet grass, without incident. But it does happen. Especially when there's a calf to protect cows can be extremely, fatally, unpredictably aggressive. Even experienced herdsmen are injured, sometimes fatally, when the cows turn nasty. (I question now whether there being two of us in the field that day would have helped.)

So... perhaps, just perhaps, Karl's lashing out wasn't so much uncontrolled aggression as appropriate behaviour? Maybe his successful attempt at Grievous Bodily Harm hadn't invalidated Zootherapy?

49

And perhaps Karl was practising Zootherapy just as I had urged him to do. He was doing just what any sensible, sensate animal – even placid herbivores - *should* do when they feel threatened. They will defend themselves.

I realise I am putting a lot of mental effort into arguing this case. I'm a true child of my times: it's not enough for me to exist in the moment, like (I assume) animals do. No, I want a system; some formula or algorithm that will guarantee that I shall always be in the moment.

So I had been the one at fault, staying in character as a human and a government employee, never expecting that a cow could exhibit behaviour other than that which I've seen in my limited exposure to them in real life, or on TV adverts for butter and cheese. I'd assumed Zootherapy would be a mechanistic procedure. A technology with specified inputs and predictable outputs. But Karl it was, who'd actually been the practising Zootherapist. I'd behaved contrary to the very principle of Zootherapy: presupposing a certain wished-for outcome; to wit: Karl behaving like any comfortably grazing cow. But (I'm high now, on whatever opiate's coursing along my bloodstream) Zootherapy is about liberating ourselves from the shackles of predetermined behaviour! It's about bypassing our intellect and giving intelligence and insight a chance to act. Our behaviours under Zootherapy cannot be foreseen; we can just trust that they will be appropriate. Hey! I've convinced myself! Good stuff!

A nurse comes by, and quietly encourages me to drink from the water jug on my bedside table. What am I doing, spinning philosophy, when there are angels like these, ministering to people with real problems, working long hours at night for very little money? She tells me it's just after 2am. I ask for pen and paper.

And this is what I write:

LESSON 4

- *The essence of Zootherapy is simple: see the world through the eyes of an animal.*

- *Don't prejudge the result. You don't know what's going to happen with Zootherapy. You can't assume it's going to be what you expect or want. In fact, Zootherapy is not at all about what the therapist or client wants: it's about suspending the 'you' for a while, and letting instinct, insight, intuition take over.*

Later I add another lesson, which I should have drawn from my first session with Jenny:

- *The effect of putting on a costume can be radical, instantaneous and startling. If you encourage someone to see the world through animal eyes, don't be surprised if they behave as an animal does.*

MORNING IN HOSPITAL

Mid-morning, and I am unceremoniously shaken awake by a nurse calling my name. A policeman stands by the bed, telling me that Karl has been cautioned. He asks me whether I wanted to press charges. I say no, which appears to be the right answer.

The next time I wake I see beside the jug of water on the stand by my bed a chirpy *Get Well Soon* card signed by Mike and my colleagues at the Ministry, featuring stylised kiwis, with grotesquely long yellow beaks, playing rugby (not my scene, but it's the thought that counts) with exuberance.

My flatmates have also been visiting. Their card says

> *"Handle every stressful situation like a dog. If you can't eat it, or play with it, just pee on it and walk away."*

They've crossed out 'dog' and written 'gorilla' instead.

With that cheerful thought, I fall asleep yet again.

I wake in the afternoon, when two nurses are discussing my case history. One of them, a trim figure, with curly brown hair and upturned nose, speaks to me. Her badge tells me her first name is Tina. 'And how are you this afternoon, Mr Sinclaire?'

I mumble that I am OK. The pager on the other nurse bleeps. She hands my charts over to Tina, and walks briskly away to the wall-phone. Tina is checking the dressings on my ribs.

''Hmmm, observation for 24 hours.' Then, more distinctly, 'So how are you doing?'

'I'm fine thanks.'

Tina looks at my case notes. 'It says you sustained these injuries in the course of your employment as an employee at the Ministry of Social Welfare. Is that right?'

'Right. I, uh, must have fallen down the stairs.'

She unwinds the bandage round my eye. I have to keep it half-closed for a couple of minutes to get used to the light. Quietly she says 'That's not very original.'

'Sorry?'

'Hey, I may look inexperienced and naïve but I've worked in paediatrics. I've seen enough child abuse cases and I'm pretty sure you don't get a black eye by falling down the stairs.'

I begin to protest. She would have none of it. She smears some ointment around my eye.

'Or walking into a door or anything like that. A black eye means someone hit you.'

'Well....' She ignores me, and begins to record my blood pressure.

'So who was it; a disgruntled taxpayer? A client who hadn't taken his medication? Or are you one of those battered husbands we see on *60 Minutes*?'

'I ..er.. I'm not married'. I've become aware of my unfortunate and utterly counterproductive habit of seeing every pretty, not-obviously-attached female as a potential life partner. But that doesn't stop me. Why is she being nice to me? Is it just part of the job, like being in retail or serving drinks on a plane? That must be it. She's doing valuable work, for heaven's sake. She's got her act together. And so the excuses for inaction proliferate: fear of being rejected and, always, the upwelling memories of my parents' marriage, the arguments, the shouting, the smashed-up furniture.

Besides, what could she see in me? Could she be feeling affection for me, after all of five minutes? But, as with the existence of God Himself, the yearning to believe in it doesn't mean it's not true. And I'm the guy with the gorilla costume; OK it's at home but I can use my imagination. Gorilla-James (or it might be the drugs) kicks in. The excuses, memories, arguments and counter-arguments, the hang-ups; I peer at her through my one functioning gorilla eye and they vanish in an instant. She's not wearing a wedding ring. I smile:

'Well, Nurse Tina, how about I tell it you all about it over a cup of coffee once I'm out of here?' Confidence faked is indistinguishable from confidence real. And so....

COFFEE WITH TINA

A few days later, it's a Thursday afternoon. I'm out of hospital and off work sick till Monday. My chest aches a little less, and I now have two working eyes; one of them surrounded by a fascinating swirl of yellow and purple. I'm at a table in a coffee shop near the hospital. Opposite me is Tina; it's her day off. She's bright and chirpy. After the usual preliminaries, I talk of the Gorillagram, of my female interviewees, and my own solo role play experiments. Her enthusiasm is a delight. Sparks fly between us.

'What a fabulous idea!'

'You really think so?'

'Well, it works doesn't it? Obvious and effective. Brilliant! Too simple and revolutionary for the medical profession to take seriously of course.'

I tell her about Karl, and how I ended up in hospital. She's ahead of me. Though she's always lived in the city, like most kiwis she knows more about farming through osmosis than I learned in my entire year on the farm.

'Well if it hadn't happened, we'd not be here now.' She says nothing for a moment. I think: wow, a woman who's brash enough to hint that she likes me. Then:

'Why don't you, you know, make people pay for it? It's a useful service. You could make a living doing it. A sort of therapy.'

'They're all on welfare – it wouldn't be right. It's not as if I studied anything for it.'

'I don't mean your welfare beneficiaries. I mean paying customers. People with cash.'

Why don't I? There are lots of reasons. I'm from the old world: of course there are.

'It's not what I'm trained to do. I'm not qualified. I haven't studied animals, nor worked with them. And it's not exactly rocket surgery is it?'

Tina laughs 'No, but then rocket surgery isn't rocket science and brain science isn't brain surgery. I'm a nurse. I know these things.'

I have another excuse: 'It's too simple. Putting on an animal costume – where's the skill in that?'

'If it works, James, doesn't matter how simple it is. Make it seem complicated if that's what it takes.'

And I'm still not sure. It had *seemed* to work with the ladies who'd been in violent relationships. It seems to work for me. But then Karl came along. OK, I guess you could say it still worked, so long as Karl had been imagining himself as a newly-calved cow, or one of her gang. There was a more solid objection; one that operated at every level of my psyche: the convenient government habit of injecting $935.22 into my bank account every fortnight.

 'I don't want to lose my salary.'

'You could rent an office somewhere cheap. See how it goes. You've got a degree right?

'Only Bachelor's at the moment, from England.'

'No problem; put your certificate on the wall. Frame it.'

'And give up my job?'

'No need. Not at first. See how you get on. Work evenings and Saturdays on the animal therapy. And take a couple of afternoons off work. You're on glidetime now? Work some nine-hour days. You can do that. I work 12-hour shifts. You get used to it.'

It was so easy, when she put it like that. I'd probably have to take longer to do my Master's. And back in England, trying to find a new career, I'd done an introductory course in podiatry. A correspondence course, sure, but I'd passed their exam and they'd given me a certificate (as well as a plastic foot). That could also go on the be framed and put on my office wall.

The old world wouldn't quite let me go: 'What about the expenses; the office, the costumes for different animals? It's a bit of a risk.'

'Listen, my ex is sharing a flat with a make-up artist. She's can get all sorts of costumes from the movie studios. We've gone to theme parties.' Her ex. This is interesting. Does it mean I'm in with a chance? 'They've got a warehouse full of the stuff. Why don't you put an ad in the paper?'

'What, for clients?'

'*Paying* clients. Just do it. Call it something like Advanced Role-play Counselling, something like that.'

It's feasible. Regulation is sparse and unsystematic. How can it be otherwise in a country with a population of fewer than 3.5 million? There just aren't the resources for bureaucratic follow through. Finance companies go bust all the time, hundreds of small savers lose everything, while the directors make off with millions. Cars routinely shoot through red traffic lights. Hypnotists are still allowed to go on stage and perform demeaning acts on audience members. Food poisonings – like Jason's campylobacter – aren't especially rare. Of course there are laws and regulations, but enforcement is patchy. And prisons are full to bursting. The upside is that there are few obstacles in the way of starting up a new business.

Tina settles the argument:

'If you don't charge for it, nobody will value it.'

True enough. This is mid-1980s New Zealand, the years of Rogernomics when free markets are supplanting heavy-handed government intervention (and, I suspect, God) as our new organising principle. New Zealand has been transformed into Adam Smith's Isles in a few short years. The whole economy is being revamped by the ideologues at Treasury who are dedicated to imposing Chicago

School economics on our small, hitherto egalitarian country. 'User pays' is the mantra; markets our religion.

We in the Ministry of Social Welfare know something about New Zealand's new guiding economic paradigm partly because we have to pick up some of the pieces, and partly because the government bureaucracy itself is being reshaped in an attempt to replicate in the public sector the resource allocation mechanisms that, supposedly, make the private sector so wonderfully efficient.

And so, in obeisance to the Zeitgeist, I step diffidently into the commercial world. I rent an office in the gloomy upper reaches of a massive hulk of a building called the Harbour City Centre in Lambton Quay. I'm just along the corridor from a homeopath, next door to an acupuncturist of Chinese origin with a sparse, spikey moustache who speaks little English. We're several floors above the more soigné offices of dentists, osteopaths and taxation accountants. I pay three months' rent in advance, and hang my podiatry and degree certificates (framed) on the wall. There's some old furniture inherited from the previous tenant (a prisoners' rights organisation): a metal desk and two tubular steel chairs, with fading blue canvas. I've bought an easy chair from a garage sale. A small ad in the *Evening Post* and I'm ready to go.

Tina has delivered on the costumes. Or rather her ex, Duane, a policeman, has, through the good graces of his current squeeze (Tina's word: '...and she's welcome to him.'), the make-up artist, and her colleagues in the film business.

There's a fair sprinkling of mythical animal costumes, including a unicorn and a centaur, but I prefer the real animals; the ones with established behaviours that I, and therefore everyone else, will know about or, more accurately, think we know about. There's only one size of costume for each animal, but that's OK. Depending mainly on the animal some, like the gorilla costume, cover the face except for the eye-holes. Others have an open face; more practical in some ways; they cover only the top of the head and neck, leaving facial features and cues visible. Either will be fine: my paid sessions will last just one hour, and the costumes aren't going to be worn for the whole session.

PETER

A Saturday morning, a fortnight or so after my advert began appearing in the Wednesday and Saturday editions of the *Evening Post*.

Sitting across from my desk is my first paying customer. Peter reminds me of Clark Kent as portrayed in the *Superman* comics of my childhood, but with greying temples and a receding hairline. A mild-mannered, bespectacled, self-employed, man in his mid-40s, sole proprietor of a business importing European (read: 'upmarket') kitchen units. We'd had our initial session a week ago: a thirty-minute free consultation. I offer those to prepare myself for the actual Zootherapy session, and to give me time to get hold of the relevant costume. I also think it's helpful to build in the client a sense of anticipation before beginning the costume work.

Peter's problem, he'd explained in our preliminary session, is that he feels insufficiently aggressive and indecisive.

'You see, I've always employed family till quite recently. And I'm pretty sure the guy who does my books is ripping me off. There's nothing that would stand up in a court of law though. But I want him gone.'

Ah! That's the immediate problem. 'Right. So you got used to treating your employees with some degree of latitude?'

'I've just got into the habit of avoiding confrontation.' I nod, sagely. 'And your ad said "Behaviour Modification", so here I am.' He hasn't actually come on his own initiative. He's here at the urging of his wife.

Last week I'd given him a pre-emptive disclaimer about how I'm not qualified to give financial or psychological advice. I'm a graduate student and social worker, I told him, trying out a new form of therapy - which is why my rates are so reasonable. I was aiming to give the impression that I had been experienced and successful in England in a different, unspecified, line of business, but am trying something new in New Zealand; this, I hope, would explain the tatty office, the mismatched furniture, and my corduroy jacket with the worn elbows. But I don't think Peter cares very much about all that. He doesn't question me too closely; no doubt as a way of avoiding confrontation. In this respect he's ideal as my first paying customer.

Now it's time to begin, for real.

'Right. Tell me, Mr McAdams, what do you know about the rhinoceros?

'Rhinos? Not much. There's not many left. Aren't they breeding them in the Zoo? They had a baby recently? It was on the front page of the *Post*.' (I'm pretty certain it was actually a baby hippo, but I let that go.)

'Ok,' I said, 'let me read something to you'.

I've photocopied something from the University Library:

> *Although not habitually violent, especially towards humans, rhinos may exhibit bursts of aggressiveness. Fortunately for their enemies, their poor eyesight prevents them from making targeted attacks, at least until they are provoked.*

I emphasise the last sentence:

Their senses of smell and hearing however are well developed.

With the confidence that only my private gorilla sessions could give me, I open the big metal drawer on the right-hand side of my desk. Built for suspended files, it contains the rhinoceros head-and-shoulders costume that has been temporarily liberated from Tina's ex's girlfriend's place of work, the warehouse in Petone wherein all New Zealand's TV and film costumes are stored. I've had to apply butter to the threads of the plastic horn, and I've had a few practice goes at it, so this time it screws on cleanly, burnishing, I hope, my professional image. Peter looks puzzled.

'What's this?' he asks as I present him with the rhino head.

'It's just a form of role play. Don't be embarrassed. Nobody's watching. You'll need to take your jacket off.' He looks quizzical, 'Trust me', I say, 'the hardest part is putting it on.'

He begins to take off his jacket, then hesitates.

'Mr Sinclaire, I'm sorry.' He laid the costume down. 'This is ridiculous; is this some sort of joke?' (Assertiveness! I think optimistically; has my pre-Zootherapy pump-priming already begun to work?)

'Could you humour me please, Mr McAdams?' More self-conscious than my welfare clients, and perhaps less desperate, Peter needs more convincing. He's shaking his head.

'Surely you've heard of the placebo effect?', I ask. A tentative nod. 'It's when a doctor gives a physiologically inactive sugar pill to a patient who then takes it, and is relieved of his symptoms.' Another nod. 'Well', I continue, 'the interesting thing is that even if the patient knows it's just a sugar pill, it still works.'

Peter looks quizzical. 'Mr McAdams, it's a real effect. It's been peer-reviewed; double-blind, randomised control trials – that sort of thing. It's well known and it's been widely replicated. So humour me. I know it seems ridiculous, but just go along with it for now.'

He's not buying it. 'I can't....'

'Mr McAdams, trust is essential to the behaviour modification process.' I expected to have to make this speech. ('Faith' would be a better word than 'trust', but appealing to faith is out of synch with the times.) 'There's total privacy here. There's no cameras, no wire, nothing. What happens in this room is between me and you. You've paid your fees and you are of course free to terminate the therapeutic process right now and at any time hereafter. It's entirely up to you. But I think it would help both of us if you were to participate in the process, whatever reservations you might have.' I smile. Conspiratorially, I hope. 'Humour me.'

He gives in, takes off his jacket, puts on the top half of the rhino costume (I don't bother with the trousers), and I help him with the rhino head, whose heavy plastic horn makes it awkward to handle.

Wellington's a small town and everybody's just a couple of degrees of separation from everyone else. So it isn't difficult to find out what transpired in Peter's office a week or so later.

Picture this: Peter and the dubious book-keeper, a guy I'll call Pritchard, are in his office, both in business suits. Peter stands behind his desk; Pritchard sits on the other side. Blue-tacked onto the wall facing Peter is a large poster I've given him of an antelope grazing in the wild. I've gone to some effort, with the help of a photography friend to get this image enlarged, from a colour plate in a used book about the fauna of southern Africa I'd picked up in Cuba Street. It shows the antelope as it would be seen by a beast of prey, grazing nonchalantly on the scrub. My pal, at my request, had inserted a fuzzy prominence occupying the lower-centre of the frame, to represent a rhino's horn, as I imagine it would be perceived by the rhino himself.

Peter begins shouting at Pritchard – he's easily heard from outside his office. Edited (by my source, rather than me), this is what is heard: 'You absolute bastard! You're evil; you know that? You've ripped me off; you've ripped off everyone in this company. I trusted you and look how you repaid me! You're a thief and I'm going to ruin you.'

Then (I imagine) he stands up, narrowing his eyes, and walking round his desk so that Pritchard and the picture of the antelope move into alignment: the picture immediately behind Pritchard and begins a slow, lumbering charge at Pritchard. He bellows:

'Get out of here. Get out and don't come back! If I see you again I'm going to gore you to death!'

At that point the door Peter's office door bursts open, and Pritchard dashes through it, blurring past the ordinarily unflappable secretary, heading straight for the staircase. In the sudden silence there is only the diminishing sound of Pritchard's footsteps as he hurriedly descends the stairs on his way to the exit.

Peter is seen punching the air before he calmly closes the door. Some time later he emerges to tell his drop-jawed secretary that Pritchard is no longer with the company, and would she please clear Pritchard's desk and send his effects on to his home address?

My first business success. Occasionally I see Peter amidst the pedestrian traffic on Lambton Quay. Client confidentiality means that I don't acknowledge him, but some weeks later, when we've both been working late, we spy each other across an almost deserted Lambton Quay. He takes the initiative, stopping me, and thanking me for my help. I already know he's appreciative, because a couple of new clients have given his name when I asked how they know about me.

But in my initial elation immediately after hearing of Peter's success, the doubts that first struck me while in hospital after Karl, resurface. Again Zootherapy appears to have encouraged aggression. It seems to have the effect of making all my clients, paying or not, more aggressive. Am I sowing dragon's teeth? The kiwi Einstein, a mini-Oppenheimer unleashing the destructive potential of the uninhibited psyche? You're on a roll, James, don't let up on the self-dramatisation! But it's true, isn't it? I turned a normally passive, genial man into a murderous maniac. Temporarily, to be sure, but then all history's mass murderers had their downtime. Do the ends justify the means? Could Zootherapy generate violence in otherwise placid people? This is not Britain, I remind myself, where I could count on my madcap ideas being shot down by the 'Establishment' almost before they get off the ground. I've got responsibilities here.

But maybe a bit of violence, strategically deployed at an early stage, is the least worst option. Targeted assassinations of Stalin, Hitler, Mao, Pol Pot could have saved millions of lives in the twentieth century. OK Pritchard was no mass murderer, but then we didn't liquidate him, did we? He'd been caught with his fingers in the till and all I've done is er... 'facilitate' his sacking from his part-time job doing accounts for Peter.

Nope: my conscience is clear. The abused wives and Peter all *needed* a bit of animal aggression. Their micro-acts of violence were defensive, appropriate and justifiable, just as when Karl lashed out at me for pretending to ear-tag him, as he was about to be molested by a government employee. Anyway, that led to my hospitalisation and that led to Tina.

And then, less unconvincingly, though more difficult to articulate, has been my own Zootherapy experience: those islands of peace

63

when I don the gorilla costume at home. The lightening of the psychic load. The removal of the screen between me and the rest of the world. The immediacy of perception; those fleeting, precious moments when my mind is quiet. And so I again see Zootherapy as a means of bypassing the stuff that gets in the way of doing the right thing. All's well in my world again. This optimistic edifice is reinforced by the (regrettable) fact that the only widely accepted measure of a product or service's validity in the New Zealand of 1990 is the revenue it brings in, and I'm doing all right on that score too.

MY ARTICLE IN THE *DOMINION*

My article in the *Dominion*. I wrote it about three months ago, but they delayed publication until precisely the time when its appearance would maximise the Government's embarrassment: the day an international comparison of youth suicide rates in the rich countries is published, showing New Zealand in its usual, shameful position near the top of the table. My article is one of two, talking about a range of diverse, innovative approaches to mental health issues that the Government could usefully consider. I give a brief mention of Zootherapy and express my doubts about the different sorts of therapy that governments favour: basically medication, rather than anything that involves actually meeting and listening to people. I don't single out New Zealand. I point out that other countries are even more comfortable with pharmaceutical fixes. I describe my early experiences with clients. And, I've ensured that after my screed, there's a statement emphasising that, though I am employed by the Ministry of Social Welfare, these are my own personal views. You'd think that would suffice.

It doesn't. The *Dominion* has given my piece a prominent position on the same page as an editorial condemning the Government's 'mean-spirited and unimaginative approach to New Zealand's mental health crisis'. Image matters at least as much to politicians as reality, and the urgent need to find a scapegoat cascades swiftly from the top. The Minister of Social Welfare berates our Director-General (new, and a little insecure), who berates Trish, the Director of our unit, who berates Mike, who calls me into his office and explains that he has to give me a written warning, the first step of the thousand-mile journey that could lead to my formal dismissal from the New Zealand public service.

Mike forbids me now from practising Zootherapy on Ministry premises at any time. He warns me against writing anything about Zootherapy or indeed anything else in any public forum at all, ever. These conditions, presented to me by a hesitant, clearly unhappy, but unapologetic Mike, are decisive. I do like Mike, and I feel a twinge of sympathy. He's upset and angry, not so much with me, I suspect, but because his superiors are taking it out on him and he is now having to behave out of character towards me. If I stay on, I'll damage Mike's career and have to give up Zootherapy. No contest. I go back to my desk, have a think for all of five minutes, then do the decent thing and resign from the Ministry.

I LEAVE THE MINISTRY, 1990

My last day, and there's a pleasant, subdued, farewell do with my group at morning tea time, the sun streaming through the north-facing windows. Mike and I make short, gracious speeches, as we cluster round the tea trolley, supplemented for this occasion, with doughnuts and salted peanuts. In the afternoon Mike treats me to a coffee and muffin at the Midland Park Café. We sit outside in the sun, a stiff breeze occasionally sending a fine rainbow mist from the fountain in our direction.

As he lights up, cupping his hand over the flame 'That's how it's always been in social welfare. We work hard, we achieve things, we help people, but if we make one slip they crucify us. You're lucky;

you're getting out of it.' He sighs. 'It's our mistakes that make the headlines.' I can only agree.

I'm sad to be missing my colleagues and the camaraderie, but I'm also partly relieved. I had my doubts about the Ministry and its ever-expanding remit. I've learned something important: the bureaucracy is quite different from the sum of its parts. The guys I worked with were all rounded, likable people. The system, though, is more interested in its survival and expansion than its goals as stated in its mission statement. Organisations, I guess, unlike people, go on for ever: they thrive by making themselves indispensable. Their over-arching goal is self-perpetuation. Job security for employees, sure – until they rock the boat. Then the system crashes down on you like a ton of bricks. Not just government bodies, I muse, but churches, trade unions, universities.... OK, I'm dramatising here, and I guess there's a hint of sour grapes. Still, I'm not too unhappy to depart the Ministry, just before it begins its eighth restructuring since I started there three years ago.

So it's time to move on. With no dependants and no car I'm not particularly worried about money: the housemates have gone our separate ways but I still live modestly, renting a couple of draughty rooms in an old house on The Terrace. I'm getting enough from my Zootherapy clients to keep me going. I still have time to work on my Master's and I now live an easy walking distance to both the university and my office. A final pint of beer at The Oxford with my ex-colleagues marks my departure from the New Zealand public service.

ACCESS RADIO, 1990

Wellington's alternative radio station, Access Radio, broadcasts every Sunday afternoon. They approach me, having seen my *Dominion* article and ads in the *Evening Post,* and give Zootherapy a slot in between the Sri Lankan Community Roundup, and the local lesbian chat show. Radio alchemy converts the 30-minute slot into 13 minutes of just the interviewer and myself, plus another 12 minutes with the interviewer, me and, online from Switzerland, a Maurice Krumzinger, apparently a professor, an award-winning author, and a cultural anthropologist. A bit of publicity can't hurt, I think. The interviewer's a keen young man, name of Hugh.

Hugh: tell us a bit about yourself.

Sinclaire: I was born and educated in England, and emigrated to New Zealand in 1985.

Hugh: What made you come to New Zealand?

Sinclaire: I wanted to live in a country of peace; a long way from Britain's, and all the world's troubles; all the talk of nuclear weapons, the miners' strike. At primary school we had a teacher from New Zealand: tall, bronzed, charismatic: I'm sure that influenced me too.

Hugh: What do you think about New Zealand?

Sinclaire: It's been good to me and especially to Zootherapy.

Hugh: Could you please tell our listeners exactly what is Zootherapy?

Sinclaire: It's a way of encouraging people to access their own animal talents and insight. A sort of role play.

Hugh: It started with a gorilla costume, right?

Sinclaire: Yes, I won't say too much because, you know, client confidentiality. But yes, I have used a gorilla costume in my Zootherapy practice.

Hugh: And how does that work?

Sinclaire: Well, for some people, some of the time, behaving as they imagine a gorilla will behave releases certain tensions and inhibitions, and the benefits of Zootherapy can carry over into everyday life.

Hugh: So how long does this Zootherapy take to learn?

Sinclaire: It's more about unlearning, Hugh. But it's not learning about unlearning. It's creating an environment within which it's more likely that you'll unlearn. You see the world through animal eyes. But you keep what's necessary of the human world. It's like (pause) I don't know (pause) you know, Robinson Crusoe. We enter a new and pristine animal world of vitality and living in the present, but with our intellectual faculties there as a bonus to be used only when necessary. But if they're over-used, these human faculties create problems. There's things animals do better than us –

Hugh: Like what?

Sinclaire: Well, animals don't torture or kill their own, like we do. That's a good starting point: if we're behaving worse than animals, then maybe we should question why that is. And also if we're more depressed than animals. We should ask why that is.

Hugh: OK. Right. And how long does it take to learn Zootherapy?

Sinclaire: I've seen good results in a couple of sessions, but most people need a few more.

Hugh: Any failures?

Sinclaire: Two or three *apparent* failures. I think it's like anything else: people have not necessarily got to want change but they do have to be open to the possibility of change. But with Zootherapy we don't always know what sort of change we'll see: only that it will be appropriate for the client. Some people resist that, but I like to think that the sessions open up new pathways in the mind that will be activated later in their life.

Hugh: Er...OK. Some people are saying Zootherapy is just a licence to behave like an animal. You, like, you know, free sex, or just grabbing somebody else's food whenever you see it.

Sinclaire: They've got completely the wrong idea. First, animals are actually quite sophisticated when they're in their own environment. They've evolved ways of dealing with sex and property and territory. Second, sure, Zootherapy is about getting rid of our inhibitions but only so that we behave appropriately. It makes us take in all the circumstances, rather than just our own desires. That's what we, as humans are good at.

Hugh: Okaaaay.

Sinclaire: Look, giraffes have a long neck, elephants have a trunk, spiders have eight legs, right? Well, humans have the capacity to over-ride our instincts for the greater good.

I find I often have a great idea, a clinching argument, but by the time I open my mouth and start speaking, I've forgotten it. This was one of those occasions. What I'd wanted to say, I'm sure, would have tied up those loose ends, but I couldn't think of the words or the gist of my argument. Fortunately....

Hugh: At this point I'd like to bring in Professor Maurice Krumzinger, on the line from Zurich in Switzerland, right on the other side of the world. Thank you Professor, and I suppose I should say good morning to you and welcome to the programme.

Krumzinger: Very good to be with you.

I imagine him as a neat, precise, figure with a pointed beard, and his voice is consistent with that. But I've done this with people on the phone before and I invariably get it wrong. He's probably a big bear of a man, with a shaggy black mane of hair, dressed in a tracksuit and sneakers.

Hugh: Professor Krumzinger, why don't you start by telling us your own ideas about Zootherapy.

Krumzinger: I think it's very interesting that Mr Sinclaire began his movement with gorillas. You see, the ape represents the human at the pre-developmental stage. So when Mr Sinclaire dresses people up as apes, he's saying 'There are unresolved issues in your early life. We're going to go back to an earlier time and will evolve properly this time.'

Naturally, I want to say something here. I mean, gorillagrams might be passé everywhere else, but in New Zealand they're a thing. If you want to send an animated human birthday greeting to someone in Wellington, you're limited to either commissioning someone to dress up as a gorilla, or hiring a young, nubile female to do a slow striptease. It's either a gorilla suit or a sequined bikini and feather boa. But I try to be understanding and put my energies instead into performing some postural neck retraction exercises. (Something I'd learned to do at the Ministry: how else to endure our Monday morning meetings?) The professor just wants to see Zootherapy through his own grid of knowledge. A common failing. A bit later, when Hugh asks about any downsides to Zootherapy, and I reveal that my transformative session with my first abused woman client (Jenny) had drawn blood, the professor is unstoppable:

Krumzinger: Very interesting. The scratch on Mr Sinclaire's face was an offering of sacrificial blood, so to speak. He was in effect offering up to the gods his career as a social worker. And in fact Mr Sinclaire is echoing what many thinkers have said before: that we need to develop a more intuitive understanding of animals. Why, back in 1928 an American by the name of Henry Beston -

Hugh: That's great, Professor. Turning to you, James Sinclaire, I believe you recently left the public service, and are now working as a full-time Zootherapist?

Sinclaire: That's right. I'm in the Harbour City Centre. You can look me up in the Yellow Pages, under Alternative Medicine.

Hugh: And how is that going?

Sinclaire: Well, it's been a slow start.

I hesitate. I want to encourage new clients, but I don't want to give the impression that I don't have any at the moment. Fortunately, Krumzinger fills the air time:

Krumzinger: Mr Sinclaire did something noble. He was prepared to sacrifice his government salary for the greater good of humankind. There are fascinating parallels with the Christian theme of renunciation. The Passion most obviously but the theme has resonances in every extant culture.

It keeps the show going, but I still I find this stuff irritating, mainly because I have a tendency to do it myself: all this rationalising something that I discovered by chance. You couldn't prove or disprove any of it. I suppose some of it could be true at some level. But so what? The whole point about Zootherapy is to ditch these theories and anything else that comes between us and the world. At least the professor isn't asking whether I'm serious. Eventually he pauses, and I deliver a summing up I've prepared beforehand:

> Sinclaire: We can't know everything about everything. We can't really know everything about anything. We all need to do a bit of screening. We do it with words and theories, beliefs in God or the free market or whatever. All useful screening devices, which save us having to make decisions all the time. But there are times when these screens get in our way. Zootherapy is a way to living life without the interference of these screens.

As after my *Dominion* piece, there's a brief but welcome flurry of interest in Zootherapy, whose most helpful manifestation is a boost in my client numbers. My clients are a mix of private individuals, and employees of smallish Wellington companies. There's some demand for assertiveness techniques, but more for general behavioural goals; mostly aimed at losing weight or giving up smoking. Despite offering a free initial consultation and relatively low rates thereafter, I am almost making my government salary. There's more book-keeping and administration for tax purposes, but I am my own boss now.

My life is changing in other ways too. Tina and I are seeing quite a bit of each other.

ELEPHANTS, 1992
'Harder, deeper. Oh yeeeesssss!'

The year 1992. It's Saturday, mid-morning; Tina's stayed over. I'm wearing the head and shoulders of a beautifully crafted glossy horse costume, peeping through the eye holes. We're having sex, and I'm taking Tina from behind; one of the more practical configurations, given the length of the horse's head.

Lying in bed Tina afterwards says 'You know, you don't need to bother with all the other animals. You could just do stallions. Make a fortune from middle-aged guys who can't get it up. Better than ginseng or oysters; more fun; no risk of food poisoning.'

Now there's a thought. Our sex life would have been good anyway, but putting on an animal costume does remove your inhibitions. Animals seem to manage without our hang-ups and performance anxieties. Hmm... perhaps that's why masks are such a feature in the world of kinky sex. Whatever, Tina does like wearing the snake costume I've had made specially for our more elaborate night-time sex manoeuvres.

After a lazy lie-in, Tina gets out of bed, climbs over the rest of the horse costume on the floor, puts on a robe, and begins to make coffee. She takes the rubbish out as the water in the jug starts boiling. A few minutes later, she returns with two mugs of coffee on the tray, and the mail from the letterbox.

'A and E tonight.'

It's the 12-hour Saturday night shift: 10pm to 10am. 'Ugh'.

'I don't mind on Saturdays. We're busy. No time to think.'

I open the mail. 'Hey, you know how I couldn't get hold of a decent elephant costume anywhere in New Zealand?'

'I thought you're getting one from that interwebby thing at Varsity?'

Yes, business has moved on, and I'd been looking for a costume for my male clients; the ones who want to tone down their aggressive tendencies. There were cow and sheep costumes at Duane's partner's storage facility, but I wanted something more masculine. I'd had the horse and snake suits made up, at vast cost, from a local theatrical supplier. But being a graduate student at Victoria University, I have access to their computer terminals. Mainly I use

73

them for word-processing and the odd bit of data-crunching but recently we were connected to the World Wide Web. Very useful for research for my thesis. I now have an electronic-mail account and access to Usenet – those bulletin boards about any subject you could imagine. On there you can buy and sell things, and I eventually found someone in New York City willing to sell me an elephant outfit.

'Yeah, well, Mr Elephant's arrived and they're holding him at Shed 4 on the wharf.' I glance down the page. 'Wow, that's steep: 149 dollars for customs and fumigation.'

WHARFSIDE, 1992

Monday lunchtime I go down to the wharf. Though crossing Custom House Quay is something of a challenge, it's striking how short the journey is from the service economy – the offices, bureaucrats, symbol manipulators, shape-shifters and psychographic market micro-segmenters - to the real world of heavy machinery, goods, and fuel tanks, where mistakes have immediate, physical consequences and blame can't be diffused. At times like this, I realise just how deeply I have been immersed in a secondary reality for...well, most of my life really. Fifty million people in the country in which I was brought up; plenty of scope for specialising in the world of words, equations, exams, memos, slide shows, spreadsheets, meetings and so self-extrudingly on and on. It's humbling, being surrounded by stacks of shipping containers and cranes and I feel a tad guilty. I've had it so easy, being insulated from nature in the raw, from the lashing southerlies and sea swells. But I'm also a bit envious: the wharfies' work is definite, undeniable, real. They get results that are visible, results that are an objective reality, not a matter of debate and obfuscation. Things don't have to work in theory; only in practice.

It's a sunny, breezy day. There's no visible security. I walk right in amongst the shipping containers, most of them stacked two high. It's quiet and there are eerily few men about. I see a guy in an orange hard hat walking around, looking at labels on the containers, talking into a mobile phone. He sees the quizzical look on my face, points to the wharf office and resumes his phone conversation.

In the office, there's a ginger-haired guy keying something into a massive computer occupying a third of the area of his desk. An orange hard hat is plonked down on a heap of pink papers on top of a metal filing cabinet. The guy looks up briefly, then back at his computer monitor, saying he won't be a minute. There's a smouldering cigarette in an ashtray on the desk, a mug of what looks like coffee and a fax machine on the floor. When he looks up, I show him the letter about the elephant costume.

'Just a moment'. He goes back to the computer, exits whatever he was doing, and begins keying in the reference number, deliberately. 'Okie dokie. It's just out here.'

Grabbing his hard hat and a mobile phone, he leads me out back onto the wharf. He seems relieved to be outside. We walk a short distance, threading a way between container stacks.

He points to a non-descript shipping container, standing beneath another. 'That's the one', he says, checking his docket. 'OK, you got a truck, or you want it delivered?'

I tell him I don't have a truck. 'Can't we open it up, find my parcel,' (In this setting I can't bring myself to say 'elephant costume') 'and I can just pay for it now?'

'What do you mean, open it?'

'It's just one item. A special outfit. Adult size.'

'Yeah; one container.' I look bemused. 'You're getting whatever's in this container. Let's see,' he reads the docket 'Fifty-eight assorted adult and children's sizes theatrical costumes in form of elephant. Country of Loading: United States of America; Country of Manufacture: People's Republic of China.'

'I thought I just ordered one.... ' My voice trails away as I realise what must have happened.

I had had to steel myself to pay the high price asked for what I thought was a single elephant costume 'in container', in what the vendor had advertised as a distress sale. I can guess now what probably happened. I'd either misread the internet bulletin board posting, or misinterpreted the word 'container'. So rather than paying too much for one elephant costume, I've paid a very low per unit price for a 20-foot shipping container full of them. I've bought myself a literal truckload of elephant costumes for what would be a bargain price, if I actually wanted all of them. That would explain the high cost of uplifting my purchase, and the customs inspection and fumigation charges.

The wharfie asks whether I want to take delivery now. Seems there's quite a steep daily charge for leaving the container on the wharf, so I ask whether I can use his office phone to make a local call.

I check the time and ring Tina. She finished her night shift at 4am, and should be awake by now.

'Tina. Listen. It's something of an emergency. Can you speak to your mum and dad?'

A couple of hours later Tina and I find myself outside the (fortunately) three-car garage at her parents' place in Khandallah. We're standing together, Tina, her mum and me, while the truck drives away with its now-empty container. (All the backing up and unloading in this hitherto quiet street is, I suspect, is going to be the

.

main feature of upcoming neighbourhood coffee mornings and bridge nights.) The elephant costumes, wrapped in layers of thick translucent plastic, are inelegantly piled up along one side of the garage. The tusks are packed separately, in long thin cardboard boxes and are stacked along the other side.

'I'm sorry about this.' For all my contrition, I think Tina's mum is quite amused by it all. I turn to Tina: 'I guess I can always use a couple of them; maybe the Salvation Army will take the rest. I know they do collect. Failing that, there's always landfill.'

'Well you know,' Tina said brightly, 'they might not be completely useless.'

'Yeah you're right. There's sure to be a re-enactment of Hannibal crossing the Alps some day now. It happens all the time. Especially in Wellington.'

She pokes my stomach.

'Silly. Let me ask around.'

PRISON

On a Tuesday afternoon a month later, I find myself standing in front of a group of about 20 convicted male felons in a large, grim, multi-purpose (there are yellow duct-taped five-a-side soccer pitch markings on the dark green resinous floor) arena of the Wellington prison at Mount Crawford. They're not the hardest of criminals – their sentences have all been for 18 months or less – so only four prison guards are there, standing about to ensure the peace. These prisoners are all due to be released in the next few months and they are the ones who've behaved themselves best during their incarceration. They've attended training programmes and, I'm told, have expressed remorse for their misdeeds. Through Duane and the good graces of the prison governors, I've been given the chance to talk to them about Zootherapy twice a week for three weeks, for which the Department of Corrections will pay me a handy one hundred dollars per session. I'm not supposed to treat the prisoners in any formal sense, which would require all sorts of permits, supporting statements from the medical profession, and qualifications that I just don't have. Because Zootherapy has no official recognition the bureaucracy has categorised my afternoon as an 'entertainment/informational lecture'. (Apparently, similarly privileged groups had been treated to sessions with a cellist from the New Zealand Symphony Orchestra, an astrophysicist from the Carter Observatory, and a reformed cannabis retailer who now runs an upholstery business in Wainuiomata.) It's an austere, cheerless environment and there's nothing glamorous about this occasion, my first group presentation, but talking about Zootherapy is a great way of reminding myself to practise Zootherapy myself. I'm buzzing with confidence.

I'm standing before this group of men with a TV and video player playing a video cassette from Wellington Library: a National Geographic documentary about elephants. (Technically, I suppose, this is a public performance, and I might be doing something illegal but, this being New Zealand, it's never occurred to me to check.) Each prisoner sits on a white plastic chair, next to which lies his elephant costume. Tina and I have prepared them all. It was trickier than you might think; the tusks are a hard, dense, plastic, surprisingly heavy, and their curvature makes them awkward to handle. It took us much of the weekend and copious amounts of sewing machine oil to get them all nicely screwed in.

On the TV screen we see elephants browsing somewhere in the African bush, and hear the earnest US-accented narration:

> Despite their enormous size, elephants are mostly placid animals. They are vegetarian and like nothing more than spending their days, browsing amongst the trees for their leafy diet.

A few minutes later, I stop the video player and talk to the prisoners.

'OK you've seen how elephants behave, just walking slowly about, gently browsing the shrubs and trees. No drama, no aggression. Now you're going to be elephants for a while.'

One of the prisoners, an unshaven brick wall of a man, trumpets like an elephant. Then so do some of the others, while others laugh. The guards noticeably bristle, then relax.

'That's fine. Now please put on your costumes. Don't worry about how you look; nobody's taking pictures.'

I'm surprised when the prisoners put on their elephant costumes without any of the resistance or bemusement I've noticed with my individual clients. Perhaps they've grown used to following instructions. They make a surreal, faintly comical scene, with the tusks pointing in all directions and the elephant mouths seeming to smile. Once the ribald comments about the length and thickness of the dangling rubbery trunks have died down I continue:

'Now just forget everything you know about where you are, or what you're doing here, or what happens when you leave here. You're elephants.' I've shucked off the role of entertainer now and, if the governors but knew it, am wandering into therapy territory, but I'm enjoying this and I sense the prisoners too, perhaps anticipating their imminent freedom, are on a bit of a high. 'You're the biggest beasts in the jungle. Nobody's threatening you. Just relax and enjoy the company of your elephant friends.'

The prisoners do exactly as I ask. They walk about, following instructions, emitting trumpet sounds, some more convincingly than others, in apparent spontaneity.

As with my other clients, I mix theory and practice in this and the five subsequent sessions. I see the prisoners on Tuesdays and

Thursdays, with excerpts from different elephant documentaries, slightly different instructions, but the same costumes, and the same overall expectations.

It's at this point that television companies outside Wellington, and even a few overseas media people become interested in Zootherapy. I'm naïve, I suppose, but still a bit miffed not to have been consulted. But the elephant costumes *are* photogenic and so Zootherapy first appears on TV as the jokey item at the end of New Zealand Television's evening news bulletin. It shows the prison governor posing with an elephant costume, then being 'persuaded' to put the headpiece on. It's a shame that Zootherapy is allotted the same slot as recently occupied by the first topless croquet match in New Zealand and the dog in Taihape that barks the opening bars of Beethoven's Fifth Symphony; but 'no publicity is bad publicity' as they say, and at least my name is mentioned. So my practice in Wellington sees a further inflow of new clients.

I do wonder sometimes how Zootherapy would fare if I tried to develop it in Britain or, indeed, any country other than New Zealand. No doubt it helps that New Zealand is going through a period of self-conscious nationalism, in the years following the 150th anniversary of white settlement, with ties to the old country fraying as the UK sees its future as part of Europe rather than the Commonwealth. Also in my favour is that kiwi willingness to bend or ignore those rules that, whatever their stated purpose, serve to reinforce the hierarchy that British settlers came here to escape. I cannot imagine that the equivalent of the New Zealand Department of Corrections in any other country would let somebody as underqualified as me entertain a group of (OK: not-that-hardened) criminals with an assorted array of elephant costumes, and *pay for it*. In the Old World, tried, tested and failed always trumps new, innovative and promising. Nothing must ever be done for the first time.

A few weeks after prison and the TV news item, some positive anecdotes make it into the *Evening Post*. A group of volunteer prison visitors have looked at Zootherapy and some of their unofficial comments appear in the newspaper. It must be a slow news day, or at least a day when all the big news happened overseas, and there's a lot of space to fill. So there it is, in the Saturday 'Lifestyle' section: *Jumbo reduction in crime* blares a headline half way down page five. There's a head shot of me posing with the gorilla head (it must have been snapped while I lived in Newtown, but I honestly can't remember the occasion). The subhead reads *Elephants soften crims*. A second subhead, further down the article says *Reoffending down*. And a third comprises the word *'Zootherapy'* in quotes. I think it's premature to be so upbeat: the evidence isn't statistically significant, but the comments, backed up by reports from probation officers, do encourage me. It probably helps that people's expectations of prisons and prisoners are unanimously low.

I try to be objective at this early result of my first attempt at group Zootherapy. I've been lucky, I think, in that my first group consisted of prisoners. Deprived of most other distractions, they welcome anything that takes them outside the prison experience. Zootherapy is so off-the-wall that they can't interpret it, or me, as representing the society that has locked them up. While superficially radical, it is also apparently harmless and so acceptable to the prison governors, just like the other last-item-in-the-newsbites (I learned the other day that there is violinist who plays Sarasate on a tightrope over Niagara Falls). Zootherapy poses no obvious threat to the existing order. I wonder too whether, being outside the mainstream, the prisoners are more in touch with their animal natures and more open to acknowledging others'. For whatever reasons, Mount Crawford was fertile ground on which to sow the seeds of group Zootherapy.

I learned a lot from doing Zootherapy with a group. Years ago, back in the UK, I'd gone to a hypnotherapist for a social anxiety problem. In a tatty room in a suite shared with a podiatrist, above a charity shop, the lady began my session by suggesting that my right arm would rise. I didn't really believe in hypnosis, so I did nothing at all; keeping my arm firmly on my lap. She grew more insistent 'You can feel your arm rising'. I began to feel sorry for her and eventually decided to raise my arm. Because I did so deliberately, I thought that must mean it's not working. After that session I never went back. But had I been wrong? Just performing the act – maybe that was enough? OK, we might not believe in God as described in scripture, but that doesn't mean that the rituals, music, prayers and homilies are devoid of significance. So it might be that prisoners were doing the same as I was doing at the hypnotherapist's: humouring me, or *thinking* that they were humouring me. Playing along in a mildly distracting way of passing their few remaining days in the nick. But maybe they got something out of it even so. I write down my thoughts:

LESSON 5

- *Putting on an animal costume at first glance might seem like an act of isolation, of deliberately setting yourself apart. But the effect is exactly the opposite. Putting the costume on, we become part of nature. Our kinship with all the animals, including human animals, becomes clear and inescapable. We are part of the vast continuum of nature. We know this, intellectually. Wearing the costume as an individual we experience it. Wearing the costume in the company of others similarly attired potentiates that experience.*

THE RISE AND RISE OF ZOOTHERAPY

The semi-official imprimatur of respectability granted by my prison work raises the Zootherapy profile. And so, in New Zealand, though so far only in New Zealand, Zootherapy becomes an increasingly acceptable alternative or complement to conventional medicine, talking therapy, or counselling. I am making a good, stable, living now purely from Zootherapy. I buy a compact new one-bedroom apartment, still on The Terrace, in Wellington's city centre. Unusually for a kiwi, I don't own or car nor have any desire to. The block of about 20 apartments stands in a grassy area. It's a well-managed setup, and one of its rules is that no four-footed pets are allowed. (Jason said 'Why don't you get a kangaroo?')

Tina is a senior nurse now, and still has a room in a nurses' hostel in the hospital grounds for when she's doing unsociable shifts. Her father's showing the first signs of dementia, and she spends the odd afternoon or night at her parents' house to give her mum a break. But the rest of the time she stays over with me.

SWANS

It's a weekday evening and we're both at the apartment. We've just had a quick bout of sex, Tina stepping out of her sparkly sequin-covered snake costume. She's in the kitchen, in her robe, making cocoa. I prop myself up in bed, facing the TV set with the remote control. The Video Cassette Recorder is switched on and humming beside the TV which is recording, I hope, the animal documentary on the TV screen. I turn the volume up.

It's a British production, not totally dumbed-down, but with the picture changing roughly every two seconds, and information imparted orally in bite-sized chunks. There's an overwrought orchestral background that comes to the fore between each datum. The in-your-face emphasis on the appealing features of the female presenter is also distracting. (It reminds me of the belly-dancer at the Middle Eastern restaurant we went to the other evening. Belly-dancing and dinner; one or the other, yes, fine, very nice. But both at the same time?)

> *You've all seen those pictures of swans or lovebirds on greetings cards.*

Soaring flutes and violins. From the kitchen, Tina asks me whether I want anything to eat. I don't, unless she's having something or feels like making popcorn. The presenter speaks again:

> *But research shows that being faithful doesn't come naturally in most of the in the animal kingdom. Studies show nine out of ten mammals and birds that mate for life cheat on their mates.*

A cello bass note to accompany the violins. This must be a complicated fact, as they give us several seconds of music to absorb it.

> *Experts found that animals that fool around are only following the urges of biology.*

'Just cocoa then', I tell Tina.

> *And while birds like swans may mate for life, they're not necessarily faithful to their mate.*

'Typical; men', says Tina.

I muse aloud: 'Difficult to wear a swan costume.'

> *The clue was DNA. Researchers looked at the offspring of the birds and found that the mother bird's offspring weren't necessarily the father bird's offspring.*

'Ha!', I say 'It was the females doing the fooling around!' The kettle clicks off.

> *About 40 percent of the swan's babies were sired by someone other than the mother's mate.*

'You believe all that?', Tina says 'Who did the research? Men I bet.'

She might well be right about that.

In fact, experts think that even for animal species that supposedly mate for life, a certain amount of canoodling goes on.

The TV camera pans from swans paddling around a lake to the presenter, whose face almost fills the screen:

It seems that for animals, as for humans, the fact that a male and a female may be bonded to each other and raise offspring together doesn't stop them fooling around with outsiders. Monogamy in the animal kingdom is so rare that the authors of a book called The Monogamy Myth *say that instead of portraying swans as our romantic ideal, greetings cards would be better to feature the flatworm.*

That's the thing with these TV documentaries. They feed you these teaspoonfuls of data, your thinking process slows down in sympathy, then suddenly they present you with a huge chunk of information that you now find difficult to digest all at once. With this series of statements the rhythm of the programme changes. The TV picture switches to the studio, where the presenter and a man and woman, the authors of *The Monogamy Myth*, are sitting at a table in front of a larger-than-life backdrop of two swans facing each other. There's a tiny terrarium on the table in which, presumably, are flatworms. Tina brings in two mugs of cocoa. The interview's about to start. I turned to Tina:

Me, casual now: 'So are you a swan or a flatworm?' There's something just a bit off in Tina's reply:

'What do you mean?'

'You wouldn't be unfaithful to me would you, slinky snake?'

I see Tina stiffen for a fraction of a second, and in that instant, my stomach lurches. The TV programme is quickly forgotten, though it burbles on in the background.

'What?' I ask.

'Nothing'

I'm sitting up now, watching her closely. I'm tense now, fully alert.

I stare at her. 'What?', she says

'Tina? What's going on?'

'Nothing', but she's not meeting my eyes. She stays standing by the bed, the snake costume on the floor beside her.

'I'm not sure I believe you.'

She knows that I know that she's not telling me something. She makes an effort and looks directly at me. The words come out as a formula, programmed: 'Why are you looking at me like that? Don't you trust me?'

'Should I?'

'James...'

She looks away for a second. Something's very wrong.

'Tina – don't avoid me; look at me'

'James... 'and now a strange thing happens. I feel sorry for her, though I know she's hiding something.

'Who is it? Someone at the hospital? A doctor? Or another patient? Like me?'

She turns away.

'Or just someone you met while shopping?'

Now she rounds on me: 'Stop it James!', half pleading, half demanding. Our cocoa, ignored, steams by the bed.

'Tina. Please don't insult me.' And while I talk like this, I'm quite aware that I'm roiling inside and that this is very much the old James; the pre-Zootherapy James. This occurs to me for a microsecond, but it doesn't staunch my righteous anger.

Tina is more dignified in her distress. She looks down, and almost whispers: 'It was only once James. It was a long time ago. And it was for you.'

I must have looked how I felt, confused, uncomprehending.

'It was months ago. And I did it for your sake.' She says again.

'Very good of you,' I say, 'I'm so grateful.' It's strange though. I'm feeling sorry for her. But I'm playing a role here; one mirroring what I've seen in TV dramas and movies. The script says: be aggrieved, and I'm dutifully going along with it.

'I'm serious. I wanted you to see the prisoners. More than anything. This was the only way.'

What is she on about? There are a few moments of silence. In the distance an emergency vehicle siren sounds forlornly. It seems like an omen. She bends down and strokes my hair.

'I had sex with Duane. Once, since we... you know.' She means, since we'd first made love and promised ourselves to each other. Duane, the policeman, her ex; I've seen him only once, fleetingly, at a farewell party for one of Tina's colleagues. 'It was before Julie.'

Julie, I assume, is the current girlfriend, the make-up artist. Can I believe her?

'Duane?'

'James. I had one fling with Duane; one fling since we met. It was months ago; before the prisoners. Nothing since. I swear. I did it for you. He promised me he would have a word with the Governor. That's the only reason I did it. '

'The Governor?'

'The prison Governor. Mount Crawford. It was for you James. I swear. I haven't seen him since. I don't speak to him at all now.''

'Duane....'

'It was only the once, James.

She's stroking my hair. I shudder. I so much want to believe her. Well, in fact, I do believe her. But righteous anger is a powerful emotion and I feel I have to recite my lines. If I were able to spit out a vitriolic, devastating retort, I'd do so, but all that comes to mind is:

'Great. Was he any good?'

'I did it for you James, I mean it.'

I can't play the role of angry man any longer. Simply: I love Tina. And my years of preaching and practising Zootherapy may finally be exerting a detectable influence outside its designated environs, giving me just a little distance, a little detachment. So: it was a while ago, it was for me and, it was once only. I melt. Tina senses this.

'Do you think you'd have got to see the prisoners without me? Without Duane putting in a word for you? It was your one chance!'

'I can't believe I'm hearing this.' Again with the script, but my heart isn't in it. I must have pulled this one straight from a soap opera. It certainly wasn't what I was beginning to feel. Tina put me straight.

'How do you think you got the chance to speak to those crims? You'd only just started out. '

'But we'd already been seeing each other.'

'We'd only just started. Look: it was the only way. And it was only once. And it was worth it.'

'Oh yes? Who to?'

'To me. To see you happy. To you James. To Zootherapy.' She's quiet. On the TV, the presenters are amusing themselves, trying to pick up a flatworm with a wooden spill. 'Listen James; you're too nice for these people. You're naïve and I love you for it. But can you imagine what they really thought about Zootherapy? About putting on animal costumes?'

'What - who do you mean?'

'Anyone! Everyone! The prison people, academics, doctors, the media! They think you're another one of these crackpots or weirdoes. They never took it seriously. They've seen it all before. Or they thought they had. They're not like you. I did what I had to do. You're one in a million James. It was a contractual arrangement I had with Duane. Almost blackmail. It was a transaction. I did a deal with him. A one-off. It's finished.'

'Duane...'

She spells it out slowly, calmly: 'Duane had a word with his chief, superintendent, whatever, who had a word with the Prison Governor.'

'And now?'

'It's over. I promise you.' She stops for a second. 'It was your big break, wasn't it? It worked.'

'What was Duane thinking? What did he get out of it?'

'I don't know what he thought. He probably thought I'd fall in love with him again. I knew I wouldn't and he knows it now. Come on James.'

I believe her. I know I desperately want to believe her. But that doesn't mean she's not telling the truth.

'He's not hassling you?'

'It was a one-off James. I haven't even seen him since then! I promise. Come on James.' There's a long pause. Has the drama played out? 'You're Mr Zootherapy, James! You don't *do* grudges! You don't *do* bygones!'

I have to smile, and as we move to embrace each other she says, softly: 'You're Mr Zootherapy.' She kisses me on the lips. 'And I want to be Mrs Zootherapy.'

Never looking back. Always in the present. Tina had a past, but it was past. She'd known me, begun to fall in love with me and then slept with Duane. But it had been a long while ago, before we'd really committed ourselves. And at some level I am aware of my hypocrisy; who's to know how I'd react if some random gorgeous young lady had pursued my body at that time? And she's right about the prisoners. It's largely because of them that Zootherapy is seen as something other than another dodgy New Age fad. (It helps, more than it should have, when after a more than usually pyrotechnical bout of lovemaking that night, Tina said softly: 'He was never much good in bed; and I'm not just saying that.')

I MARRY TINA, 1993
So after a mostly happy few years of being an item, Tina and I have a brief, low-key wedding ceremony, which pleases, or at least relieves, her mum. She gives up her room at the nurses' hostel, and moves into my flat on a more permanent basis, and very soon after that, or perhaps a while before, Tina becomes pregnant, this time to the unambiguous delight of her mum. We both want Tina to look after the baby full time, at least for the first year. So we are going to need a decent, stable cash flow. Could Zootherapy generate enough

income to keep the three of us? Wellington isn't a big city, and personal growth, while trendy, might not be lucrative enough to support me along with homeopathy, acupuncture, naturopathy, tantric yoga, sacro-cranal massage and the rest. The prisoners had been an isolated event: a select group of docile inmates, approaching the end of their sentences. That happens rarely, and there's no guarantee that I'll be in demand for a repeat performance. Not, at least, unless and until I achieve a scientifically robust success rate. I do, though, graduate to a more upmarket and swisher office, still in the Harbour City Centre, but on a lower floor, which I share with dentists and osteopaths. It's big enough for me to do sessions with small groups – usually friends of former clients. But these are neither frequent nor very lucrative. We could probably survive on my current income. But we'd not thrive. So I do what anybody else would have done in my situation, and what Tina is encouraging me to do. I go corporate.

ZOOTHERAPY GOES CORPORATE

I have a flier done, in which I try to market Zootherapy as a consciousness-raising, team-building, bonding opportunity for individuals and groups of employees:

- *If you are an employer, consider Zootherapy for training purposes. It can round out the personality of your staff members, making them more cohesive, more productive, and happier. If they are too shy and passive, Zootherapy can make them more confident and assertive. If they are too aggressive, Zootherapy can soften and smooth out those rough edges. Whatever the personality of your employees, Zootherapy can foster team spirit. A short course of Zootherapy can motivate and energise your employees for that new marketing push, or that vital restructuring.*
- *Zootherapy can be good for your bottom line. If you have an issue with personnel, or you want to impress a client, a Zootherapy-induced change in perspective can pay off. After a few sessions with a qualified Zootherapist you or your employee will find you*

can apply the technique discreetly in the workplace. You may find that your particular personality problem, whether it involves yourself or an employee, requires some investigation. Talk over you or your employee's issues in a free initial consultation with the founder of Zootherapy: James Sinclaire, who has worked with individuals and groups in various settings.

- *Employees: If you are invited to participate in a group Zootherapy session:*
    - o *Be open-minded: be sceptical, but not cynical*
    - o *Go along with it, even if you don't think it's going to work*
    - o *Don't worry about how you look. Remember: everyone else is wearing a costume too*

There's a black and white photograph of me. Tina and I debated which one to use. We don't want to frighten people by appearing too radical, but nor do we want to underplay the reality of Zootherapy. We settle on one taken on the harbour front, with a backdrop of Wellington's 15-20 storey office buildings (corporate, reliable), and I'm holding the head of the original gorilla suit (innovative). My corporate launch comes at an interesting time: just as employers need to offer retraining to typists and others about to be replaced by computers. Self-indulgently, Tina says, or factually, I think, I expatiate on the role of intelligence in the workplace:

- *Systems and automation, processes and procedures: all can get in the way of efficiency and safety. Human beings aren't well suited to monitoring or sitting and staring at a computer screen, but that is what jobs many jobs have become. Ticking boxes, multiple choice tests, and automation of manufacturing jobs leave very little room for alertness, originality or ingenuity. Systems give us security: but they mean we can switch off our active intelligence and initiative. Zootherapy switches them on again!*

There's enough interest to keep me busy. Word of mouth works, and the income from full-day sessions with small groups of employees from organisations like the Department of Trade and

Industry (about to be folded into the Ministry of Foreign Affairs), insurance companies and banks (moving their head offices to Auckland or Sydney) allows Tina, who tires easily now, to end her contract at the hospital and stay home for the last two months of her pregnancy. I'm still seeing individual clients and groups of two or three at my office in the Harbour City Centre, but Wellington has a decent choice of hotels with function rooms for my seminars. Life is more difficult for the several Zootherapists I've trained who've gone on to practise elsewhere. Most of them give up after a while, or quietly drop Zootherapy and ply their clients with other alternative therapies.

SAMANTHA BORN, 1993

We arrive at Wellington Hospital in the early hours of a winter morning, with a howling southerly blowing up Adelaide Road, tree branches and plastic bags scudding across the parking lot outside the maternity unit. A few tense hours, with me resisting the trend du jour, staying out of the unit, and Samantha is born. All is well; Tina's tired and sore, but we're both immensely euphoric. Once the flurry of brief, elated visits from some of Tina's ex-colleagues subsides, it's time to go back to the flat. Tina's father is now in an 'assisted living facility', but her mum insists on driving us and then, attuned to our wishes and body language rather than our words, leaves us to spend our first evening as a family. After gazing in adoration at Samantha sleeping in her cot in our bedroom we flop down on the sofa in the lounge, exhausted, happy. Precious, precious moments.

A few days later, after the afterglow has diminished a little, we are still experiencing the joy of our creation, but the practical aspects and anxieties don't overwhelm us quite so much now, and we can indulge ourselves in a little speculation.

'I just want to protect her from everything,' says Tina.

'She'll be fine. She'll make her own way. Like we did.'

'I'd love to know how she'll turn out...'

'You know I'm an expert on this?' I say, not at all seriously.

'Oh yes, my majestic, know-all husband, Zoo man extraordinaire?'

'I can tell you absolutely, Sam won't be what we want her to be. But neither will she be what we don't want her to be.'

'That doesn't leave many options.'

'And she won't do what we tell her to do. And she won't do what we forbid her from doing.'

'She'll do what she wants'

'Not exactly, no.'

'Now I'm really lost.'

'She'll be what we expect her to be. Children are smart: they pick up on our expectations. All we have to do is *expect* Samantha to be OK, to be a good daughter, a good citizen, kind, compassionate, caring, well behaved and, I guarantee, that's what she will be.' Tina looks puzzled. 'You don't believe me, do you?'

She doesn't, so I tell her about Clever Hans, the German circus horse who could apparently do simple arithmetic calculations by stamping his right fore-hoof. So when asked what two and three added up to he would stamp his foot five times.

'Ok, but what's that got to do with Sam?'

'I'm getting to that. How do you think he was getting the answers?'

'The trainer signalled to him.'

'No, he gave the right answer even when the trainer wasn't there.'

'Someone in the audience...?

'No, but here's a clue: there did need to be an audience, and the audience did need to know the answers.'

'I don't know. He read the minds of the audience?'

'Almost, and almost as amazing: he picked up cues from the audience.'

'Cues?'

'The guys in the audience knew the answers, right? And they were tensing their muscles until Hans got to the correct answer. They didn't know they were doing it. Tiny muscle movements, slight changes in breathing, which we probably can't detect ourselves. But Hans could pick up on them; he knew when to stop thumping his hoof.'

'Right. Interesting. And the relevance to Sam is?'

'You see what I'm saying? Think about it: if a horse can do it...you see?' Tina gets it:

'Sam will pick up on ... our expectations for her?'

'Right. Even if we don't know we have them. Even if we can't say exactly what they are.'

Tina's ancestry is as white New Zealander as they come, but she works and socialises with Maori and Pacific Islander colleagues, and I've tagged along to some of their parties. Without wishing to idealise, I find her pals less susceptible to the 'You've got to be cruel to be kind' philosophy of child-rearing that permeates much of New Zealand and (I suspect) the west. I used to muse on this when I was doing my economics module. Our economic system takes it as axiomatic that we always want more. Our needs shall never be satisfied. And I wonder: is that because we're denied affection and love in our earliest days, and for the rest of our lives we're always seeking them? Does it 'spoil' the child to supply the necessary affection and attachment requirements when they're young? Maybe kids brought up with their full quota of affection don't need big houses, fast cars, gadgets. So animals are OK then - in their natural habitat they have everything they need, so they don't bother to imitate us? More thought required and besides, all our dissatisfaction, this constant wanting more, more, more; in trying, trying (but always failing) to achieve satisfaction; all this yearning generates material abundance. Everybody benefits from decent medical facilities, nice warm houses with electricity and beds and popcorn makers. Health is good! Gadgets are fun! Well I don't know. It works both ways: denial of love generates economic surplus which along with all the good stuff means a military, bombs, invasions for territory or whatever. Anyway, I do know that I'm very glad that, the second Samantha begins whimpering or crying, Tina picks her up and comforts her.

SETTING OUT MY STALL: THE THEORY OF ZOOTHERAPY, 1997
I am now the personification of Zootherapy not only to Tina, but also to the New Zealand media. Partly because Zootherapy has become my full-time occupation – I dropped my Master's without a second thought - partly because the other practitioners, the ones I'd trained, have all drifted away from Zootherapy leaving me, again, as the only (official) Zootherapist on the planet. My chosen career is now giving my little family a better-than-average New Zealand living. A two-bedroomed flat in our apartment block on The Terrace becomes vacant, and I snap it up before it's even listed. As well as a second bedroom, which we convert into a nursery, it has a tiny room that I can use as an office.

And at this point I think of codifying Zootherapy, giving it a bit of intellectual underpinning. This I do at home, mostly in the evenings, when Tina and Samantha are playing or asleep. I do it partly for my own satisfaction, and partly because, to be honest, I have an aspiration to win respectability amongst the more orthodox healing professions. As well, I am increasingly fed up with the 'Are you serious?' question asked explicitly by the media, and implicitly by just about everyone else. A bit of theory could go a long way to dealing with that. There's one more reason: Zootherapy is so simple, that I need to fill out both my individual and group sessions, and my course materials, with theory. Not because the theory's necessary for a full understanding (it isn't), but because packaging is the first thing people notice. It's emphatically not the experience, but it can tempt sceptics to partake of the experience. I say all this as though it were my idea, but in fact it was Tina's:

'You know how those computer companies put their software in a box much bigger than the disk? It's the packaging that makes people buy it.'

'Like breakfast cereal?'

'Like everything. Clothes maketh man. Make the packaging big and attractive and colourful. Expand it. Make it wordy, talk about your life story.'

Oh, and, as Tina also says, if the packaging is attractive 'they'll pay more for it.'

So this is what I write:

> *Zootherapy functions at different levels some or all of which will be experienced in different combinations by different people at different times:*
>
> *1. At the most basic level the client getting into the animal costume takes on the characteristics that he or she associates with that animal.*

This is how I thought Zootherapy worked in its post-Gorillagram early months, and how it appeared to work with clients like Jenny and Peter. I've come to believe that there's more to it than that.

> *2. Zootherapy can also work at the same level as other complementary or alternative therapies, counselling, or talking to supportive friends in a relaxed and non-judgemental environment. The consultation and dialogue between an empathic Zootherapist and his or her client are important in establishing trust and creating an environment within which the client feels free to bring to light and explore issues; that process itself can be healing.*

> *3. By the mere act of putting on a costume, clients show a degree of humility, a willingness to accept that there are limits to the value of knowledge and rationality, and that a person's remembered narrative does not define who they are nor pre-ordain their response to memories or future events. Ritual and imagination can be liberating.*

What I don't say is that it helps if you're guided by someone a bit wacky, in the sense of being outside the system. The system? The conventional way of doing things: working, earning, the house, the car; the pressures to conform. The Zootherapist embodies an alternative to all that; the earthly manifestation of an alternative universe.

> *4. At its highest, most abstract level, it's not the outward form of the animal costume that matters; it's that which all animals have in common with the entire animal kingdom, including us. This is the universal animal. Zootherapy works by stripping away our human-ness with all its guilt, shame, anxiety, ambitions and fears. Zootherapy connects us with animals, nature and the cosmos. It liberates us from our past and our future but allows reconnection to the vast wealth of human knowledge when appropriate.*

This sounds complicated in theory; but it happens perfectly naturally in practice. It also sounds as though Zootherapy were the result of rational thought: it wasn't, of course. Like much scientific discovery, it began serendipitously. The experience came first, the rationalisation after. That doesn't invalidate it: penicillin still works.

> *5. We don't lose our humanity by becoming animal: we put it to one side, and use it when, and only when, it's helpful. Our accumulated memories, because we constantly reference them, play a grossly exaggerated role in our lives. But there are times when we need them. When we practise Zootherapy we don't actually become animal: we are just putting aside our accumulated memories when we don't need them. But we have access to them for when they are useful to us – and only then.*

At times, I'll elaborate on this latter theme in early sessions with my more highbrow clients: every moment, every thing, every event has its animal and human features; that is features that are unique to itself, and features that are replicated somewhere else. Two sets of aspects: one that is unique and ever changing and one that is constant and can identical with others and so amenable to our acquired knowledge. Equations and algorithms are too human, static. They stand for vested interests, and reinforce existing structures – and hangups – as much as enlighten. Zootherapy opens our minds to the particular, the ever-changing, the immediate.

'You don't think this is too abstract and theoretical?', I ask Tina.

'It's just packaging; you have to tell people a story, and sell it to them. You're talking to middle managers, supervisors. They've got to get their bosses to sign off on it.'

Well I hope so. But looking at the history of the world's religions, I do see a pattern: inspiration, codification, institutionalisation, corruption. Still, having put down my thoughts in this way, I've got something to counter the cynics who say that Zootherapy is taking the Mickey, coming the raw prawn with the populace and I'm laughing all the way to the bank, deceiving everybody – including myself. There's still scepticism out there, which is no bad thing; but there's bitterness and envy too. I don't dwell on all that: my practice is busy now and there's something about having a young daughter at home that dissolves such negativity. Magic moments. I remember one evening a client cancelled at the last minute, and I was home early enough to help Tina put four-year-old Samantha to bed. If we go into space, she asks, 'Will we see God?' 'No, but we'll see what God made,' Tina replies.

PANDAS, 1999

A mid-Atlantic, male voice, blares out from the TV:

> You all know what Giant Pandas look like with their round black ears and black eye patches standing out against a white face and neck. But did you know what they eat? As much as 90 to 98 percent of the panda's diet consists of the leaves, shoots, and stems of bamboo, a large grass available year-round in much of China's forested regions.

It's 1999, and I am still the world's only official, full-time, Zootherapist. 'Number one in a field of one', as MAD Magazine would have it. I still see individual clients at my recently refurbished office in the Harbour City Centre office, but today I'm doing a session in one of the smaller conference rooms at a three-star hotel in Wellington, on Oriental Parade just across from the beach.

It's a small group: just six, with a couple of the clients (or their employers), paying my full charges themselves, the others being subsidised by one branch or other of Social Services. We've just come in from a lunchtime break. They're all men, but otherwise diverse: between 30 and 50 years old, dressed smart casual. I think of them as satyrs, that is, lustful, lascivious men, highly sexed, with a not-quite-criminal record of being too overt and forceful about it. They're guys who've stepped over the boundary once or twice, and will face serious trouble if they do so again. Two have referred themselves to these sessions. The others have had complaints made against them in their workplace and attendance here or at more conventional counselling has been made a condition of their continued employment. They sit in a semi-circle around me, in this windowless function room in a soulless building; a trolley with tea, coffee and biscuits on one side, a trio of large pots of bamboo grass and shoots on the other. Our shirts sport sticky paper labels bearing our first names. There's a table next to me, on which sit a TV set and Video Cassette Player.

The setup for my group sessions hasn't changed much over the years. But the TV is much bigger, and this time my 'public performance' of the (Australian) wildlife documentary is legal, or at least my lawyer says so; I have to take such precautions now that I'm significant enough to attract the malevolent attention of intellectual property lawyers. Besides, I have more to lose.

> But Giant Pandas still have the digestive system of their carnivorous ancestors. They can't actually digest cellulose, a main constituent of bamboo. So what do they do? They eat enormous quantities of bamboo grass every day. As much as 16 out of every 24 hours of the Giant Panda's life is spent feeding on bamboo.

I've already given this group my spiel about how, even if they were directed to come here as a last resort, they should see this not as a punishment but as a privilege; I've talked up Zootherapy and laid out some Zootherapy lore. So far this afternoon I've played excerpts from the panda video, interspersed with each guy's tale of how he ended up here. Now it's time for the last of the men to give his story. From my list of their full names I recognise him as someone I've heard on National Radio.

'Ian?'

'Yeah.' He gestures to the others, 'Very much the same as everyone else. I work with women, some of them very young. I'm never sure whether they're up for it or just teasing.'

The others grunt their agreement. I nod encouragingly.

'I was recording *Rural Report* with a new girl. I dunno, maybe because it was a stud farm we'd been reporting on in the Wairarapa'. The others snigger. I try to remain po-faced. As Ian tells it, ice and wind over the Rimutakas meant that the radio team, rather than all return to Wellington that evening as planned, had to stay overnight at a motel in Greytown. After a boozy evening, Ian had been overly lecherous to his new colleague, a recent graduate from journalism school. 'One thing didn't lead to another. Well, it led to a slap in the face. And this.' He gestures round the room. We nod in understanding. 'I didn't actually do anything but...you know. "We're giving you one more chance", they said. "We're going to keep you on, under probation. One more incident, even a small one, and we're going to have to let you go. Do you understand?" I couldn't hide it from my girlfriend. I didn't want to. We want our relationship to work. We've got a two-year old daughter. So... here I am.'

Essentially the same as the others. I speak to all the men.

'OK. So you've all got your own experiences; you come from different backgrounds but you've all got something in common: you've all acknowledged that you have this problem – and I'm going to be frank now – this problem of uncontrollable lust for women. That's good: you recognise you have this problem and you want to solve it. That's half the battle. Now I want you to try to forget everything you might have heard about Zootherapy, even what I was talking about this morning. Just sit back again and learn some more about pandas.

I get the VCR to play the final short extract from the documentary. While it's playing I go to a large trunk and take out my Giant Panda costumes – well-crafted in, appropriately, China.

> Giant Pandas are one of the least sexually responsive of all animals. Getting it to mate in captivity has been incredibly difficult. In one zoo in Thailand they separated their male and female pandas to spark a little romance. They even introduced panda porn - videos of other pandas mating - to get the pair in the mood. Here we see the male being completely indifferent to the advances of the female. He's far more interested in the bamboo at the other end of the cage!

I stop the VCR and switch the TV off.

'Now I want you to put these costumes on.'

It doesn't take long, and now I ask them leading questions about what they've learned about pandas. They've all taken on board the message I've been bashing home with a sledge-hammer: pandas aren't into sex.

And now, as I urge them once more to put aside any preconceptions about Zootherapy. I knock three times on the inside of the door: a signal to a fit and nubile part-time martial arts instructor Linda, and equally lubricious 'Crystal', an escort procured from one of the innumerable agencies advertising in the *Evening Post*, who have been waiting outside. I launch into my usual Zootherapy patter:

'Now don't be self-conscious. Nobody's taking any pictures. It's just a sort of role play. And don't worry if you don't believe in this. Only the result matters. Nobody knows who you are; nobody cares who you are. You're going to be Giant Pandas for a while.'

I am moving the pots of bamboo to a more central position in the room, trying convey with my expression and body language that I know they might think it's a bit silly, but I want them to humour me.

With a flourish, I open the door and in come my temptresses, who move seductively amongst the men.

'OK pandas,' I cry, 'you know what to do! There's some lovely bamboo in the pots here.'

The satyrs in their panda costumes ignore Linda and Crystal, and move towards the bamboo pot.

The next day but one, we go through a similar exercise, with the two ladies in a more provocative state of undress. It's a simple, simplistic, even crude method, but I'm confident that it will continue to work in the world outside the hotel. Maybe it's the camaraderie, maybe it's the ever-growing reputation of Zootherapy in Wellington combined with the placebo effect. Or maybe it works and Zootherapy does actually open up or block the appropriate pathways in my clients' neurological systems. Plus the fact that most of my over-sexed male clients desperately want and need it to work. Whatever, it feels I'm doing something ethical and positive, helping to save relationships and keep families together. It's a nice earner too.

DIALOGUE WITH JASON, 1999
Jason and I still meet for the occasional drink after work. Now that we both have families and my working days are getting longer, our meetings are less frequent and more hurried.

'I'm not sure you got the timing right with your Zootherapy, you know: it's so retro.'

'Huh?'

'Everything's computers now. All the typists – remember them? Gone. Phut. We've all got our own terminals and do our own word-processing and printing.'

'I like them. Gives us autonomy. Saves a lot of hassle.'

'Yeah, well music's gone digital too now. And now there's broadband. Nobody comes to see our gigs anymore. They're all on the internet playing those stupid video games, or watching porn. I don't know. You might have missed the boat with those costumes. Too low-tech.'

'I don't know, Jason. Could work the other way.'

Even a short-sighted city boy like me had some childhood experience of the world of nature: the back garden, a pet tortoise, centipedes and millipedes under rocks, worms, the cold damp soil, playing football in the local park. But technology has moved in. Today's equivalent of me as a child has a TV in his room, with dozens of channels. The natural world outside my room is another movie, even a threat. It's called 'The Environment', now, as though it's a separate entity. Maybe New Zealand is a little different; there's a much more immediate access to nature here. But who's got the time? I'm one of the lucky ones yet my life is about getting to work, logging on to computers in the office, dealing with clients, flopping down at home and preparing for the next day's ordeal. Staring at screens at the office and at home. I'm just as busy as everyone else, lucky in that Tina manages the housework, does the shopping and is raising Samantha single-handedly. I don't want to think too much along these lines.

'It could work the other way, though.' I say, 'There could be a reaction: a return to nature. My business is doing all right. OK, it might be retro, but that means people appreciate it more, putting on something real like one of my animal costumes.'

As always, I'm glad of Jason looking at things from a different angle. He sees Zootherapy as the pet project of somebody he knows well: inevitably flawed and homespun, rather than the fully-formed, polished, quintessentially kiwi creation of a talented New Zealander, as trumpeted by the local media. To Jason, Zootherapy is still something I do in my spare time; more of a hobby than a business, much like his musical sideline. He doesn't begrudge my success, but he's more puzzled than reverential about it. Salutary as, I will admit, the more worshipful comments I get from clients and the media do go to my head sometimes.

'They're moving into composing now.' He means computers. We're walking in the cold of the night, along Lambton Quay. 'They do everything, you put in a basic melody; they have programs which add in the counterpoint and rhythm. Dreadful, digital, synthesiser sounds. You don't have to read music or know anything about music. It's all automatic. And the internet's getting faster. Broadband. You can download videos. Face it, my band, your animal suits: they're retro. It will all be interactive computer holograms in a few years.' On that note, we go our separate ways: Jason heads to the railway station, I begin the climb up to The Terrace.

Kitty, 2000

Zootherapy becomes my life. Tina looks after my home life, and does it very well. Samantha suffers only the usual toddler and childhood ailments and accidents: Tina's nursing skills keep everything under control. Tina's father dies soon after the beginning of the new millennium, and Tina's mother eventually moves to a smaller house, still in the wealthy (but somewhat sterile) suburb of Khandallah. We move to a house in Wadestown with a not-too-hilly section. And I become a commuter, catching the bus to work, or the occasional minicab, when there's a foul southerly blowing in. I could, and should, walk to work; it's downhill all the way, but I need to get to the office early. Tina buys a little runabout. We keep the flat on The Terrace for rental income.

We try to instil in Sam a love for animals. Tina bought a spider catcher one day: a long-handled, yellow-green plastic stick with a cone-shaped brush at the end for circling spiders and picking them up from corners and walls without injuring them, and then depositing them outside. We've used it several times in a few months, which works out at four New Zealand dollars per spider saved. Expensive? But to each spider it was surely worth immeasurably more. You can get all philosophical about this sort of thing. Does lavishing so much care on spiders mean there's less compassion left for the human race? Or rather, is the sympathetic reflex a muscle that atrophies when it's not exercised? Tina and I go on instinct: we do what feels right at the time. And the delight we see when Samantha releases a spider she's captured into the garden makes it worthwhile.

For Samantha's seventh birthday she wants a puppy. A hamster, guinea pig or even goldfish would be more manageable, but her heart is set on a puppy. Tina and I sit on the sofa, late one night:

'A dog's too much work,' says Tina, 'We have to be practical. You're often not here in the evenings: dogs need walking twice a day. And it might bark and annoy the neighbours.'

'And we'll have to clean up after it.' Remembering the dogs we used to keep, I tell Tina about Sadie. I'm in England 22 years old, but a young 22. The family I had been born into was breaking up. We had to sell and move. Amidst the winding up and the desolation nobody knew what to do with Sadie, a sassy Dalmation that we'd had for eight years. I went away for a while then I came home and she'd disappeared. I asked my mother who told me she'd gone round to one of our neighbours, a dog breeder, with Sadie, then knocked on the door and claimed to have found Sadie running loose. 'Is this yours?' she asked, 'I saw her on the side of the road and think she might have escaped.' The lady did the decent thing and took Sadie in. My mother recounted this episode with pride. Dog gone. Job done.

It's been a while since I thought of all that. A realisation comes to mind: 'And she'd have done exactly the same with me,' I blurt out. I've never before voiced that opinion, but it's probably accurate. Understand, I'm not blaming my mother. Her generation had no choices about marriage and children. It's just sad.

Tina strokes my leg. A bit more discussion of pros and cons and:

'A cat it is then,' announces Tina. And the three of us go along to the Cats' Protection League which is fortuitously holding an Adopt-a-Thon that weekend, and are immediately drawn to an abandoned, affectionate black (mostly) kitten. Her wish for a puppy, only a puppy, nothing but a puppy, evaporating instantly, Samantha falls in love with her new furry friend and names her (she's only seven!) Kitty.

THE NEXT FEW YEARS: KIWI ICON, 2003

With Tina being a stay-at-home mum, and with some help from her own mother, Sam, Kitty and the house are well taken care of. I am free to devote most of my waking hours to my Zootherapy clients, and the ever-proliferating administrative burdens of running a small business. My office suite has a small vestibule, and I hire an assistant, Kate to come in three mornings a week to help out. She's quietly efficient and confident (she used to be a legal secretary but found it too boring); a real help, but even so, there's quite a bit of admin stuff that only a proprietor can do.

I'm also kept busy promulgating the Zootherapy gospel. As I become better known around Wellington and, increasingly, the rest of New Zealand, I have to field questions from the media as well as would-be clients. Example: 'You say that all you really need to know about Zootherapy is that you put on a costume and imagine you are an animal, or stop thinking that you're a human....' (What I don't say, but want to is *Just stop thinking!* It works for me!) '...yet your consultations or training sessions take hours or days. Why, if it's so simple, not just sell your patients costumes, or rent them out, and leave it at that?' I give various explanations, depending on who's asking, but the important one is that society is full of distractions. We need constant reminders that Zootherapy is an option. It would save time to rattle off prepared answers to queries like that, but saying the same thing in different ways gives a more three-dimensional picture than saying the same thing multiple times.

Wellington's white-collar establishment mostly comprises bureaucrats and people servicing bureaucrats. So it isn't a place where you absorb risk-taking and entrepreneurship from the air. It's no big surprise then that Tina doesn't exactly encourage me when I say, returning home after a late evening session with a particularly grateful client: 'You know, I could easily export Zootherapy to the rest of the world.' 'That's nice,' she says. I don't let Tina's lack of enthusiasm stop me. I'm a man with a mission. I have carved out a niche market in the Wellington therapy scene. On a respectability rating, I'm not (yet) up there with doctors and dentists or psychologists or accredited counsellors. But I like to feel I'm a notch or two above the naturopaths, tarot card readers and the other travellers in the New Age cavalcade.

There are, inevitably, disappointments, many of them clients who ostensibly want to lose weight or give up smoking. They come to me as a last resort after more conventional counselling, acupuncture, diets or hypnotherapy. I rationalise their failure by wondering whether they really did want to give up cigarettes or moderate their calorie intake. They are gratifyingly outnumbered by my successes, coming from all socio-economic backgrounds. Some work in the private sector, but many of my clients come from one of Wellington's myriad government bodies. I also do a bit of *pro bono* work for those who are referred to me, informally, by people who know me from Social Welfare. Their sessions are subsidised by an illustrious few who occupy the most exalted levels of Wellington society: Directors-General, Chief Executives; even one or two senior politicians or their partners. Most likely it is one of these who, without my knowledge, nominates me for Kiwi Icon of the Year, 2003.

A Friday in summer and I'm in the office just after 7am: a typical morning start for me these hectic days. I like to sweep away some of the administrative debris before my first clients, due at 8am, arrive. The phone rings in my office. It's on silent but I hear the click, and it goes to voicemail:

'Mr Sinclaire, could you get back to me urgently regarding your flight to Auckland this evening?'

It attests to the size of my ego that, when I return the call and am told I'm a finalist in this evening's Kiwi Icon of the Year presentation ceremony, I believe it. It seems they did send an email to that effect, but either Kate or (more likely) I didn't bother to read it. My non-response appears to have been taken as acceptance of their all-expenses paid invitation to the finals in Auckland that evening, and I need to get to the airport for the 5pm flight. A limousine would pick me up at the domestic terminal there and whisk me to my suite at the SkyCity Hotel, in time for the award ceremony in the hotel ballroom at 8pm. Panic! Yes, they can organise a dinner jacket, bowtie and fresh shirt for me for this evening. I'll have to reschedule my evening clients: there are two after 4pm today. The first thankfully, is amenable. The other is not so happy, but accepts my offer to waive her fees for a rescheduled session. It's nearly 8am when my first client's due; I leave a message for Kate to reschedule Saturday's clients, explaining that it's urgent but not an emergency, and hinting that it's good news.

It's all a blur: my clients that day, then the taxi to Wellington Airport (we go past the Ministry of Agriculture building – I've come a long way since that Gorillagram, I think to myself), the flight to Auckland, the limo on arrival, the dinner (I get there just as the main course is served). It is a long, warm, humid, festive evening in the run-up to Christmas. After dessert is the award ceremony, with the celebrities, the microphone feedback, the bright TV lights, and the concentric penumbrae of acolytes and hangers-on; and then comes the protracted micro-drama of the envelope opening. I'm one of the four finalists, competing against the owner of a Hawkes Bay winery, a Maori playwright, and the founder of the Auckland Erotic Bakery, which specialises in the creation of bread, cakes and muffins in the shape of genitalia. I don't expect to win: the Maori playwright had a rough upbringing (to put it mildly) and, if I'd been a neutral observer, I'd be gunning for him.

But I do win; the awards are given, live on TV, at the tail end of the alcohol-fuelled banquet, and I find myself giving an impromptu acceptance speech, trophy in hand. I'm standing at the front of the convention hall with various New Zealand celebrities and high achievers; the other finalists, their partners, the pundits, fashionistas, CEOs and philanthropists. I've made no notes of course, I've had a couple of drinks and am a bit disorientated. But I've spoken in front of many audiences now and am borderline coherent.

'When I started Zootherapy some people thought I was taking the Mickey. That it was some sort of terribly sophisticated spoof on psychology or psychotherapy. Putting people in animal costumes: it seemed too easy, too simplistic. But I kept on, partly because Zootherapy works; but partly also because of New Zealand, this great, beautiful country; my home for the past twenty years. It is the New Zealand spirit that urged me on: the spirit of "Go for it", the optimism, the hope and aspirations that carry us along. This is not my trophy: it belongs to all New Zealanders, kiwis everywhere!'

As I hold the trophy up in triumph, there's applause and the staccato flashing of cameras. A few reporters hold up their hands.

The Master (or Mistress – I'm not paying attention) of Ceremonies picks out one of them:

He-or-she's saying something but I can hardly hear. Then a bit of feedback and the roving microphone on a pole finds him and now his voice booms around the hall:

'Roger Curtis, TVNZ. Congratulations James on winning the Kiwi Icon award. How do you feel about it and how do you plan to use it?'

What is the award? Apart, that is, from the trophy I'm holding – a 30 centimetres tall, light, shiny gilt pillar on an Art Deco plinth, topped by a stylised kiwi in jade. Perhaps there's some cash too, but I can't be sure.

'I'm absolutely delighted of course. I want to use this award to help spread the benefits of Zootherapy even wider. I mean, within and beyond New Zealand'. One or two similar questions that I can answer without stopping to think, then:

'Sue Callaghan, *New Zealand Herald*. Congratulations on your win. I'd just like to ask: what's the animal costume that you put on most often?'

That throws me. I hesitate for a brief moment.

'Well, you might not believe this, but I've been so busy, I can't remember the last time I actually did that.' Some laughter and (strangely) applause cover my embarrassment. I recover quickly 'Only joking of course', (I'm not) 'It's a kiwi.' (Not true, but it's the first creature that comes to mind.)

The truth hurts. My body is right up there, drinking champagne with the glitterati, the media magnates, the hype merchants, being feted, lauded, and regaled with the flattery and flummery. But inwardly? I realise I've been 'too busy' to use my own therapy on myself, even as I've been urging my clients always to just do it, regardless of whether they really feel like it or whether they even believe in it. 'Don't think too much about it', I've told them repeatedly; 'Build it into your daily life'. My real message might just as well be 'Do as I say, not as I do'. So smug I've been; 'A long way from the Gorillagram'. Sure.

MEANWHILE, BACK IN WELLINGTON

Tina and Samantha stand at the front door of the house. The sun's just set. Tina's been to the supermarket having picked up Sam from school, where she's been practising with the Under-12's netball team. On the front lawn there's some not-very-expert topiary, in the form of an elephant and a hen. Tina is agitated, opening the front door to the house, eight or ten supermarket carrier bags at her side, just unloaded from her car in the driveway. The mobile phone in her handbag's ringing and the ringing of the landline inside the house is just audible. Samantha's anxious to get inside: she wants to watch a British TV programme about the Amazon rainforest. Tina fishes the front door keys from her handbag, ignores the mobile, and hurriedly opens the front door. She shoos Samantha into the house, leaving the front door open and the supermarket bags outside. As the mobile stops ringing, Tina rushes in to answer the landline.

Tina is stressed, hassled, panicky.

'Yes? Oh hi Mum - I'm fine. I, yes...everything's wonderful. Just wonderful. No, nothing. Nothing's wrong. On the television? Now? .... Everything's fine. .... She's good.... It's all all right! I promise!.... Yes. Thank you Mum.'

Tina ends the call and sighs.

'Come and see Sam; your daddy's on television .... You know who I mean? Your father. The lodger. The guy who comes here at night to sleep.'

She goes out to bring in the shopping, while Samantha turns on the giant plasma TV set in the living room and flicks through a couple of channels.

'And the winner of Kiwi Icon of the Year is.... James Sinclaire, the man from Wellington who invented Zootherapy. The world's one and only Zootherapist!' Cheers and applause.

'Mummy – Daddy's won! Daddy's on telly!' Tina calls from the hall: 'Marvellous', she says.

Sam points to her father on the screen 'there's Daddy!' Tina stands at the door to the living room, glances at the screen, then goes out to bring in the rest of the shopping. Samantha's a sensitive soul; she's caught between excitement at seeing her father on the telly and the anxiety that goes with the knowledge that something is very wrong with her parents' relationship.

Suite 1424, SkyCity

It should be my dream night. Instead I'm rattling around on my own in my overlarge suite. I've been presented with the trophy, plied with drink, and now my head's buzzing in the silence of the bedroom. The loneliness is brutal after the crowds and acclamation. The hotel suite is the usual five-star combination of opulence, sterility and various shades of beige; on the wall there's a framed print of Auckland harbour, showing white sails on a calm turquoise sea. On my desk lie numerous congratulatory messages, my Kiwi Icon award, and flowers. They say alcohol's a depressant, but it's not that: what's happened to my marriage? I didn't even mention Tina in my speech. The empty acreage of the king-size bed mocks me.

Through the fog of alcohol and the razzmatazz ringing in my ears I'm frantically pressing 'redial' on the room's landline, trying to ring home. I suspect Tina's pulled the plug out. I've tried her mobile, but it goes straight to voicemail. My cellphone's full of congratulatory texts from pals, clients, former clients, but nothing from Tina. No message, no phone call from my wife on this day of my public triumph? And I know exactly why: I can no longer kid myself. I've spent months, deliberately avoiding it, but now I can't think of anything else; I see it all now.

When was the last time Tina and I had discussed anything real, or shared any sort of emotional experience? We've been living like affluent suburban housemates; Zootherapy – the business, that is -

has taken me over; we do nothing together. Tina takes Sam to school, takes her to netball, does the shopping, the cleaning, mows the lawn, feeds the cat. I work long hours and spend what's left of evenings and weekends either seeing clients or catching up with book-keeping and admin. When was the last time I read a bedtime story to my daughter? There's been no shock, no drama; just a slow remorseless divergence between my work and home lives, and the gap is now so wide that, groggy, half drunk as I am, even I can't fail to notice it. The distance between us ... can I bridge it? Is it too late? My stomach is pitching.

Around 2am I give up trying to phone Tina, not sure what I'd say anyway. ('Er...sorry about the last year or so, Tina. From now on I'll try to be a good husband.'?) I take my shoes off, lie on the bed and suffer a few fitful episodes of alcohol-induced drowsiness before getting up. Tired though I am, I know I'll not get any proper sleep. I splash water on my face. I don't shave, but brush my teeth with the flimsy brush and miniature toothpaste provided by the hotel, then change back into my own old clothes. My head aches and I'm as low as I've ever been. The morning sun and long shadows, the quiet outside; normally they'd calm me, but not today. I get my things together quickly, leaving the formal wear on the armchair and shoving the Kiwi Icon trophy in my briefcase. Alone in the lift going down, I see that there's no thirteenth floor; the 'fourteenth' floor, the floor of my suite, is the one above the twelfth; it's really the thirteenth. Yeah, that would be right. No queue at checkout this early in the morning, but I still can't face talking to anyone at reception. Everything would be paid for anyway by the Kiwi Icon people. Luckily, even this early in the morning, there are a couple of taxis parked on the forecourt. I get into the back seat of the first. Luckily too, the driver – a chap of Middle Eastern appearance – doesn't feel like talking either. Traffic's light, and I find myself at the airport in time to check in for the first flight to Wellington at 6.30am.

The air inside the plane is crisp and cold, the passengers and crew all are young, snappily-dressed, slim, efficient. They look well rested. The plane lofts us briskly up into the clear early morning air, and I have little to do except wonder how I have come to this. No distractions here. I have to look at myself. Without flinching.

I can't kid myself any longer that talking about Zootherapy is a spiritual quest. That promulgating Zootherapy is more noble than, for instance, spending time with my wife and child. That it's been a laudable sacrifice. It's as clear as the early morning air around me that I've been single-mindedly pursuing money and status. Well I got money, and I got my Kiwi Icon award. Great. But I may well have lost my family. And, oh yes, what happened to my spirituality? I might have access to some spiritual truth if I actually practised Zootherapy. But I don't. Instead I get the shiny brassy trophy – which I'm tempted to take out of my briefcase and just leave under the seat in front of me. (Do it James, do it... But I don't. I'm too deflated even for that.) Now all I can hope is that that Tina and Sam are still at home, still willing to give me another chance.

It's a short flight. I get into a taxi at Wellington Airport where there's a stiff wind and a chill in the air. Seems I've neglected my marriage for years without a thought and now, because there's a half-minute delay as traffic builds up around the Basin Reserve, I'm inwardly going berserk. My family life hangs on a thread; any major traffic hold-up and I just know I'll be too late. Mercifully, in clock time, the taxi ride takes just a few minutes; no longer than you'd expect for a Saturday morning. I give the driver two twenties, tell him to keep the change. As he drives away, there's only the sound of the birds. It's just after 8am; the sun's up but the front lawn's in the shade and covered in dew. Now Kitty emerges from the bush, sees me, miaows and accompanies me to the front door. All is outwardly serene, but my heart is fluttering as I fumble for the keys.

And there, in our bed, are my wife and my daughter. They've heard me entering the house, and are starting to sit up, bleary eyed.

'You're back,' says my wife. I take in the words, the tone, and Samantha's anxious look, which breaks my heart. 'Nice of you to come and see us.'

'I...' I want to say 'I'm sorry', but it's too trite, too easy. I need to do more.

Samantha quietly leaves the room. A small part of me marvels at her intuition. She's only ten years old.

Twenty-four hours was all it had taken to show me up as a failure. Sure, I've won one of those glitzy Mickey Mouse awards, been feted and idolised, for one evening anyway by a ballroomful of free-loading achievers. (Big fish – and don't we know it! – in the New Zealand pond.) But Tina knows the truth. In the things that matter, I've failed. I kneel on the bed and try to kiss Tina. She turns her head and makes a weak attempt to push me away. This I see as more hopeful than no reaction at all. Then, a lightning flash: I experience another fleeting Zed-moment and the futility of my Zootherapy career again strikes me once again with a stark clarity. But this time there's no raucous crowd of celebratory drink-sodden dinner guests. I can't avoid the question and I can't lie: how long has it been since I actually practised Zootherapy? I've been teaching it to others, organising seminars, talking about it, writing about it, taking money for it, and now have received an award for it. But I've become too busy to do it. Too 'busy'. My time's too precious! I'm such an important guy! My clients need me! They've put me on a pedestal, but its foundations are built on mud and sand. I'm just another of those guys who think they validate their philosophy by trying to convert everyone to it, rather than actually living it.

It's not all lost. Not yet. Tina gets out of bed. Top priority is to feed the cat to stop her yowling. And then over coffee, we talk. To Tina I'm no icon – just a workaholic husband, an absent father. The rest of the world (well, no, let's not exaggerate, a few high-society people in one corner of it) might have raised me up, but Tina knows me better than any of the luminaries of last night, who voted me the winner of that gimcrack trophy, now lying on top of the papers in my briefcase by our front door. My entire body and soul become an apology. It's like sloughing off a layer of skin – Mr Zootherapy, the snake, moulting, humbled. But it's not irretrievable; this is what I've been telling straying husbands and wives, bereaved parents, drivers done for manslaughter. Practise Zootherapy! Give your animal nature a chance! And so I do. To do anything else would be dangerous. And now I'm in Zootherapy-mode. Instinct takes over; my decision is made. We're going away. Right now.

The next couple of hours we're both on our phones: I'm ringing Kate asking her to put off my clients – again – and postpone training sessions for the next week. 'Tell them it's a family emergency.' Tell them the truth, in other words. Tina rings her mum who says she'll cancel her hair appointment that morning and responds agreeably to our request for her to come round as soon as she's dressed so she can stay at our place and look after Sam and Kitty for at least the next few days. Samantha senses the change in mood and emerges from her room. 'We're going away for a few days – grandma's coming to stay,' we tell her. 'Remember Kitty needs food *and* milk *and* water'. Sam can't know all that's going on but she sees us talking and doing something together. It's a start.

Now we're packing, urgently, almost randomly. Tina's mum arrives; some quick hugs; I ring for a taxi that arrives within minutes. Cases in the boot, doors slam, and we are off to the airport. In the back seat, I put my hand on Tina's thigh, and she doesn't withdraw. However this turns out, I know I'm doing the right thing. It's not a matter of seeing things in perspective, or nibbling a couple of hours off my hectic weekly schedule so that I can spend a bit more 'quality time' with my wife and daughter or perhaps make room for a date night once a week. Everything needs to change. Urgently. Right now. We have to get away.

AKL-BKK

For the second time in twenty-four hours I touch down at Auckland Airport. A quick walk to the International Terminal, a quick decision over our destination: 'It doesn't matter! Wherever the next plane's going!' I say to the clean-cut guy behind the first ticket sales desk we encounter. The faintest flicker of a quizzical look, a glance at our suitcases and he tells us we have to check in; the quickest he can do is Bangkok, departing in 90 minutes. We pay for Business Class tickets, and wheel our baggage over to check in, where we are told that we've been upgraded to First Class. Through passport control, security and on to the First Class Lounge, shared by Thai Air and a few other airlines. I can feel our marriage being reformed as we sit on a sofa, looking out over the tarmac, and beyond to Manukau Harbour, sipping drinks: complimentary champagne for Tina, fizzy mineral water for me. I should really have a shave, but I don't want to leave Tina's side. After half an hour, a neat young man sporting a dark blazer comes to our sofa and discreetly tells us that our flight to Bangkok is ready for boarding. He escorts us to the gate; another passport check and we're on the plane. Tina takes the window seat. We're not talking much but we do hold hands during the take-off roll. Nearly 3pm; difficult to believe that twenty-four hours earlier I was in my office, with a client, contemplating my evening in Auckland; and that early this morning I was hurtling down the same runway bound for Wellington.

At cruise altitude we are served canapes, and then an elaborate lunch; the only sound this close to the front of the aircraft is a faint hum from the engines and the rush of air sweeping past the cabin.

Exhausted, and still suffering from the effects of the previous evening's alcohol, I eat little, forgo all the wines and the sticky-chocolate dessert, recline my seat and fall into a deep, not-quite-contented, sleep.

I wake up several hours later; Tina's asleep and the cabin's mostly in darkness. The petite oriental flight attendant helps me return my seat to the sitting position, hands me a hot towel and asks if there's anything I want from the galley. I ask for tea and, while sipping, think about one of the less dramatic aspects of the last day or so: the ever-so-slightly lingering looks from the people who've encountered me in the airports. Even the taxi drivers in Wellington, the ticket agent; nothing too overt, just a few unnecessary microseconds of their staring beyond the time of our interaction. And I realise it's exactly how I respond when I see the face of someone I think I recognise, but I'm not sure from where, or whether it's really are the person I think it is. Simple really: they must've glimpsed me on TV last nighty or seen a picture of the award ceremony in the morning papers.

I get up to wash and shave in the capacious bathroom, then return to my seat and ask for more tea. And so, as we fly north and west through the extended night, pools of light illuminating the somnolent cabin I think about what I have become: basically, a salesman. I've allowed Zootherapy, the career, to distract me from Zootherapy, the practice. I've let Zootherapy be corrupted, commodified. The Market, that alternative to God as the great organising principle of our age, has digested Zootherapy and converted it into a brand, a body of knowledge, another dish on the lifestyle buffet, a vehicle for selling courses, costumes and, most sadly of all, my time. I have become Zootherapy Inc, the personality, whose whole life – at the expense of his loved ones – is devoted to Zootherapy, but who doesn't actually get round to practising it. I've

120

been beguiled by the baubles. Kiwi icon? Don't make me laugh. I've let everyone down, and not just the people I love most.

Perhaps it was inevitable, and so excusable? I mean, what hasn't been converted into a commodity these days? The environment, the arts, relationships...the list goes on. What chance did I have? So I try to persuade or excuse myself, in the swoosh of the forward cabin of the 747, my wife asleep by my side. It could have happened to anyone. Well – it *has* happened to everyone, more or less. We've all got our excuses; ourselves and our families to support.

They say you have to hit rock bottom before you can climb up again. They say a lot of stuff that sounds wise but makes no sense when you think about it. Nobody rings a bell when you've hit rock bottom, any more than they do when the sharemarket hits a low, telling you it's time to buy. But it *seems* like rock bottom, and sometime between my second and third cup of my second pot of tea I forgive myself. It might not be permanent, but it is instant. Zootherapy without the animal costume. Sure, I've failed, in the past. But what is the past? Some neurons amongst billions; like a few unusually shaped and not particularly well-formed grains of sand on the beach. An irrelevance. Zed-mode is the same whether you're a beginner or a Zed-master or even the founder of Zootherapy.

All I have to do is raise my eyebrows a fraction, James Bond style, and our flight attendant comes over. I ask for a pen and paper, and this is what I write.

LESSON 6

- *There's no progress in Zootherapy. You're either doing it, or you're not. The notion of progress in Zootherapy is just another impediment to Zootherapy. You can no more decide to do Zootherapy than you can decide to fall asleep. All you can do is remove obstacles.*

- *If preaching it, selling it, promoting it, talking about it interferes with even one minute's practice, drop all that stuff and just do it.*

- *If you feel better afterwards: fine. If you don't: also fine. Zootherapy is not about fulfilling hopes or dreams or achieving anything. It's not a system or a technology. If it doesn't seem to be working be aware of that and of your reaction to that and just see it all as an animal would: something you need to ignore, so you can be alert to your environment.*

- *Don't spend time trying to convert other people to Zootherapy: don't think that preaching Zootherapy is the same as practising it. You validate Zootherapy not by teaching it, preaching it, or writing books about it, but by living it.*

Eight hours into the flight, another three and a half to go. A few miles above Borneo, according to the flight tracker map on the screen in front of me. The window shades are down, but I sense the blackness outside. All the passengers in the cabin are asleep, but the ever-attentive Thai crew members keep a discreet eye on us.

BANGKOK

Having overdosed on luxury, we eschew the airport limousines and wait in a fast-moving queue for a public taxi; the humid heat's like a warm enveloping blanket. It's close to midnight; whistles and shouts, doors slamming; the line clears quickly. Our luggage loaded, the driver asks, in fractured English, where we are staying. I say 'We don't know'. I haven't travelled overseas for a long time and this counts as a beginner's error. I add, remembering a feature in the inflight magazine, that we want to stay near the Grand Palace. I say I'll give him some cash if he finds a place we like. We're in his hands, and through a combination of his erudition and happy chance we end up in a three-star hotel in the old core of the city, near the backpackers' haunts in Khao Sarn Road. Despite the random choice of destination – Bangkok was the destination of the first feasible plane out of New Zealand – it feels right. I'm glad we're not surrounded by the English language, which would hook us into distraction and recrimination.

We're up early; the sun rises quickly and walking around the area after breakfast we find that we're well away from the sleaze and the shopping malls and over-the-top luxury. The tourists here are a wholesome, diverse bunch; lots of youngsters from Europe and Australia, many of them, judging from their wide-eyed curiosity, experiencing Asia for their first time. For the first couple of days we hardly stray beyond a few hundred metres from the hotel. Within that densely packed circle we experience a richness, luminosity and chaos that is as bewilderingly diverse as rainforest. The analytical part of the mind switches off when surrounded by a world it cannot comprehend. You can't take it all in. There's the street market; the vendors selling tee-shirts, saucepans, dodgy watches, software disks, food stalls and internet cafes. A monastery spire glows golden in the sun. But it's the Thais who charm us the most. The laughing chambermaids, the lively stall-holders, hoping for a sale but never pestering; courteous, peaceable, beguiling people.

OK, that sounds patronising, but don't be too hard on me. We've gone through a rough patch. It's excusable, isn't it, for us right now to be seeing things in their most favourable light? So we do the usual tourist things. We join a motley crowd, including several orange-robed monks, boarding one of the public ferry boats that ply the tea-coloured Chao Phraya River with its lugubrious rice barges. We do the Grand Palace, Wat Po and see the reclining Buddha. And in this setting, surrounded by so much literal warmth, and an entirely different and impenetrable culture, we fall in love again, not only with each other, but also with ourselves. Perhaps it is the stray dogs, torpid by day, who just lie near busy shop doorways, or in the monasteries, undisturbed. The Thais would walk around them, letting them be. Or perhaps it is the images of the Buddha in repose or in silent meditation, or the people, or the heat, the fumes, the traffic, or the whole exotic combination, but what rubs off onto us is the *jai yen*, 'cool heart', cultivated by the Thais and the absence of judgement, the acceptance of it all including, above all, our own flawed selves.

We're aware of the rubbish piled high on the streets (though I don't point out to Tina the rats poking around therein, always at the edge of the frame), aware too of the cement blocks that most Thais live in, the undistinguished skyscrapers the murderous traffic, the flyovers. And we read in the *Bangkok Post* about the dramatic and (to westerners) unpredictable eruptions of violence. The guidebooks tell about corruption and sex tourism and human trafficking and all the rest. But for Tina and I, now, privileged visitors, our days are filled with wonder. Sure, Bangkok on the surface is an unlovely big Asian city: dirty and dangerous, staggeringly unequal, noisy and chaotic. But we love it.

Our last evening; the street market of tee-shirts, bras, shoes and just about everything else has packed up for the day to be replaced by busy streetside food stalls. We sit at blue plastic tables on plastic stools beside gas canisters and flames licking up the sides of enormous woks. We're having dinner, along with tourists, ordinary Thais and a businessman who drives up in a Mercedes and orders rice and various servings in clear plastic bags to take home. We're sharing a large bottle of Singha beer, while seafood platters and rice are being brought to our table. A couple of skinny dogs, more active in the cool of the evening, are prowling. Competing for a scrap of something that's swept off a table, one of them gives a brief bark. Around us people are speaking in Thai, so musical, so foreign. It strikes me then that dogs bark and growl - and birds call and cats miaow - in Thailand just the same as they do in New Zealand. Such familiar sounds in such an alien environment.

'How come,' I muse to Tina, 'animals speak the same language everywhere, yet we humans can't manage it?'

Tina smiles and puts her hand on top of mine, 'Maybe it just sounds the same to us. Just like they probably think we're speaking Thai'.

'I wonder whether they know they don't understand what we're saying. You know, how does Kitty feel when we're chatting to each other?' I point to the dogs waiting expectantly by our table, 'Do they know there's something going on that they can't understand? Like we do, hearing everyone speak Thai?'

Animals practising Zootherapy. Hardly surprising. There they are diffusing their sense of self into their surroundings, unmediated by language, not bothering to try to understand. Do they know that attempts to comprehend are not going to get them anywhere, so the only sane response, the only thing that comes naturally, is for their minds to become silent; to observe without trying to work it all out or judge everything? With no purchase on the babble of voices around them, there's nothing between them and their environment. Tina strokes my arm, 'I wouldn't overthink it James. It's more a case of "If I do this, I'll get that."' A long pause: 'I wish we could stay here longer. I miss Sammy though.'

'We don't have to go back you know.' And right now, this strikes me as true: the cost of living is low here, and we're probably wealthy enough. We could keep our properties in New Zealand and the rental income would be more than enough for a decent lifestyle in Thailand. Subject to bureaucratic uncertainties, I reckon we could stay in Thailand as permanent tourists.

Tina sighs, 'Mum? Sammy?'

'We get your Mum and Sam on the plane here. We rent a serviced apartment, with a swimming pool. Sam would love it. You've seen how Thais love kids. There are lots of expatriates, English-speaking schools. Your mum can stay too if she wants. We can learn Thai. Let the house or sell it. Close down New Zealand. Your pals would visit. We can stay here as long as we like.' I gesture around, at the plastic chairs and metal tables, the pots and dishes of curries and rice. You'll never have to cook again.'

'Your work, your clients; and it's too hot for mum.'

'I'll get new clients. Lots of English-speaking expats here. Anyway, work doesn't matter. I've done Zootherapy. If people want to know about it, they can find it.' This is true: with a bit of help, I've put the essential Zootherapy teachings on the internet, free to read, free to download. I point to the empty plastic bowls on our table. 'Food's cheap here. So's everything else. We can travel round Asia.'

'Kitty?'

'She can come with us. Maybe. Or we'll find her a good home. Your mum, if she doesn't want to live here. Not a problem.'

But we've booked and paid for our flights and we do the automatic, sensible thing, and the next afternoon we pack our bags and take a taxi to the airport for our night flight to Auckland.

BKK-AKL

Back in the world of luxury. We're upgraded again, and have time for a free massage in Thai Air's sumptuous First Class Lounge. We decline the offer of a trip on the electric cart to our gate, and only on our walk through the shopping malls do we get an impression of the sheer numbers of flights and travellers using the airport. By the time we get to our gate, the holding pen is almost deserted. We're nearly the last to board. The cabin's almost empty: maybe three or four other passengers, and the same number of flight attendants.

Tina takes the window seat again. A glass of champagne, then all the announcements, take-off, more drinks, dinner. We recline our seats, and doze off. I wake up maybe a couple of hours later, to find that we've been covered with fleecy blankets. The lights are dimmed. It's still dark outside. Tina's fast asleep. An attendant brings me a hot towel. I get up to stretch my legs, and stroll through the curtain into Business Class. The engine noise is a fraction louder here, but still subdued. This cabin's maybe half full. Everyone's asleep, except for someone sitting upright, his shiny bald pate reflecting his reading light. Another night owl. I take in the orange robes of a Thai Buddhist monk; but the man's pale, with European features.

He looks vaguely familiar. At first I can't place him. Shorn of hair and eyebrows: no... surely not? But New Zealand is a small country and these things do happen. It is indeed someone I have met: it's Karl. Karl who, several years ago punched me in the ribs, gave me a black eye, and sent me to hospital. Karl, now dressed in Buddhist robes, silently intoning from some exotic text in a large format book propped up on his tray table. He looks up, a faint, flickering smile of recognition. He gestures to the empty seat beside him, and explains everything.

His assault on me transformed both our lives. It propelled me into hospital and towards the love of my life. It led him to a police caution, which went onto his record, so the next time he struck someone (a month or so later, outside a Newtown bottle store) he was sent to trial, charged with assault at the end of which was revealed his long history of violent assaults, cautions, arrests, suspended sentences. But this time he was given a short jail term. Not the most sympathetic character, nor the most receptive to new ideas, he'd been left alone by all the chaplains except the Buddhist monk from the Stokes Valley monastery north of Wellington. With abundant time to contemplate his life and actions, and with the inexhaustible patience of the mentoring monk, Karl had studied

Buddhism and begun to meditate in his cell. After his release, and several years of being a Theravada initiate at Stokes Valley he had, just a few days earlier, been ordained as a monk in a forest monastery in northeast Thailand. He's heading back to Stokes Valley, where he will wake at 4 am every morning, chant in Pali (he glances at the text in front of him), meditate and do menial tasks, more studying, and giving talks about Buddhism to visitors and schools in the region. (And, perhaps, he says smiling, he'll be a prison chaplain at some point.) What's he doing flying Business Class? Ah, he answers; his Economy Class fare was donated by lay people, but Thai Air upgrades all monks as a matter of routine.

It sounds unbelievable, I know. But we're both kiwis: reinvention is a possibility in these new countries, bereft of the ballast of history. Karl had been a persistent truant, born into a feckless family in one of the North Island's smallest east coast towns. He'd been luckier than some. His parents had simply ignored rather than abused him. A natural loner and often absent from school, in his early years he'd spent much of his plentiful spare time amidst nature; nature, which may be red in tooth and claw, but is also a great deal less wantonly cruel than the worst of kiwi culture, with its gangs, drugs, and violence. They came along later; late enough, anyway, that Karl's life wasn't irredeemable. His silent aggression, his lack of empathy and humour – all apparent in our one and only Zootherapy session - have miraculously metamorphosed into a serious Buddhist serenity.

At my request, he talked a bit about Buddhism. Tina and I had seen its superficial manifestations: the walks taken by the monks in the comparative cool and calm of the early mornings, to receive the food offerings of ordinary Thais, the amulets for sale, the birds in tiny wooden cages, to be released as an act of merit in return for a cash payment, the horoscopes and lottery numbers for sale. Karl's dismissive.

'The real Buddhist practice,' Karl says, 'isn't in the city, but in the forests, meditating, chanting, and learning.' He talks about the uncertainty of life, the fact of suffering, the way we cling to things that cannot satisfy us. Karl's gentle manner, his grounded goodwill, and his benevolent tone, while we talk against the background of faint engine noise and air rushing past the plane, affect me. A bit of turbulence, a faint gong, the seatbelt signs come on and I leave Karl to be with Tina. I think she might have woken up, but I find she's still sleeping peacefully. I ask for a beer.

I've never sneered at religion, and much of what Karl said makes sense. Perhaps donning an orange robe works in the same way as stepping into an animal costume. But Zootherapy seems much easier, though, and more immediate, than poring over voluminous tomes of esoteric scripture and waking up before dawn. Still, Karl's assured manner is humbling. In the solitude of the cabin, I wonder why I feel this need to believe that Zootherapy is the sole solution to the human condition. Isn't there room for alternative approaches? Are they really so different? Had Karl leapfrogged over me into enlightenment? How does that make me feel? How should I feel?

So this is what I write:

LESSON 7

- *Zootherapy doesn't have to be a complete answer, nor does it compete with any religion, ideology or philosophy. Ritual, chanting, organisation, hierarchy, distinctive dress, scriptures and ceremony; they all have their place, perhaps, but so too do immediacy and accessibility. You don't need to study or meditate or perform elaborate rituals to practise Zootherapy or even to teach Zootherapy. You just need to realise – that is, to make real - your animal nature. Anyone can do it. Children can do it. Animals are doing it all the time.*

Funny thing, the human mind. I think about Tina and me. How the distance between us began as a minute crack, as on a dinner plate, then imperceptibly (to me) widened over the past year or so. But it's been mercifully easy to close. We both know the theory of Zootherapy and can practise it, not all the time, but enough to repair the damage. It's best, isn't it, to have an animal memory? Starting out with facts, we humans then part company from the other animals: we generate narratives out of facts, then find the evidence that justifies our narrative. Language becomes a commentary on the narrative, then a commentary on the commentary. It's what we do and it can be fun – it's culture! - but not when it poisons the present. Every relationship has bad patches. Recalling them is expanding them; then there's no hope. Before I left the Ministry, we had a meeting with chap with glasses and a ponytail talking about the spiffing new Relational Database that he was going to set up. A what? He explained: a Relational Database is like a big bucket of data that we can access with different dippers. As with human history, an individual's life is so complex, so rich we can selectively choose a set of facts that will justify any story we want to narrate. Which comes first? I'm sure I saw it proved somewhere that we start with the conclusion and then rationalise how we got there. Motivated reasoning, it's called.

We're all doing it; me, everyone on this plane, crew, passengers, all with our histories. And, again, I'm reminded that animals aren't haunted by their past: sure, there are inherited instincts, and extreme early-age experiences whose recurrence they will fear and try to avoid. But their narratives don't define animals as they do us. All right. It's a matter of degree. But objectively, animals strip out more of the nonsense. Neither, though, do they fly planes, write books or compose piano concertos. Is the trade-off worth it? To animals? To us? Maybe their smaller brain is a choice they made when they saw where their big brain would get them – somewhere like where humans are today. We seem dominant now, but maybe the animals are biding their time; they've seen our future and it doesn't work. Or it could be that they're really smarter than us and have seen what we do to smart humans. Maybe they'll outlive us. All right; enough with the high-altitude speculation. Tina stirs and within seconds our flight attendant brings her a hot towel. Tina lifts up her window shade. I lean over. We see at the edge of the inky black sky just a hint of the beginning of a new day. Time for breakfast.

WELLINGTON, 2003-04

Thailand has worked its magic on us. Our marriage is strong again. A new departure for me: I turn away clients when I think I'm overdoing it: it's difficult at first but, with Kate's help, becomes easier. Tina starts work at the hospital again, part time, day time shifts. We don't need the income; it's more that Tina wants to keep her hand in and escape the emptiness of daytime suburban New Zealand. I am still earning a decent living, by New Zealand standards. And Tina and I make an explicit, binding commitment to practise what I preach. It was absurd that I, Mr Zootherapy, had stopped actually practising Zootherapy. So every Friday evening and every Sunday morning or afternoon one or both of us will now put on an animal costume for at least 20 minutes. It doesn't matter which animal – we have a big range in the wardrobes in our spare room; and it doesn't matter what happens while the costume is being worn. (Very often, it's sex.) Our rock-solid commitment becomes the behavioural equivalent of the rings we wear. And we introduce Samantha to Zootherapy, with child-size costumes and open faces. She loves it, and she loves animals in general. She is growing up fast, and wants to be a vet.

Tina, Sam, Kitty and I are happy together and, with my Kiwi Icon fame, I can charge more for my time. This I do, partly for Samantha's financial security, partly because higher rates enhance any placebo effect, and partly also because I do not want to be put into a box labelled 'idealist' or 'do-gooder', and thereby written off by ordinary folk. With the limited number of individual clients I see, I spend more time on lucrative corporate training sessions and motivational seminars in Wellington and, occasionally, Auckland. Zootherapy begins to become a part of the New Zealand mainstream: recognised, or at least, tolerated, by some in the medical profession who had disdained it in its earlier days. Sam, even as she becomes a teenager, continues to practise Zootherapy with us every Sunday and promotes it to her school pals. (I even give a talk at her school to the older kids - complete with a demonstration using open face costumes.) We can afford private tuition for Sam (for flute, ballet and maths), and we are living well.

Dolphins, 2008

We've had a good few years living, I guess, the New Zealand dream, despite my unconventional occupation. Samantha is a young woman now. She and Tina, if anything, grow closer. Kitty is the same as ever, only bigger and now she wears a little bell to warn birds of her approach. She still delivers presents to our back door: usually dead fieldmice. And Zootherapy? It meanders on: no big breakthroughs, no drama, but I'm in my 50s now and want others to carry the torch for when I retire. So I begin training human resource personnel and counsellors to become Zootherapists themselves. The ambivalence I used to feel – I created Zootherapy; it's my baby! and I want to control it – doesn't entirely disappear, but in my moments of clarity I realise that this is the only way forward: to light the flame for others, and trust that in their practice they will ensure that the core teachings remain uncorrupted.

Training people to become Zootherapists is going to be subtly different from just teaching people how to practise Zootherapy regularly. With Tina's help, I try to anticipate likely questions. For instance: what about Zootherapy outside the main centres – won't people living there challenge my trainees, saying Zootherapy's elitist – something that only rich people do?

Tina and I agree that I'll advise them to say something like 'It works for me', and leave it at that. We don't want them to start talking about their individual problems. It's one reason why I've never really shared my past with anyone in New Zealand, except Jason and Tina. Certainly none of my Zootherapy clients. Whatever I've gone through will be different from what they've gone through. Maybe worse, maybe better, but certainly different. And that would give them an excuse to think that Zootherapy is not for them. There are always any number of good, plausible reasons not to do anything, especially including something as superficially outlandish as Zootherapy. At home, Tina nails it:

'Your trainees can do what you do when you give these radio interviews. Tell them some people are always going to see Zootherapy as either new age nonsense or a threat. Tell them to keep it simple. We all suffer because we're human, and Zootherapy may be of help in some cases. That's all.'

And so, in 2008, I conduct my first training session for aspiring Zootherapists. This takes place in another of those windowless conference rooms but this time, in keeping with our family finances and the upmarket image I aim to project, I'm in the rather swish Park Royal Hotel, a stone's throw from my office. I'm standing at the front of the room where there is a billboard-size plasma screen wireless linked to my laptop, showing frames of my presentation. Four men, four women: six kiwis, two Australians, from 35 to 55 years old, looking for an alternative to the more ordinary careers with which they've become disenchanted. They've gone through Zootherapy themselves, with me: most of them not out of any urgent need, but as a precondition for my training. They have paid quite a bit for my tuition and will have to submit to additional scrutiny by Mr

Zootherapy himself before they can become registered as practising members of the professional body I've created, which, in a moment of megalomania I've named: The Oceania Society of Zootherapists. We've had ten days of fairly intensive lectures and tutorials, all conducted by myself. I intend this group to form the nucleus of new Zootherapy centres around New Zealand and Australia. My presentation is just ending, and I ask whether there are any questions. There's an awkward pause while I pretend to be busy with my laptop.

Anna, an ex-lecturer in finance at Auckland University, raises her hand.

'What if a client is a bit self-conscious and they absolutely refuse to dress up as an animal?'

Ah; the recurring question; the one I've been asking myself for years. The others nod and murmur: they want to know the answer too. Anna continues: 'Or maybe physically – they're just too big or claustrophobic or something. They think as long as they *imagine* they're an animal that will be OK.' More expressions of support for this question.

'This is one of the most common problems. Ultimately it's about humility. The client has to acknowledge that change is possible and desirable. At least for part of your first dress session, you should try to insist on your client's wearing the entire animal costume. You're opening up to new behaviour patterns, and the client will have some idea anyway what to expect. I can't stress this too strongly.' I pause. 'I had problems in my early days; there were no quick computerised costume fabrication shops then. I took short cuts; head only, imagination only, whatever; it works with some but not with others, and you can't know in advance which will be which.' I pause, while they take notes.

'After the first session, or maybe the first few sessions, and you have to play it by ear, you can probably dispense with the costume body. At that stage, some reminder, even some symbolic reminder, of the animal they're supposed to be – and actually are - will be enough. You'll be the judge. That's where your experience will come in.'

'What if they're claustrophobic?'

'If they really can't...to be frank: it depends. I've had reluctant, *extremely* reluctant clients. But if there's a real phobia about being enclosed, then you can allow either the head or the body, rather than both. Maybe a bit more talking than the norm will help. But almost always you'll find that resistance to putting on the costume is an indicator of a personality problem, and you go some way to solving that by getting them to agree to the whole costume. You do what you can.'

A few mundane questions about tomorrow's schedule, then the trainees gather their materials. Most of them are staying at the hotel (some have doubled up, it's low season, and I've negotiated a special rate) so they haven't brought coats or backpacks. I turn off the power to the TV and begin closing down my laptop.

'All right that's it for today. See you again tomorrow, 9.30am.'

They file out of the room. I tidy up my things and switch off the plasma screen. One of the trainees, Sarah, asks me for a copy of some of today's notes. She's spilt coffee on hers. Outside the doorway I see a sombre-looking policeman and policewoman in uniform, holding their hats, waiting patiently. This can't be good: do they want Sarah or me?

I riffle through my papers and hand a copy to Sarah, who thanks me and leaves. Then they enter the room. Oh. One policeman? It could have been somebody slashing my tires, a burglary at home. But two? My first thought is some frivolous but career-killing accusation of sexual harassment. (But I'm innocent!) Their expressions hint that it's worse even than that. They're awkward, grave. Something is very wrong. I can feel the blood draining from my head. I feel faint. They gesture to a chair. I move over to it, but don't sit down.

'What's happened? Tina? Sam?'

The policewoman looks down; the policeman looks directly at me, with an obvious effort. They are silent, neither confirming or denying.

'How bad is it?'

The policewoman meets my eyes now. 'I'm afraid it's the very worst.'

Tina had picked up Samantha from school, taken her home, where they'd had a quick tea. Back in the car for the drive into town for Samantha's ballet class. Samantha was sitting in the front passenger seat. Tina had to turn into the main road to Wellington from the north. The details were vague, or I wasn't taking them in, but the gist of it was that a truck came along at high speed toward Tina as she was turning right, into the traffic. That was the end. Horrific. Instant for Tina, almost instant for Samantha. The finality is devastating. It seems the police have been to Tina's mother's house, waited for her to return from some play or movie or whatever, and told her. Having done so, they rang a friend to make sure she's not alone.

I'm numb, overwhelmed by a sense of futility, tinged with relief that they're not still suffering. A recognition that from now, and for ever, I'll be on my own. And I feel for the two people standing awkwardly before me.

'OK, thank you.' I hear myself saying. 'You can go now.'

They look at each other.

The policeman speaks 'We do need you to make a formal identification.'

The policewoman nods and says 'We'll drive you to the morgue, and then take you home.'

'Home?' I say, my throat dry. Get a grip 'OK, could you wait outside for a minute.' They look at each other. 'It's all right, I'm not going to...' I almost say 'do anything silly'; the maddening euphemism, but I am just coherent enough to say '...kill myself.'

They look at each other then leave the room, closing the door quietly behind them.

I shall have to get used to this solitude.

'Tina. Sam.'

I stand, then sit down again, for fear of fainting. I close my eyes, breathing deeply. The tears begin to flow.

Beside me on a table are some dolphin costumes we've been using for role play. Their smiles seem to mock me. I give a shout, a brief howl, and punch one in the face. Its teeth graze the back of my hand; I'm glad of the pain.

And now I take comfort in ritual: as if in a dream I take another dolphin costume and step into it, first the body, zipping it up at the front. Then the head.

Wearing the costume, I sit still; for how long I don't know, with eyes closed. At some point I open my eyes, and see my reflection in the laptop screen. I see the dolphin smiling and my bright eyes peeping through. That one glimpse of myself as a dolphin, through the eyes of a dolphin, gives me hope. For a fraction of a second I know I'll never stop mourning, but nor shall I ever be without a way of seeing it through. I see neither the past nor the future, but only the crystal clarity of the present. The worst has already happened. It can't happen again. It can't get worse.

The dolphin smile, which just minutes ago was mocking, leering, sinister, reminds me now of something vaguely familiar, wise and benign. It takes me back to the temples in Bangkok, the Buddha's quiet smile, acknowledging our suffering and life's uncertainty.

I remember the rest of the evening vividly: unzipping the dolphin costume, packing up my things, leaving the training room and seeing the police officers still waiting for me outside. I remember how they instantly stop chatting when my opening the door interrupts their conversation. We go down to the hotel reception and I tell the uniformed concierge about a 'family emergency' so could they please send my laptop and all the other stuff to my office? I accompany the police to the morgue. Outwardly I'm calm. Inwardly I'm empty. There's no precedent for this. The police officers take control and I'm relieved not to have to make any decisions.

I find myself behaving as I imagine Tina would want her Mr Zootherapy to behave. How she would behave. Has her soul somehow been redistributed amongst those who were close to her when she was living? The policewoman helps me by taking me home and, when I most need it, walking with me into the empty house. Well, not quite empty: an unfed Kitty is yowling incessantly on the front doorstep and scurrying quickly inside once the door's open for her delayed dinner.

FARM DOGS, 1973

One summer weekend afternoon, soon after we'd left the city, I am mooching around in the field adjacent to our back garden in the rolling dairy country of the Cheshire countryside. Our little 'Jack Russell type' terrier Louie and cat, Misty, are there with me. Then I see the dogs of the neighbouring farm through the fence. Ugly brutes. I've done some vacation work on the farm and know these dogs are vicious. On the farmer's premises they had to be shouted at by the family to stop them attacking strangers. There are at least three of them, but I see only an amorphous seething mass. With no little anxiety, I begin to walk towards our house, about 400 metres down the slope, trying not to attract the dogs' attention. I'm new to this rural lifestyle and, frankly, scared. The farm dogs sense my fear. I begin to run, Louie runs with me and I'm holding Misty awkwardly in my arms. The dogs chase, closing the gap; Misty squirms and I release her. Panicking now, Louie overtakes me. The dogs are gaining on us, fast. No chance of making it to the house. I know they'll go for my throat. A quick glance back; I'll never make it to the house on time. I'm going to be mauled, maybe to death.

They say at times of crisis you become capable of extraordinary feats. I have no choice. No time to think. I stop, turn and flap my arms and in a voice louder than you'd think my ectomorphic physique could produce, I shout and shout and shout. The farm dogs – amazingly – stop! I'm sure the expression on their faces is that of puzzlement. I keep shouting, and gesticulating, gaining in power and confidence, as the hounds from hell now look – surely not – embarrassed. At this point, Louie also sees how things are going; he runs back to me and, emboldened, joins with me and barks at the dogs, each one of which is three times his size. We take great pleasure in seeing the dogs slink away. We even give chase, and they hurry back up the slope and through the fence. Misty, sensibly, is up a tree, and comes down now that all is clear. A vast relief, intruded on only slightly by the totally unreasonable thought that Misty's been a little dishonourable in not wanting to share what looked like my inevitable violent ending. Louie too; he came to support me only when victory was assured. Where was their loyalty? Where was their team spirit? Ridiculous thoughts of course. And Louie, let's be fair, *had* eventually sided with me against his conspecifics.

An unforgettable experience for me, but an everyday one for Louie and Misty, whose survival beyond the next second or two is never guaranteed.

LESSON 8

- *Zootherapy won't stop bad things happening to you, but it can change your perspective. To have an animal's perspective means not to think about things about which you cannot do anything. To feel only what your animal self feels. Example: there's something really fearful in prospect; can you get away from it? If yes, do so. If not, if it's something unavoidable, don't waste energy trying to deny the facts, even if they seem overwhelming. Turn toward the facts and confront them. You're ill, you're going to die, your husband or wife has been killed, your child is dying: confront the facts, engage with them as they are.*

- *Zootherapy can help: as an animal you focus only on what you can do now, not in the future, not in some ideal world, not by going back in time and fixing things retrospectively. You can't do any of that; thinking about doing so is a waste of energy. Practising Zootherapy suspends that thinking. When we practise Zootherapy we're not suppressing or acting: we're just being true to our animal nature. We focus on the moment. You cannot make the future problem-free. But in practising Zootherapy you deal with your current problem – and only your current problem. Zootherapy focuses you on the present moment. No more, no less.*

NOBODY NEEDS ME, 2008

It doesn't work. I don't just put on an animal costume when I feel depressed, and magically recover. I can't imagine that I can get better so I don't even try and, besides, there are times, to put it harshly, when I actually want to feel *something* and wallowing in self pity does that for me. But I also don't want Zootherapy to fail; to be tried and found wanting. And sometimes I just don't have the energy to do anything I don't have to, and putting on an animal costume is too much bother. Yes, I'm an animal, but I'm a human animal. Suffering is something I need to do.

That old familiar parental voice from childhood mocks me. Where's your enlightenment now, Mr Z? What a crock. Zootherapy shows its true colours: just another pseudo-therapy, about as helpful as a Christmas cracker quotation. And me? Another deluded New Ager who got lucky selling platitudes. I deserve to be happy? After a lifetime of privilege? Defeat on all fronts – somehow it seems more palatable than just one or two serious problems. No hope is better than some hope.

So I consider suicide: not out of despair or fear, but because of the emptiness. I see clients still and sometimes go round to Tina's mother, and we take a little comfort from sharing our grief. But it's not enough. Now that nobody needs me, not being alive seems a perfectly rational goal. I've had a good run. But how to end it? The simplest, most reliable, least painful way would be by gunshot to the temple, but I don't have a gun; I don't even know how to get one. I have a few dodgy ex-clients whose contact details are in my files. But no, what would it do for their anxiety levels - or to my whole Zootherapy edifice - if their therapist goes about killing himself? Still, you do wonder about the motives of those spoilsports who don't want us to own guns. They just assume that suicides by gunshot are always a bad thing. But what if they're a benefit? Surely a quick pull of the trigger's less painful than hanging or jumping in front of a lumbering locomotive. Perhaps the answer is a one-way trip to Thailand where, in a previous life, Tina and I got chatting to an Australian expat at a bar in Bangkok. If you want somebody bumped off, he said, your first move is to have a word with the motor-cycle taxi guys hanging around at strategic corners at the end of the *sois* leading into the main roads. Shoot me dead one night in the roofless concrete shell of one of the hundreds of abandoned building sites in and around Bangkok. I'm sure they'd do that for a few thousand baht. Maybe a few thousand more to pay off the police if there were ever to be an investigation. But the idea stumbles at the first fence: the thought of retracing our journey to Thailand, this time alone, is too painful to bear.

'It's a pity there's no market for life.' After a member of my family committed suicide many years ago, that's what one economist said to me. (It sounds cold, but what *can* you say?) And that's something else that makes me think again. It would be such a waste. Physically I'm OK. If I had a medical problem I imagine I'd feel perfectly fine ending it all. A cruel joke ... my good health condemns me to carry on. There's no means of transferring it to somebody who actually needs and deserves it. There must be hundreds of thousands in New Zealand alone. Mary, one of my less fortunate clients, for instance, afflicted with motor neurone disease, who has to be wheeled into my office. Perhaps, if I plan carefully, I could wear an organ donor card round my neck and get myself into a car accident near the hospital. No, too chancy and (probably) painful. It would traumatise the car driver and anybody in the area of the hospital. A gunshot somewhere on hospital grounds would be ideal. But no; no gun, and besides, what happens to my body if they have to do an autopsy? I'm just flying kites now. I won't do it. Even as a lapsed Zootherapy practitioner at the edge of the abyss my animal nature asserts itself. I don't really want to die.

THANK GOD FOR THE COUNTERFACTUAL
I think back to my time at the Ministry. Every so often statistics would come out showing certain social welfare indicators getting worse either absolutely, or relative to other developed countries. As well as our shameful record on youth suicides there are outbreaks of meningitis in children; domestic violence, drugs, gangs, inter-racial

strife. Sometimes a particularly tragic incident would make the news: one in which some unlucky, probably stressed-out, exhausted, Social Welfare employee had slipped up. The blowback from the media would be vicious. Frontline workers got the worst, but we'd feel it too. Over the tea urn or in the margins of internal meetings we'd chat amongst ourselves: 'We might as well go out of business'. Or 'The more we do, the more we get blamed when something goes wrong'.

One particularly bad day there'd been an almighty uproar in the morning papers about a child abuse case in which two social workers in the far north of the North Island had missed red flags on multiple occasions. Mike came out of his office during morning tea and tried to cheer us up.

'You know the newspapers: "If it bleeds, it leads". They never report on all the positive stuff. And they never consider the counterfactual.' Some questioning looks. 'What would be happening if we weren't there. That's the counterfactual. The papers don't care: we do our job and 99.9 percent of the time, we get it right and no-one pats us on the back. Nobody talks about that. Without us it would be worse, believe me. So *I'm* going to pat you on the back. Don't lose heart, and don't get defensive if you're challenged on this. Just ask them – where would the country would be without us? I know you're doing a good job. You know you're doing a good job. The newspapers, the media: they're not in the business of accuracy.'

It didn't exactly cheer us up, but it became something of a mantra on bad days: 'Thank God for the counterfactual.' In the counterfactual was our salvation. It kept us going. That, and the small matter of the fortnightly direct payment into our bank accounts from the Government payroll office.

The counterfactual was a comfort then, and it's become a comfort now. I'm in a dreadful state. But without Zootherapy it would be worse. I'm not practising it, but it's there when I want it. And it's my job. My escape from a bleak home life. Without clients and training sessions I'd have nothing at all. Zootherapy right now is a necessary and plausible reason for going on living. This has the great merit, not necessarily of being true, but of being unfalsifiable.

ALONE
Don't you hate it when you're suffering and the people you speak to – well meaning to be sure – basically just say things that validate the choices they made, the lifestyle they lead? 'Your problems are a result of your not doing this.' (The subtext being: 'which is what I did'.) Or 'It's because you're doing this.' (...'which I was smart enough to avoid doing'.) Or they come up with some slight variant of 'Count your blessings.' Or 'Just don't think about it'. Or some apparently more sophisticated, but similarly fatuous variant of 'Don't worry, be happy'.

Or they tell you to put on an animal suit.... I look at my course materials and I'm embarrassed. I see Zootherapy now as just another of these vapid, think-positive, thank-your-lucky-stars, there's-always-someone-worse-off-than-you, programmes. That's the trouble with a system: if it doesn't work all the time, it's a failure. What on earth had I been thinking? I can make people feel better? Maybe miserable people are miserable because they are doing the best they can, under the circumstances. *Their* circumstances, which no-one else has experienced nor can ever experience. We see a problem, we want to solve it or escape from it. But just perhaps, even if we're miserable; even if, as I have been, on the verge of suicide, that's the best, or the least worst, we can be. *There really is no better option.* At that minute anyway.

So, once again, practice and theory diverge. I work long hours: doing Zootherapy sessions, training would-be Zootherapists in Wellington, and making business decisions and helping Kate cope with the endless administrative chores. I don't dwell too much on the paradox that here I am, Mr Zootherapy himself, preaching and teaching happiness, fulfilment and success, dealing with my despair not by confronting it but by throwing myself into my work. I don't see anyone socially. I've been alone most of my life, so it's a return to the familiar. I craved solitude as a child, and lived in solitude as soon as it became feasible, so I can handle the practical aspects. Yes, the temptation to immerse myself in self-pity, misery, and righteous anger is always there, and sometimes I indulge it. I can't be bothered putting on an animal costume – how juvenile it seems to me now! Easier to be extolling (and marketing) Zootherapy's benefits than reaping them. I still like the *idea* of Zootherapy. It is there, as a discipline, a belief system, a body of teachings, and a source of income. It's there, waiting for me to actually practise it. I still get some tiny comfort from that. It's my choice to have it there on the shelf, rather than open it up and risk its failure.

Experienced as part of a couple, Wellington had been a pleasant bustling backdrop, filled with others like us; sharing our experience of working and living and family time. But now I see it only as a collection of cheap and nasty office buildings, empty most of the time, and isolated households, pools of domesticity. Enclosed. Alienating. People's interests narrowed down to paying back the loans on our drafty little houses, running a car.... How did we get like this? The more money we make, the better we are at fencing ourselves off from everyone else, especially misfits, such as me now. The guys who fall through the cracks. Temporarily wise, I see the pathology right there: the more attention I give to my sense of victimhood, the more I isolate myself. Even as I do it, I see it: thinking separates. That old cliché: 'he lives in his own world.' Worlds separated by constant, endless thinking to no purpose, walling us off from each other. The more active are our minds, the higher the walls.

So Zootherapy has left its traces. And, as if my body were that of an animal in my care (Kitty, less a companion than an irritable housemate, still gets top-notch dental treatment), I look after it, not succumbing to alcohol or other mind-altering substances. Unless you count television.

Cows 3

Late one night, I'm microwaving some frozen lasagne after work; I can't bear to sit and dine at a table, like we used to. Instead I invariably have my dinner in front of the TV, which I switch on as soon as I get home. While scoffing the lasagne, I chance upon a programme about how New Zealand's lakes and rivers are being polluted by dairy farming. The opening panoramas show the New Zealand countryside which, undeniably picturesque or even spectacular, doesn't do much for me. I wasn't brought up here and while it looks wonderful on calendars and chocolate boxes, it's mostly empty of people, houses, villages, humanity and history. Pals would occasionally take me through the landscape, up the coast road to the townships north of Wellington, or over the Rimutakas to the Wairarapa. Or I'd fly over it en route to and from Auckland. But I've never really felt a wish to explore it. Brought up in Manchester, I thought being in Wellington was like living in the country anyway. I could see green hills by looking out of the window at home, and the harbour and beach at Oriental Bay are just a short stroll from my office. Why leave the city? Besides, I never wanted to compete for road space with New Zealand's appalling motorists.

Sometimes you have an epiphany when you least expect it. There's stock footage of a mob of black and white cows grazing beside a stream, tails swishing. The grass is full, lush, emerald green. I sense the fresh, warm, humid breeze. A youthful, eager, male voiceover:

> Two years ago, the United Nations said "Livestock's contribution to environmental problems is on a massive

146

scale and its potential contribution to their solution is
equally large."

For maybe two seconds, the TV screen fills with the face of a cow, chewing; it flicks its tongue toward its nostrils, sticky with sweet-smelling cud. In that moment, between mouthfuls of lasagne, I'm transformed. As if a curtain is raised, I see the world as the cow sees it; with a full awareness of her environment, curious about the guy pointing a strange contraption at her face.

And Buttercup here is a large part of the problem. As we saw
last week, when she belches methane, she contributes to
climate change. But this week, we're going to look at water
pollution....

As the camera pans away toward the programme's cynosure – the back end of the cow – I switch off the TV (an unusual event for post-family me). In the quiet, I understand why the cow became an object of worship. The soft brown eyes, the gentleness, the gift of milk. Their placid acceptance. Of course, then the formalisers came along, the codifiers and the priesthood, imposing themselves between ordinary people and the animal they value. They make worship into an ideology with an attendant power structure upon whose pinnacle they sit. Then come the anthropologists with their rationalisations: the cow gives us milk, butter, meat, leather. But we can still look into the cow's soft big brown eyes, unmediated by in-depth knowledge, or philosophy, or the cynical guys who organise religion. An amazing thing happens. Well, two amazing things: First: I don't switch the TV on again. Second: after months and months of endless, useless, mental activity, I find myself in Zootherapy mode. A rare, precious, time of being at peace. Perhaps there is something in Zootherapy after all.

I could speculate on why the TV cow affected my perspective, and not real, live Kitty. Maybe it's just that I'm ready for it. Doesn't matter: Kitty, perhaps sensing the atmospherics, leaps up onto my lap and, for the first time in months, licks the back of my hand. In that minute, she ceases to be solely a poignant, resented, reminder of a golden past (she was always Samantha's pet) now gone for ever, and becomes a living thing in her own right. I never thought that she must be missing Tina and Sam too, in her own way. But she carries on, doesn't she?

All right; other people's pets are right up there with topless darts, the Linux operating system, and fake-moonshot conspiracy theories: of consuming interest to those involved; of zero interest to everyone else. But we can extract a broader meaning from them; we can learn from them, can't we? Well, this is what I learned:

LESSON 9

- *The unimportance of being rational and the unimportance of being smart: Animals don't go through life imagining how things could be different. They're not built for happiness and neither are we; we're built for survival. Don't force Zootherapy. Don't do Zootherapy as a means to an end, because you don't know what that end will be – and you don't want or need to know. In Zootherapy-mode we drop our accumulated memories and expectations. They represent a distraction from the world of nature. Don't panic! They'll be there when you need them.*

IN THE WORLD AGAIN

I'm diminished, hugely, to be sure. But I'm back in the world again, with a role to play. If I can no longer meet the needs of my wife and daughter, I can take on some of the world's problems and do my best to solve them. But I vow never to forget those recent desolate days, weeks, months, because loneliness, with no hope, is what life looks like for so many. Being alone made me see what cities have to offer those without a family or tribe for support; the people who can't take time off to write books, or start a business, or go on courses, or think of self-development, or who can't afford to look after animals, or who are damaged in countless other ways. People like my interviewees at the Ministry of Social Welfare, or some of my *pro bono* Zootherapy clients. Those who fall through the cracks. All I see are the bleak, blank suburban streets. A city being remodelled for cars, billboards appealing to one's greed. Society's single, loud message to the individual: 'We want your money'. Yes, my head knows of the free health care, free education, rule of law, subsidised housing. At some level too I know of the phone lines manned by volunteers, whom you can ring up if you desperately need to talk. But the default setting for those without family is emptiness, with some temporary human contact so long as you keep buying things. At Social Welfare I was told never to judge my interviewees and especially not to encourage women to leave abusive partners. Now I understand. Where would they go?

Death, survival and the animals

Kitty's become my companion. She sits on my lap and kneads my chest and grooms the back of my hand every evening. We're a team now, Kitty and me in our big empty house. I'm unsure of the quality of her relationships with others of her species in the area – my impression is they're of the love/hate kind – but I'm glad she is happy to spend time with me. She'd be fine without me, no question, but even if she were truly on her own, there's no chance she'd contemplate getting the lift up to the top the BNZ Tower (or whatever it's called now), climbing out onto the roof, and jumping off. Or some feline equivalent: teasing an aggressive dog, perhaps. She chooses life, every time.

You ask yourself sometimes whether cats, or any animals, are really lesser beings. Maybe they went through something like the human phase, with enlarged brains and thought processes like those that took us over, conjuring up visions of perfect worlds that we could reach only by destroying each other and the rest of nature. Or perhaps they didn't have to go through it to make their choice. Right at the start, they saw the agonies as well as the joys of being human. They took a planetary view; perhaps all the species consulted amongst themselves, did a cost-benefit analysis and used reasoning to decide that they didn't need reasoning. Maybe they knew humans would come along and try to wreck everything, but saw beyond us, to a time of human extinction or just possibly to a time of human enlightenment, when peace and the natural order of things would reign.

One Friday evening, Tina had speculated whether Zootherapy could work in reverse: could putting animals in human costumes make them more like us? We never actually did this. Partly because it was just one of many of our less practical (putting the bell on Kitty had been a three-person ordeal) wine-inspired ideas. But partly also because it seemed cruel.

We need some entrée into the world of nature. Something else from my induction course at the Ministry: a talk given by a lady who'd risen high in the ranks of psychiatry, before she became disillusioned and left that profession to work with a counselling service. 'My clients don't want answers', she told us. 'Yes, if there's something they're not aware of - a source of information, a new welfare benefit - that's fine; tell them about it. But if it's about their suffering, their circumstances, their state of mind, don't leap in with your bright ideas, or your solutions. Or what worked for you when you were in a similar state. Even if you were in exactly the same circumstances - which you never are - they don't want to know what worked for you. They don't want whizz-bang answers from some brilliant mind. What they want, what they need, is for you to listen.'

She's right, I think, and until Zootherapy came along, I thought that was all anyone could do. And maybe that is how Zootherapy works, for some people, some of the time. But I'm beginning to see now that Zootherapy, like any little or large engagement with nature, also works by reminding us that, as living beings, we are part of something much bigger than ourselves.

WASTING TAXPAYERS' MONEY

One lunchtime, in the Lambton Quay pedestrian rush hour, I bump into Rob, my rogue outsider ex-colleague from the Ministry, now close to retirement. There are a few seconds of awkwardness when he tries (and fails) to find the words to express his sympathy. Then he insists that we meet for a drink after work that evening.

'There's a pricing anomaly and we're not taking advantage of it!' We're half way through our first pint at the Oxford and Rob's trying to cheer me up. He's succeeding.

I say, 'I don't get it. You're saying you should be going to Paris instead of Sarah?'

'She's half my size!' This is almost true: Rob has a large frame and a paunch, while Sarah (much younger, but a Senior Analyst) is slim and toned; she bikes to work from Ngaio and competes in triathlons. Rob tells me she's going to Paris for a meeting of some committee or other of the Organisation of Economic Cooperation and Development as the New Zealand representative next month.

'It's not as glamorous as it sounds', I say, 'Trudging through security, taking your shoes off, putting liquids into plastic bags.' But Rob won't hear of it.

'They fly Business Class to these meetings now. Think of what they'd be saving if they sent me instead!'

'Well I don't see how they'd actually be saving anything....'

'Think about it; air fares are per person, right? They'd charge me the same as Sarah. And if they send me the cost per kilogramme would be half what they're spending. Irresponsible; that's what I call it. Spending taxpayers' money like there's no tomorrow. Typical government behaviour.' He gulps his beer. 'There's a pricing anomaly and we're not taking advantage of it. Doesn't have to be me. Could be Lynn.' (Not quite as heavy as Rob, but still much heavier than Sarah.) 'Other people's money,' he says, with a mock grimace. 'Disgusting.' At that point, we see another of my former co-workers, Maia, PA to Mike, showing plenty of cleavage, walking through the door and joining her boyfriend at the bar. She's obviously been working late; a common occurrence when I was there. 'Ah, the lovely Maia,' says Rob, whose long and fractious marriage had ended a few years previously amidst much bitterness, 'We don't know what we'd do without her.' Another gulp of beer, 'We know what we'd like to do *with* her.'

For a fleeting moment, I miss my old job. The banter, the camaraderie. But a couple of the other more colourful old-school characters had left, and Rob would be retiring soon, and it would never be the same. I order another round of beer and some kumara wedges from the bar. Walking home later, I'm touched by how Rob, in his unceremonious, kiwi, way, gave up his evening to brighten mine.

ZOOTHERAPY TODAY, 2009

With Tina and Sam gone, and having banked Tina's life insurance payout, I have no need to generate much income. I'm running Zootherapy on autopilot. I can afford to take stock and think about the direction Zootherapy's taking. Most of my depleted energy reserves are being channelled into running courses of varying length for government employees or corporate executives. I suspect that my seminars are mainly seen as a way of treating employees to a couple of days out of the office, in the guise of 'training'. Not very edifying.

Worse, though the 'Zootherapy' name and my professional organisation are legally protected, various unofficial, opportunistic offshoots that have nothing to do with me have sprouted around New Zealand. So, as well as my small, Wellington-based Zootherapy empire, there has been a trickle of courses, internet forums, and websites all inspired by Zootherapy but zealous in calling themselves something different. Some of the people behind these spinoffs are no doubt sincere. Others, more shady, devious. I hear rumours about short-lived practices being set up purely for exploiting the vulnerable or as low-level power plays in some of New Zealand's smaller towns. I have a word with my lawyers, who say that some sort of 'Cease and Desist' instruction, appearing under their letterhead will do the trick. Other weed-like growths that I can do without are the obscurantist intellectuals, mostly in New Zealand, who have written about Zootherapy for academic journals, and brought in a new and daunting vocabulary: words like umwelt, zoo-ography, animalistic ontology, therionistics, existential bestiology, ... I'll spare you the details. All this by itself would be enough to motivate me to relaunch Zootherapy, and to reorientate it into something greater than a way of paying my office expenses, distracting Wellington's middle management, and keeping Kitty in cat food.

But there's more. I've often suspected my welfare beneficiary interviewees at the Ministry and my early Zootherapy clients of holding an unvoiced accusation: 'It's all right for you'. I saw then and see now that it can function as an excuse not to take Zootherapy seriously. There's truth in it, of course. Materially I was and had always been comfortable. But like every other human being, I have actually suffered. There's no need to talk about my childhood, the more or less constant emotional abuse, the occasional beatings. They didn't last for ever, and my life in New Zealand is a long way from it, in time and space. So nobody would know about all that, nor would I want them to.

But now they know that I have suffered. The fact and manner of Tina and Sam's deaths had been dramatic enough to make the headlines in New Zealand. Not for long, but long enough for everyone in Wellington, at least, to be aware of them.

Death of a much-loved spouse and a child: they're pretty big issues, as they say. Without my even mentioning it or willing it, the deaths of my wife and daughter could open the hearts of hitherto unsympathetic millions to the message of Zootherapy. I would never claim to be a victim. But if knowledge of my sorrow would help people overcome their prejudice against Zootherapy, then why not? It doesn't have to be cynical. I could use people's sympathy as a bridge to their soul, enabling me to help people who would otherwise chafe against any perceived privilege and condescension. It shouldn't be like that, and it's a bit distasteful even to say it. Then again, knowing Tina, she wouldn't hesitate to tell me to go for it.

So, with this opening into people's hearts, and with no financial pressures, I am free, ready and able to sweep away some of the dross that, owing to my passivity, accumulated around Zootherapy. I'm ready now to unleash Zootherapy – real Zootherapy – onto the wider world.

I get in touch with the Wellington branch of an international Public Relations company, and ask them to activate their constellation of global contacts in English-speaking universities and think-tanks. I'm aware that a PR company can say things about me that I can't say myself. So their dozens of outgoing faxes and emails extol the life-enhancing merits of Zootherapy (true), say that I am an 'accomplished speaker' (not true) and similarly embellish my few other credentials.

Their efforts yield precisely two, unpaid, potential speaking engagements. One, at a veterinary centre for farm animals in Bangladesh, which would be interesting for me, but I doubt a talk about Zootherapy is what they are really looking for. The other, more exaltedly, would be at the London School of Economics - quite a coup, though I'd be part of their 'Summer Talks Programme', where their public lecture schedules are opened up to lighter-than-usual fare. I'd pay for my own flights, but that's OK. We're coming into the New Zealand winter and the northern hemisphere summer so I gladly accept. I fulfil my immediate Zootherapy obligations in New Zealand, postpone the later ones, and arrange for Kitty to be fed by a neighbour.

DIALOGUE WITH JASON, 2009

I'm less anxious about flying alone for roughly 26 hours, than by my returning to a land that holds so many unhappy memories. But it feels the right time to confront those demons. I meet up with Jason for a quick drink the evening before my departure. It's been several months since we last met. He and his partner now have a little daughter ('unplanned, but not unwanted').

We talk about how we're glad that we've spent most of our working lives in New Zealand rather than the UK, and reminisce about the old days at the Ministry of Social Welfare. I tell him about my evening with Rob. 'Ah yes, part of New Zealand's strategic reserve'.

'What?'

'You remember those ads in the British newspapers in the 1970s? You know, submarines, skulking around in the oceanic depths, and the caption, big and bold underneath: "If they were ever used, they'd be failing in their purpose". Britain's nuclear deterrent. Polaris.'

'Yees...'

'Well that's Rob. Part of our secret defence: a good mind, ready and waiting.'

I remember the terminology, and quote: '*Be unpredictable. Create an uncertainty in the mind of the enemy as to our retaliatory capability.*'

'Exactly: that's Rob. New Zealand's independent deterrent. Our Ace in the Hole.'

Later: 'You'll have a good trip anyway, but I really hope the lecture works. It's a good thing you're going to England. They might not be as nice to you as they are here, but they'll give you a fair hearing.'

That's all I can ask for.

FROM NEW ZEALAND TO THE WORLD, 2009

Jason is right: New Zealand has given me a gentle ride. Tolerant, and nationalistic in the mildest, kindest sense, it has nurtured Zootherapy, encouraged me, rewarded me, and when it's challenged me it has done so in an open-minded, supportive way. Sure, there has been bemusement, and occasional opposition, but it's been for the most part muted and respectful. Mostly, those kiwis with no direct experience of Zootherapy are either indifferent to it, or look on it as a home-grown New Zealand creation: quirky and harmlessly eccentric.

The rest of the world is more of a challenge. In Wellington you'd hear of high-flying kiwi government officials and politicians, who, adept as they are at achieving their goals in the New Zealand environment, would fail miserably in the wider world. They just can't handle the corruption, the cynical horse-trading and ruthless power plays of the people who govern two-thirds of the planet. It doesn't matter to me any more: I have no family to look after, no need to kowtow. Success or failure are less important than trying. The world needs Zootherapy, and my role is to meet that need. Well, what else can I do? I board the 737 for the quick hop to Auckland, then it's a relaxed flight to Singapore, in a cabin just one-third full. I eat, read and doze all the way.

The flight from Singapore to London is more serious and every seat in Business Class is occupied; it's a businessman's route and in the seat next to me is a purposeful-looking man in a sharp suit, about my age, with Oriental features. We smile and exchange pleasantries but still part of me wants to blame him for not being Tina. He probably has a wife and family in Singapore. A long take-off roll for this fully loaded jumbo, and up there in the tropical night, thousands of miles from any place I could call home, in the aftermath of a boozy dinner, and against the background anxiety I have about returning to England, I get quite lachrymose. And I think maybe Tina's dying was her final service to me; part of some divine plan, freeing me to solve everyone else's problems, or at least to have that as my goal. Mr Zootherapy, the comic book hero! As I recline my seat, and prepare to sleep for the final eight hours of my day in the air, I recall that none of the super-heroes of my childhood, certainly not Superman or Batman, were married. Ah, a bit of self-aggrandisement before I dream can't do me any harm. A small voice reminds me that none of the super-villains seem to have had wives either... Lex Luthor, Brainiac, The Joker....

I wake up a couple of hours later to go to the bathroom. Everyone in the cabin's asleep. The volatility of the mental state of a single guy like me is extreme and it's at this point that the reality (or the downward slope of the alcohol curve) hits: I'm suspended above the Earth, everyone's comatose around me, nobody knows or cares where I am. Even the flight attendants are invisible. The sense of isolation is total. Back in my seat, I fleetingly wonder whether I really did once meet a young lady who loved me, and lived with me, and had a daughter by me....

Q AND A AT LSE

Summer in the northern hemisphere; a two-thirds full lecture hall on, a warm, airless, sticky evening in London, and I have just given my presentation at the LSE to a polite audience of about sixty, casually-dressed, mature students, with a sprinkling of academics. The ethnic diversity on show pleases me. To beef up my credentials with this intellectual crowd, I've referred to quite a bit of recent research, all showing the hitherto unsuspected complexity and intelligence of the animal kingdom, from dogs to jellyfish. And it's the London School of Economics, so I've talked too about biophilia and the fiscal benefits of easy access to nature.

Time for questions. The Chair takes them in groups of three, which allows me to answer the first one, the inevitable *are you serious?* with a single word – yes – and to move swiftly on to the others.

> *Don't you think, with respect, that you're being pretty naïve? I mean, New Zealand isn't exactly representative: it's clean, green, with more sheep than people and a long way from the world's troubles. Zootherapy might work there, but here we've got unemployment, drugs, crime; do you think what you're saying is going to help people in Hackney, or Sheffield, or Bangladesh?*

You're assuming New Zealand is somehow without social problems of any kind. Believe me, we have drugs and crime too, and domestic abuse, gangs and violence, just on a smaller scale because we're a smaller country. There's poverty and drugs in New Zealand! You're also implying that if people have material wealth, that's enough. But I'm talking psychological liberation. I mean, we're all doing all right aren't we? We're well fed, well clothed, have enough time and health to spend an evening here, right? But are we happy? Don't we have problems? And listen to this: if Zootherapy works for us, don't you think we'd do a better

158

job of creating a society that would work for all of us –
people everywhere, Bangladesh, Hackney... Animals too!

I guess people understand things differently. Jenny, my other
Ministry interviewees and primary school kids understand the animal
mind without having to be convinced by theoretical justifications for
it. They put the costume on, and instinct takes over. These guys and,
let's be honest, I, have to see a reasoned case for it before we can
take it seriously. Well, I can speak that language too.

> *Animals kill each other. Can't we as humans aspire to something
> better?*

> You'd be surprised by how many people *don't* ask this
> question. Probably because even if we did simply become
> like the rest of the animal kingdom, killing just for food and
> defence, that's actually an improvement over what we are.
> But there's more to Zootherapy than that. I think if you
> actually practise it you'll see that you're not just pretending
> to be an animal. Zootherapy is another way of using our
> minds. If we became like all the other animals sure, we'd stop
> killing for pleasure or using our brains to kill millions. But
> we'd lose culture, music, literature and everything else. My
> point is that we can have the best of both worlds: empathy,
> compassion *and* culture.

I can, and do, continue in this vein without thinking. My mind drifts
back to my last presentation in an academic institution: namely
Elizabeth St Primary School, Mount Victoria, Wellington, where I
demonstrated Zootherapy with a group of nine-year olds. I had
brought with me a mixture of different, open-faced, child-size
costumes: two each of cats, dogs, turtles and ladybirds, and I'd
brought a kiwi costume too, with its long kiwi beak projecting
downwards from the rubberised-felt head covering. The children in
their costumes were delightful to watch; one shy boy, dressed as a

cat, went up to a girl in a dog costume and, to her amazement, kissed her on the cheek. The kids had questions too: 'Can I be a dog and then a cat?', 'Can we keep these?', 'Have you got a pony costume?' Those questions, I couldn't anticipate. Now, though, it's easy:

> Zootherapy is about getting rid of all the accumulated stuff, the fears and all the barriers to our perception that *we think* go hand-in-hand with being human. What I'm saying is that with Zootherapy, we can have the good things about being human, without the bad. We don't have to drop all the literature and music and culture and everything else that make us human; science, medicine and all the rest. Zootherapy will tell us when all that stuff, the memories and narratives, are distorting our lives, and when they're OK.

Too much knowledge: I could go on and on about whether animals would become 'like us' if they had the choice. Or whether they've superseded us. But no need to show off: there are plenty of hands up now:

> *You talked about getting rid of our narratives but don't you think that it's our narratives that give us our identity? We just don't want to lose all that. It's who we are.*

I remember once when our cat tripped me up in the kitchen. As I was falling she ran in front of me and I ended up slamming his body onto the floor. She yelped and yowled. But she got over it in about two days. But I still feel awful about it a few years later. You see; we've invested so much in all our memories and ideas and prejudices. But when you practise Zootherapy you see knowledge for what it is: useful some of the time, but most of the time it distorts our view of the world. It's great for writing novels or memoires. But don't you think there are times when it just gets in the way? It's a

160

barrier between us and other people and between us and reality. But you're right: we're so invested in all our accumulated knowledge that it's difficult to put aside even when it's just adding to the confusion. It's a sunk cost. Or rather, it can be.

At this point I sense the audience is warming to my words. I seem to feed off this, and relieved that things have gone reasonably well, I get a little intoxicated and come up with this:

> I am sure everyone in this room knows this about arithmetic: infinity minus the biggest number you can imagine is exactly the same as infinity minus one. There's so much knowledge out there you might as well be ignorant of all of it. The universe, reality, it's all so complicated and big that in the vast scheme of things is our understanding of the universe significantly more than our cat's, or dog's or goldfish's? Maybe this is God's answer to Job: all our suffering is minuscule; as consequential or not as great joy. Different shapes of sand grains on a wide, wide stretch of beach. Look: we know enough to survive; we need survival skills. But the important ones are hard-wired anyway.

An enigmatic end to my digression, but the Chair adroitly jumps in, and takes more questions, one by one now:

> *You claim that you're serious. Somewhat dismissively I think. But it still sounds sketchy, and I'm not sure whether you're taking the Mickey or not. You're talking about real psychological problems and saying you can solve them by playing around with animal costumes. Some would say it's insulting. Dime-store positive thinking maybe. Is your Zootherapy really any different?*

> Look, talking about it isn't doing it. However I respond to you, it's just words, which you can then dismiss as just another formula. I'm not going to change your mind. All I

would say is just try it. It is a simple thing to do. Kids do it! But often the simplest things are the most subtle.

Just to take you up on that: it's simple, and you basically summed it all up in one of your first sentences: see the world through the eyes of an animal. So how come the need for sessions and courses?

Sometimes it helps to see things from a different angle. And we've got a lot of unlearning to do. Often it helps if you say the same thing in a different way. But basically you're right – and that's why I think children should be introduced to animals and Zootherapy. The younger the better. They won't complicate things like we - adults - do.

If it's as simple as you say, and easy to practise, how come nobody's thought of it before?

It's like what they say about finding a £20 note in the street: you'll never find one because somebody will have always picked it up. You know about that, right? The Efficient Market Hypothesis. Well Zootherapy is simple, and since it entered the public arena people have been saying it's all been done before, by philosophers eastern and western, and by scientists looking into quantum theory, and you know what? I'm sure it has. Zootherapy might well be just a repackaging of ancient wisdom. Maybe the wisest people just never felt the need to go public with it, like I did.

I loosen up a bit, now we're approaching the end:

Ladies, gentlemen: I've been giving an intellectual explanation about why intellectual explanations are grossly overrated! And I've been doing it to some of the most gigantic intellects on the planet! We're like a gang of adolescents discussing sex: those who talk about it most do it least.

A few laughs, and the Chair winds up the formal session. There's some brief applause.

DRINKS AT LSE

Their ignorance of New Zealand society aside, the LSE audience, at first indifferent, seems to have been won over by my talk – or at least to be have become more open minded. It's been bracing: I had to be at the top of my game and, responding to the questions, I think I helped the cause of Zootherapy. *I* certainly have emerged more convinced than ever.

Drinks afterwards, in a faculty lounge, and the atmosphere's mellow. I get chatting to one of the older guys, an emeritus professor, well spoken, wearing a bow-tie, smelling of fresh cigar smoke and sipping red wine. He tells me he has a daughter, married to a dairy farmer living in Taranaki and has been to New Zealand several times.

'The problem you'll have in England is that people won't like putting the costumes on. They'll feel silly and self-conscious about it.' He gestures around the room, 'This is a country where you kill people through embarrassment. The worst thing you can say to an Englishman is "Oh, come off it!". They'll be too embarrassed to dress up as an animal – or even to think about it.'

We've been joined by a lady, whose name and precise affiliation – something to do with the LSE – I immediately forget. She's nodding. 'It's one of the reasons you never got a serious fascist movement here. All that strutting around in uniforms. It was all seen as being so...' She puts on an upper-class accent '"...terribly vulgar".'

'To be honest,' I say, 'I don't think the costumes are really necessary; not all the time. It's the things that go with the costume: seeing the world differently, through the eyes of animals: that's what's important.'

The lady replies: 'So the costume, is a ritual. It's the side benefits that really matter.'

'Like fasting,' the professor says, 'or not eating pork in the desert when it goes rotten. You do it to stay healthy; the ritual is just for show.'

I say: 'Well, it's a sort of discipline. It keeps you doing the right thing.'

'It's like McDonalds or Burger King or all those fast food places,' says the lady. I'm glad to see the professor looks as mystified as me. She goes on: 'They advertise their hamburgers and cheeseburgers and chicken bits, but the real profits come from selling those fizzy drinks. Just a load of ice, water, and a spoonful of syrup. Imagine the margins on them!'

'I'll have to think about that one,' says the professor.

'Me too,' I say. It's been an enjoyable evening.

Born and brought up as I was in the north of England, I never spent much time in London: it was the stuff of short breaks including one memorable FA Cup Final when I was 11 years old. But still it's England, where I was born and spent the first decades of my life, and has the comforting familiarity of an old shoe, and I enjoy, for the first time, being based in a central hotel. Having cash to spare, I have booked myself into the Dorchester Hotel, in Mayfair. (Even so, online at home, I'd balked at their rates and ended up opting for their least costly room, without breakfast.) Mooching around the West End for a couple of days after my talk, I'm impressed by the city's energy, which amounts to more than the summation of the countless thousands of people and their individual strivings. The parks in the summer heat are a blessing, but when I venture eastwards to the financial district the atmosphere changes. The energy is still there, but it's a hungry, bloodless energy, detached from nature and history. Enthralling in its way, but also hyper-individualistic, anonymous, chilling. They're a cosmopolitan lot, the people here, yet seem to have emerged fully formed from this steel and glass urban landscape, their brainpower directed into esoteric, trading activities. Even those in less exalted positions – dispatch drivers, caterers, window cleaners – seem to share in the spoils. It is only when I leave London, on a day trip to Margate, on the Kent coast (I need to see the sea!) that I encounter the less fortunate: the ordinary folk, working for ordinary wages or not working at all. Those left behind. There's an air of hopelessness, a faint scent of grievance, a muted, thwarted demeanour. There's no desperate material poverty, but there's decay and defeat in the air, the sense that things will at best, never improve. The town centre's down-at-heel; all boarded-up premises, charity shops selling second-hand goods and furnishings, the detritus of lost lives.

In Bangkok, the horrors of the modern cityscape have been imposed on people; they didn't want it, but they live with it and, like flowers growing through concrete, survive despite it. In England the people, in their exaggerated individualism, are utterly urban. They belong inescapably to their environment. If it's thriving, prosperous and optimistic, so too are they. If it's hopeless and inert, well then.... In Margate I take comfort from seeing the dogs being walked; a ginger tabby sitting on dilapidated bird bath stops washing herself to stare at me as I walk past. Only the animals and birds are bright-eyed and alert.

So much for my superficial, and no doubt, unrepresentative, impressions. I don't really want to be one of the many kiwis who, having experienced the buzz of being in London, the UK and Europe, seek to justify their decision to return to our antipodean islands by disparaging the more exciting option. I do have to admit that, on the day of my night flight home, the endless rain descending from the canopy of thick grey cloud is uninspiring. But there's another aspect to this, and one that I'd shut down very quickly when I realised that it is not appreciated in New Zealand – perhaps not in any of the New World countries: the culture of complaint. It permeated life in Britain when I was growing up, and it's still here: everything is hopeless, but not serious. Even the people with whom I interact casually, the taxi drivers, bar staff, the people I overhear in coffee shops, join in. On the surface, it's a negative, cheerless outlook. But I see it now more as a dance, or light opera. Everybody can participate at some level, and it's a way of uniting an increasingly diverse population against the weather or the government or the infrastructure or the media or life and fate itself. It's a bonding ritual and, after the sometimes grating, pervasive, insistence on being (or appearing) upbeat that is a feature of New Zealand life, I enjoy it. (It's a national joke when the England football team puts in its usual lame performance. But, when the All Blacks were knocked out unexpectedly early in some rugby competition, Victoria University of Wellington set up counselling sessions for its students.) I'm pleased that the minicab driver who takes me to Heathrow, of subcontinental origin but brought up in England, has fully embraced this British cultural form, and we pass the 90 minutes it takes to get to Terminal 3 in contrapuntal whinges about the road works, the consequent traffic congestion, the rain, Brussels bureaucrats and the recent massive bailouts of billionaire bankers.

THE UK, AND THE LONG FLIGHT BACK

In my youth, short trips to London had meant excitement, furtive visits to 'Adult' bookshops, hot chestnuts bought from street carts, and a greyish pallor on the skin. But growing old means you project backwards longer and, as I settle into the long night flight to Singapore and the screen in front of me shows our track over

Europe, I see London and the UK as the heroes of World War Two; that rare war in which good and evil were clearly distinguished and, moreover, in which good triumphed. Sometimes you think that any good that happens is just a by-product of doing what you're going to do anyway. If that's true, then so's evil. This sounds nihilistic, cynical and hopeless. But isn't the real message that we're all the same? Even as I think this, the inflight magazine emblazons on its glossy front cover the delights of Rome, to which the airline is putting on an additional weekly flight. Italy, hundreds of miles to my right, according to the map on the screen in front of me. Italy: land of chianti and opera, art, culture, homely cooking, and the Italians: smart in every sense, a touch buffoonish, difficult to take seriously. Fond of good living without pretension. *Sono tutti figli di madri*, they were heard to say, as the defeated Nazis scuttled out of Rome. 'They are all sons of mothers.' Those big-hearted Italians. Oh yes, and they massacred Ethiopians by the thousand in 1937. So. Enough with the stereotypes and narcissism of small differences. We're all basically the same aren't we?

It's not as if we're hurtling through the night over an especially bloodstained continent towards lands of peace and tranquillity: all being well our trajectory will take us over central Asia, Afghanistan, Pakistan, Tibet. Human history, from this perspective anyway, is all about war and its consequences. What is the root of it all? Mr Zootherapy would say insecurity caused by a brain that is big enough to rake up past hurts and conjure up new ones. Animals are insecure, but not about the past or the future. They're insecure, but they don't feel insecure. They face enough immediate threats not to need to generate imaginary ones. Now humans...well, we can easily use our vast store of memory and knowledge to justify the killing of just about any group of people who are, or may be, in our grotesquely overactive human imagination, about to kill us. Or perhaps we just want to be violent and use our beliefs to rationalise what we want to do anyway. They're serving the main course now and, sipping red wine, I recall the computer expert with the ponytail, who talked to us at the Ministry several years ago. Is history, like our individual lives, another Relational Database? I mean, history isn't what happened. It's a record of what happened. We can look at anything half-complicated – our own lives, western civilisation, family members, whether I should marry this person – take a view on it and then dip into a rich history and find plenty of evidence to support that view. Or the opposite view. Or any view at all.

So anyway, war is something animals don't do. Neither do they seriously think that if they are nice to everybody, then everybody will be nice to them. That seems to work most of the time in stable, evolved human societies, but not at all in others. Animals have no qualms about deploying violence when they need to. Yes, there's plenty of violence in the animal world. Animals have to eat, and they like to defend themselves too. But can anything in the animal kingdom equal the horrors that we humans inflict on each other? Instead of using our humanity to transcend animal violence, we use it to multiply and magnify it.

Such morbid thoughts. Long-haul air travel, with its copious (for me) quantities of alcohol, and bass drone of engine noise, will do that to you. Maybe also the lower air pressure up here; you become a bit light-headed. I'm sure I read that once, somewhere on the internet. The upshot of all this? Zootherapy is for everyone.

And another great insight (or so I think) comes my way: the endless merry-go-round: thinking is the mind's equivalent of a government bureaucracy: the endless restructuring; just as if you hold a hammer, every problem looks like a nail, and just as for government, every problem looks like an opportunity to intervene, so to the mind, everything – every moment, even every thought – is an opportunity to kick off another thought. The mind's activity is, for the mind, not only an end in itself, but the only end it can comprehend. At this point some tiredness, an alcoholic haze and Zootherapy work synergistically to come up with another zinger: thinking has to switch itself off, as with the animals. Knowledge is not insight. Insight is not knowledge. Maybe knowledge prevents insight. It makes you think you don't need insight.

Such are my musings on the 12-hour night flight to Singapore. Flying over Pakistan and India, the plane floats high in the sky, having burned off most of its fuel. Rushing into a new dawn, I see scatterings of light forty thousand feet below. An immense sense of privilege overwhelms me. It would take them years of scratching a living out of bare soil to make enough to spend on a plane ticket. It's clear that I am the well-dined embodiment of Narrative One: the luckiest person in the world. No attachments. Perfect freedom. A soft electronic gong, a bit of turbulence. And there were times I believed in Narrative Two! My tea in its china cup threatens to spill over into the saucer? That's what I have to worry about? What a hard life I have. You can't kid yourself that you're a victim when you're sitting in luxury, looking down several miles at people who have to wake up at first light to scrape out a meagre living.

I'm offered a hot towel and the breakfast menu. And two hours later, we begin our descent into Singapore. Flowing water inspired Tao philosophy, if I remember my Alan Watts rightly. And the Jews have a custom on their New Year, of symbolically ridding themselves of their sins by casting them into a river. Flying through the air is much the same. All motion is relative, and peering out of the window, I see the places over which I flew just moments ago, receding fast. So with my old resentments and thoughts, ideas and narratives. Perhaps I could go into business selling First Class cabin simulators for home use, complete with video, a soundtrack of engine noise, gongs and captain's announcements, meals and wine, and a reclining chair vibrating at the same frequency as in the air: an aid to

169

meditation. But why? Just practise Zootherapy. Much cheaper and you can do it anywhere.

At Changi, evening is already falling. I check out the bookshop: a massive proportion of the books for sale are devoted to management, investment and financial trading. Well, this is the way of the world; and why not? They have spouses, kids, to support, air-conditioners to buy. College, apartments, gadgets. There aren't many of us who can – or feel they can – take time out to do what needs to be done. Only I, Mr James Z Sinclaire, have total freedom. Saving the world? Only I can do it.

A hitch: some 'technical difficulty' delays my plane to Auckland. A replacement aircraft, is found, but it's a narrow-body so they look for volunteers to fly next lunchtime. Well, why not? I'm in no hurry and Singapore Airlines will put us up at a five-star hotel in the city, give us a free half-day tour of the city in the morning, and upgrade us one class on the flight. I'm curious to see Singapore, imagining it to be something like a blend of Bangkok and London. I'm wrong. It's Changi Airport in macrocosm: compact, well ordered, efficient, bursting with greenery, safe. A heavy emphasis on shopping and eating. A functioning, immaculate underground system. Polite, efficient, and English-speaking. Not a trace of anarchy. Everything works. Everything is monitored. Everyone's accountable.

We stop off at a mosque; the imam comes out to greet us: 'I am a Singaporean first, a Muslim second.' Well, why not? Better would be 'I'm a human first, a Singaporean second'. But best of all would be 'I'm an animal first, a human second.' I'm no idealist brimming with compassion, nor do I want people to think that I am. It's just that I want the world to live in peace and harmony. Nothing personal: I'm aging and I have no kids. It would just be a nicer, more efficient world. That's reason enough. Some guys close to power did once talk of creating a secondary reality; a place where the myths and lies that they propagate have an independent life. And that secondary reality can last for generations. Rough, if you were born in Russia in 1910. Actually, Singapore is a bit like that. An island whose prevailing ideology tells us that the harder we work, the more we'll be rewarded. There's no room for questioning that. Conform, conform, conform! If you want randomness, the freedom to be slipshod, or to see stray dogs and cats nosing around discarded cans of condensed milk in monastery grounds, or just to go somewhere where time isn't money, to let off steam: well, Bangkok's just a short flight away. Ideologies are like scientific models aren't they? They're all wrong, but some of them are useful. We need them to fail at times, so we don't take them too seriously.

After the mosque, there are food courts, a housing estate in the suburbs and, inevitably, a shopping mall. Back to the airport and I board my plane to Auckland hardly breaking stride. Again, you can't but be conscious of privilege. People are struggling out there! Beyond Changi and rarefied airline cabins, humanity needs a shake up. And only I, it appears, can do it. Everyone else has their own agenda by obligation or choice: loans to pay, children to feed, cars to maintain, expectations to fulfil, the accumulation of more money, more security. Even the very wealthy, judging by the tabloids back in London, have their lives scrutinised and freedoms curtailed by reporters with their telephoto lenses and lurid imaginations.

Yes, it's all up to me. It's my job to save humanity. (I could never have thought along these lines if I'd stayed in England. That old professor bloke in the bow tie had been absolutely right.) So, as my first decisive gesture on this mission, settling into my well-padded home for the next twelve hours, I nobly refuse the glass of champagne offered to me by the steward and ask for pen and paper instead. And this is what I write:

- *You don't 'do' Zootherapy. You don't advance in Zootherapy. There's no movement, just a change of perspective. The fact is: I'm an animal. Anything else, words, ideas, the notion of progress, the notion of change, improvement, is just so much chaff. Don't do anything. Get the doing, the words, the ideas out of the way. Be animal.*

- *You can practise Zootherapy – enter Z-mode - without a costume. Once you have acquired the knack, it is possible to see life through animal eyes without a costume.*

A long taxi to the runway, a long wait at the threshold. Probably everyone at some point thinks it's up to them to save the world. For me, though, there's no alternative. There'll be opposition, I'm sure. I've been too small a player, at the very edge of the world stage, to attract much malign attention so far. No doubt there'll be drug manufacturers sponsoring research showing Zootherapy in a poor light. Religious fanatics – who know a threat to their power base and institutional privilege when they see one – will preach that donning an animal costume is blasphemy or idolatry. Arms merchants, narcotics gangs...there may be death threats. But so what? Nobody would be devastated if I die. Not any more. And now we spool up for take-off, and begin to thunder down the runway, I seem to draw power from the engines. Sure, there'll be times of adversity but - we rotate upwards - I can handle it.

Climbing above the clouds now, in darkness, and there are lightning flashes in the distance. A touch of anxiety as I contemplate returning to my lonely life in the Land of the Long White Cloud. My confidence falters a little. There'll be nobody to meet me at Auckland. Or Wellington. I'm on my own. Desolate. Like a rainforest, you can't recreate a family life: once it's gone, it's gone. A market opportunity there surely: we have libraries for books, compact disks.

We rent dinner jackets and cars: why not wives, children? Or at least someone to meet us at the airport. The Japanese do it for weddings, don't they? No, that won't do. Several miles above the earth I see my own memories and my indulgence for what they really are: a shield against the pity of it all. Feeling sorry for myself lets me off the hook; for the abused kids, the battered women, the fathers who fail to put food on the table or defend their daughters, for all the wretched casualties of this world. 'I can't deal with it. I've got my own problems!' No longer. Up in the sky, flashes of lightning all around, clarity reigns. I can take it all on. Everything.

This is how it is with me: doom or transcendence. And now I'm living both narratives at once. A fact I deploy to soothe my clients comes to mind: Some species of fish need stressful triggers like drastic water quality or temperature changes in order to spawn. Animals need stressful situations to thrive. Calm down James. Zootherapy is about facing the facts and being open to all experience; including those that make us vulnerable. On Sunday morning – was it really just a couple of days ago? - I'd crossed Park Lane over to Speakers' Corner in Hyde Park where, amidst the political hucksters and ranters, the conspiracists and UFOlogists, there was a shabbily-dressed but well-spoken lady, impressing on a small, sceptical audience, her biblical knowledge. 'We must circumcise our hearts!' she says. It must have struck a chord with me. Drawing down the window shade and reclining my seat, I think I know what she means.

I don't want Zootherapy to become just another voice competing for attention from amongst the visitors to London in Hyde Park. It has to be universal, with no in-group or out-group. I think I can do it or, more realistically, if anyone can do it, it's me. I've no loyalties, no pecuniary needs, no puppet masters. And I'm a New Zealander: I'm no threat to anyone.

I wake up when I hear the soft sound of the gong and the captain announcing that we are ninety miles north of Auckland and about to begin our descent. I ask for tea. The tone of the engines falls a bit, and the sunlight is intense as I open the shade and see we're on shallow downward glide, and there's the shadow of the plane against the banks of white cloud. I've done just enough physics to recognise the rainbow-like halo around the shadow of the plane cast on the top of cloud as a glory, and to know that, though it appears to be centred exactly around where I'm sitting, it's not about me: everyone else seeing it will have the same perception. Good! We're all in this together. I'm not some super-special gifted, holy being. That takes the pressure off. It seems a happy omen.

And as we descend into the cloud layer, I think: OK, maybe there is something retro about Zootherapy, as Jason said years ago, and maybe there's also something retro about soaring ideals and the belief that things really can change for the better. That some new – call it a spiritual practice – can create a perfect world. It goes against the spirit of the age. But I can live with that.

My mission: I choose to accept it

Well, what else can I do? Zootherapy is my life now. At home I shall have to be content with Kitty, and a few reminders of Tina (including the jumper she wore on our first date and the snake costume) and Samantha (all her drawings, pictures and schoolbooks). I keep them in a cupboard, which I never open, in Samantha's room. Almost everything else, after a long while, I've had picked up by the Salvation Army. I wouldn't have chosen it but the entire world will have to serve as my family now. I could conceivably look for another relationship, but (I tell myself) I don't want to be disloyal to the people who need me: the lonely, massed millions of lonely men and women, rich and poor, the misfits, the ones who fell through the cracks, the ones for whom childhood means – like it used to for me – terror. How could I let them down? OK, that's one explanation. The

174

other is that I just don't want to go dating, or whatever it's called these days. The emotional cost is just too high. Who could possibly replace Tina? More cogently, who would want to? My neediness would scare them off. Besides, I'm a public figure in New Zealand, even now, and not all the attention I get is benign.

I suppose there had been a logical progression: changing myself, changing my clients as individuals, then groups of people; convicted criminals on to business executives. But my brief trip to the northern hemisphere, where the scale and urgency of our human problems are enormous and inescapable; the sense of privilege, bordering on guilt, as I'd lorded it in Business Class and at the Dorchester in Park Lane, all goad me, as too did the way I'd won over at least some of the LSE audience and, crucially, myself, into seeing Zootherapy as the solution to the world's problems. No longer could I, need I, confine myself to New Zealand and Australia. Logic and emotion cohere. Everything I know, all my experiences ecstatic or grievous, everything upholds Zootherapy as the universal cure for mankind's ills. It's become clear: the time has come to launch Zootherapy onto the world stage.

How to go about doing so? So many thoughts swirling around, enjoying the freshness of my arrival in Auckland, the green, the space, the friendliness at passport control, the genial older volunteers making tea and coffee for the pax waiting by the baggage carousel; the chatty guy manning the X-ray machine for checked baggage, explaining that the logo next to the WELCOME TO AUCKLAND banner above the exit from Arrivals is something to do with 'Bigwigs from Asia meeting here in summer.' After the anonymity of London, New Zealand feels like one big village. It buoys you! And at home that night, not at all tired, I climb into my gorilla suit, feeling any remaining layers of doubt, conflict, pain and ego float away. Nothing to resolve, no need to intellectualise. The animal knows what it has to do.

Tom Wilkins MP, 2010

It's now 2010, 18 months since the car crash that killed my wife and daughter. I'm in the Beehive, in the vestibule of Tom's office suite. Yes, Tom, or rather the Honourable Tom Wilkins, my bright but not-very-diligent ex-housemate and temporary gorilla impersonator has gained his law degree, spent a decade or so working for an Auckland law firm, and ended up in politics. Now he's a backbench Member of the New Zealand Parliament for the opposition National Party. I'm not sure whether he's a list MP or was elected by one of those large agricultural, constituencies in the central North Island. Either way, he's been in Parliament for years. He's on the eighth floor, and I've been sitting in his bustling ante-chamber, while he's hosting another guy in his office. His gravel-voiced private secretary sits at a desk, fielding phone calls while starting at a monitor, a smouldering cigarette in her ashtray. She's told me he's running late, but that's fine with me. I see through a glass panel next to the door that Tom is still a smoker. After a few minutes, Tom ushers out a ruddy-faced besuited man, wearing a visitor's badge like mine, all smiles and bonhomie.

Now Tom comes to me with outstretched hand. We haven't seen each other for years; he in his cocoon, me in mine.

'James. It's been a long time. I was so sorry to hear about your wife and daughter. '

He gestures me to enter his office, then turns toward his secretary: 'Jo; hold my calls would you?'

The door closes softly behind us. There's a palpable hush, the office bustle being left outside. A fine view of the harbour; blue sky, turquoise sea and lush green hills in the distance. Tom eschews his desk and gestures towards the couch and sits on an easy chair facing me.

176

'It's great to see you James, after all this time. How are you doing?'

'I'm fine now Tom. I'm keeping busy. Business is good.' Taking in Tom's overloaded desk, the butts and half-smoked cigarettes in the heavy glass ash-tray, the phones and buzzers faintly audible through the door, I wonder whether his style of progress has changed much over the years: as a student he'd always got by substituting his brilliance and charm for hard work. A winning combination of intelligence and *apparent* insouciance.

'The Zootherapy? I know. I've been reading about it.' The publicity about Tina and Sam's deaths had, in its macabre way, stimulated interest.

A minute or two more of chit-chat (Tom's about to become a grandfather) and I say 'Tom, I've come to ask you a favour.'

No doubt it is Tom's familiarity with such a preamble that enables him to combine an enthusiastic tone and open body-language with words that are far more guarded 'I'll do what I can James.'

I put my request to Tom. He lights up a cigarette, walks up to the big window and looks out to harbour. Through the window I see Jo, putting the phone down and getting up to welcome a well-dressed elderly couple. They look like they could be rural constituents in Wellington for a short visit. After a while, Tom turns to me:

'James, I'm just a backbench MP, you know that. Not even in the Government.'

'You've got some seniority, some responsibilities.'

'Vice Chair of the Committee on Regulation of Video Game Parlours?' He gestures at one of several piles of papers on his desk, 'Legal advisor to the team drawing up the voluntary code of conduct for retailers of nasal tobacco? That's how senior I am. I've got nothing to do with trade or international affairs or ASEAN.'

He means the Association of South East Asian Nations, of which New Zealand is a member. Its forthcoming Summit is to be held in Auckland. I persist:

'Word has it that you're close to the PM.' For an opposition MP anyway; it was Wellington gossip. Apart from the odd earthquake, traffic accidents and dairy hold-ups there isn't a great deal of real local news in a city this size so political tittle-tattle gets wide coverage in the media.

'I'm not on a single one of the foreign affairs committees.'

'It doesn't matter. At least try. Mention it to her. That's all I'm asking.'

He slumps into an easy chair, puts his cigarette to his lips and inhales deeply. He sighs.

I press my case: 'You know the Government has been using Zootherapy for a while now.'

This is true, insofar as I continue to do *pro bono* sessions with selected groups of prisoners.

'In the prisons? Sure. I know. You've been doing that for years.'

'It's becoming mainstream.'

Tom's well informed:

'-in New Zealand .'

Well, I had established bridgeheads in Australia, but their rules about new commercial therapies are more stringent than New Zealand's. Official Zootherapy has yet to take off there.

I say 'This is a chance to move on.' He looks sceptical. 'All I'm asking is to mention it. Informally. She's into conflict reduction.'

'True.'

'Hasn't she said she's going to resign soon after ASEAN? Quit while she's ahead? And there are all these rumours about being nominated for the top job at the UN?' The job of Secretary-General at the United Nations, and our Prime Minister's possible candidacy is the subject of no little speculation in Wellington.

'She doesn't *have* to resign. No term limits, as you know.' This is true. Tom inhales deeply on his cigarette.

''It would give her a pretty high public profile around the world.'

'What if it doesn't work?'

'She'll thank you, all the same. No publicity is-'

'-bad publicity. I know.'

'And it *will* work.'

Tom blows smoke up at the ceiling, and gestures at me to stay quiet. His expression changes and at that moment I know he will do as I ask.

I press home my advantage: 'And you started all this.'

He raises his eyebrows a fraction, then grins, 'The Gorillagram. I remember.'

Another pause, and then:

'OK, I'll do it. As it happens, her PPS is retiring this week.' (He means her Parliamentary Private Secretary.) 'There's a drinks do on Friday evening. I'll have a word with her when we've all had one or two.'

'Thanks Tom.'

'I can't promise she'll go for it.'

There is a discreet knock on a glass panel by the office door. Jo is gesticulating urgently at her phone. We stand up and I notice an orange light flashing on the phone on Tom's desk. The interview is over.

'I know that Tom. Just whatever you can do. And thanks, Tom. You're a star.' I say.

Standing, we face each other. Tom stubs his cigarette out in the ash-tray and, rather than shake hands, we hug, briefly and awkwardly. Pakeha New Zealand men aren't known for being open with their emotions, nor for standing on ceremony. It comes from the heart. I leave the office; my work done for the day. On the bus home, I ask myself 'What next?' Tom would do as I asked. That's the only certainty. At home, with a sense of 'I've done what I can', I feed Kitty, and pour myself a beer.

THEY'RE ALL GOING CRAZY OUT THERE
'Out there' being the world outside New Zealand, or at least the parts of the world that feature in the media. Single and alone, it's all too easy to become emotionally involved in the television news. Your world view becomes one long horror story, a never-ending tale of anxiety and woe, a litany of war, civil war, suicide bombings; the piling up of nuclear weapons, the rise of extremist attitudes, the mad obsession with identity. This is a world quite alien to my experience of England and New Zealand. These days, you don't sit down and negotiate a compromise over whether to, say, ban smoking, or guns, or abortion, or to promote women's rights. The thinking today is 'I'm right, you're wrong. I'm good, you're evil.' Everyone's doing it. Politicians, priests, pop stars, sportspeople. Even vegans.

You might think something needs to be done. Nah. That's old-style thinking. Things are so bad now that anything anyone does will be corrupted or deliberately misinterpreted and used as a club with which to beat you or anyone related to you. We need less mental activity, not more. So really: something needs to be undone. That's more like it. I flatter myself that it's up to me.

PHYSICIST

Normal life continues. Zootherapy is still very much a New Zealand phenomenon, but I do receive the odd enquiry from overseas. This, an email from a graduate student in physics at MIT:

> *Dear Mr Sinclaire: I am interested in the parallels between Zootherapy and quantum mechanics. Specifically, the transition between what you call Z-mode and our normal psychological state. When our conscious mind is operating, ie not in the Z-mode, then our thoughts condense, as it were, around words. But in Z-mode, as you term it, our thinking is suspended and, as with subatomic particles in quantum mechanics, all locations are possible. I'd be interested to know what you think about this....*

What I think is that I don't want to go down this rabbit hole. Where could it lead? Sure, there might be parallels, but that's all they are. Very likely there are parallels to Z-mode in physics and in classical literature, opera and eastern mysticism too, but pursuing them would just create a cloud of chaff around the core Zootherapy teaching. You see what happens don't you? I do it myself. We want to make Zootherapy safe by containing it in a cocoon of verbiage and knowledge. I respond to this and similar enquiries by urging my correspondents to practise Zootherapy, and devote their intellectual energy instead into making a living, fixing computers, or filling in tax returns: dealing, in short, with those aspects of reality that are comprehensible without insight. Zootherapy isn't about accumulating more knowledge. Just the opposite. Everybody is trying to lasso the unfamiliar, and drag it into their corral. It's what we do, I suppose. Economists want markets for everything, and go round monetising and securitising whatever they can. Accountants care only about the short-term interests of their employers. Lawyers have their 'I speak your rule book' mentality. I guess vacuum cleaner salespeople see dust or its absence everywhere. It goes on and on. I like to think Zootherapy's different: animals have to be alive to immediate threats and opportunities.

As sad, in a different way, are the heart-breaking messages I receive from people whose dog or cat has recently died. I suggest group Zootherapy to these correspondents on the basis that mixing with others will help them more in the early stages of their bereavement, and that the Zootherapy will give them a perspective that will be of longer-term benefit. I can't convince myself that there is an afterlife, but I can truthfully say to my more distraught correspondents that even what we know – life in its millions of manifestations – is already so improbable that an afterlife wouldn't be that much more surprising. Reality is a mixture of the things we can pin down and the things we can't know. So, I try to reassure the bereft.

I'm more helpful, I think, when I get messages like this:

> *I'm happy with my life, but it sometimes freaks me out that I will not live another life and my experiences are in many senses very, very limited. I'll never know what it's like to be another person or live in another country or think in another language. I'll never see all the movies, read all the books or visit all the cities and countries that I want to in the time I have to live.*
>
> *Before you point out that it can be done, that there are people who move countries and learn new languages ... sure, I've tried that and I grew up in a multilingual household. But I also mean it in a more abstract sense, that I'm really only going to know what it's like to be me, and I'm only going to ever know a limited number of people and places. One cannot be a local everywhere (unless perhaps one is also an outsider everywhere). We don't pick the era we are born into, or the body that we are born into. One cannot read all the books in the library. And so on.*

Do you get this sense from time to time? It seems to me that animals don't have those worries. Did Zootherapy help you deal with this feeling? Are there any books or other readings or movies that speak to this feeling?

I reply along these lines:

Zootherapy can help you feel connected with all living things. When you are focused as animals are on the present you are sensitive to all experience. Your sensitivity is so heightened that anything other than what you are experiencing is irrelevant. You are plugged into the whole realm of life, suffering, sorrow and death.

In Zootherapy-mode, and maybe only in Zootherapy-mode, life begins to make sense: for the lone individual, there's no sense at all. Babies die in earthquakes. Wars kill millions randomly. Diseases.... OK, you know the story. If we are lucky and escape the worst, then we kid ourselves there's something we did to deserve it. As if we're entitled. But with Zootherapy, we see that we are part of a whole; we don't have the same suffering as others, but their suffering is real to us. It becomes our job to do something to alleviate it. It strikes me too, though I don't say this, that we can share joy as well as sorrow. I'll never have a child who will grow up and have her own children. But other people do. They don't have to be *my* children and grandchildren.

DIALOGUE WITH ALAN, 2011: BEHAVIOUR ENRICHMENT

People assume that I'm knowledgeable about animals; I never really was, but have made an effort since I became more of a public figure. It comes in useful when I talk with some clients or the media, but also sometimes socially. One damp winter lunchtime I bump into Alan, an ex-colleague from the Ministry, on Lambton Quay. At my level when I worked there, he's now ascended to the position of Group Director (Mike's old job). We chat for a few minutes under a shop front while a gale blows and the streams of office workers walk

183

past, hunched against the wind. We talk about comings and goings in the Group and funding cutbacks and the inevitable burden he has to carry now he's been promoted: more administration.

'We're moving again...' I look incredulous for a second. 'To the sixth floor.' He registers my disbelief: we moved floors a couple of times in my short stint there. 'Crazy, I know.'

'Well, you could always think of it as an exercise in behaviour enrichment.'

'Huh?'

'Face it Alan; we sit in a warm, sterile, environment all day. I'm just the same. At the office, at home. We don't have to hunt for our food. It's just the same for zoo animals. They get bored. It's not natural, for them or us. Have you ever owned a dog?' He shakes his head. 'Well, if they don't get enough stimulation, they chew anything they can: newspapers, cables, shoes. We're the same. We need stimulation: problems to solve, aims to pursue, difficulties to overcome. It was on the news, didn't you see? They're doing it at the Zoo, with the zebras and elephants and the chimps: giving them puzzles, tyre swings, hiding their food, rearranging their enclosures. Behaviour enrichment. That's what the government is doing; restructuring, moving you around. They're all doing it.'

He laughs, 'And they claimed it's for earthquake strengthening. Well, I won't question it. I'm senior management now.'

The entire thrust of our civilisation has been in the direction of behaviour impoverishment. More automation, more of us switching on computers, entering bits of data, and watching, monitoring, at work and at home. Nothing very challenging. If we kept our cats or dogs - or cows and sheep for that matter - in apartment blocks or offices for 23 hours out of 24 we'd rightly be condemned for cruelty. Cats and dogs are not meant to sit around all day. They're born to move, to work for their food, to be alert. So are we. Under-stimulated animals develop weird behaviours, like over-grooming, tormenting their companions. Or they overeat, mutilate themselves or lose their appetite. Isn't that exactly a description of human pathology? Hence this perpetual restructuring, remodelling. Seeking danger in the form of rugby, gambling, gangs and, I don't know, wife-swapping. It's all behaviour enrichment. They showed a Dutch chap on TV the other night, having an ice bath, then leading a band of followers up the snows of Mount Kilimanjaro, all of them in bare feet and shorts. He says our immune system needs more work to do, otherwise it turns on us. Sounds plausible to me.

ASEAN Summit, 2011

Three months after my audience with the Honourable Tom Wilkins MP, and at the end of a routine day, I'm at home watching the start of the 9pm New Zealand TV news programme, a mug of tea by my side, Kitty on my lap. The opening fanfare, and there's just one item portentously announced as the headline story: the culmination of the Summit meeting in Auckland of the heads of state of the ASEAN countries. Something must have happened, I think to myself for it to come before the cricket or rugby. The newscaster says kia ora, smiling, then as he begins to tell us about the final ceremonies, the footage shows scenes from Auckland. And we see lined up on the podium, under a banner reading 'ASEAN Auckland 2011' the ten ASEAN Heads of State and the Deputy Prime Ministers of observer nations China and India, wearing identical short-sleeve shirts. That's the usual way ASEAN summits end, but this year there's something different. The shirts are scaly and sandy-coloured and, as the camera pans across the line-up, we see the leaders – the Prime Minister of New Zealand in the centre, taking the lead – putting on head-pieces, with open faces. We can see the leaders grinning and putting their arms round each other's shoulders. But let the newscaster tell it:

185

The ASEAN Summit in Auckland concluded with the leaders going went one step further. Instead of the usual ethnic tee-shirts, here they are wearing tuatara costumes. And despite the many tensions surrounding the regional arms build-up, this 'animated' meeting seems to have ended on a conciliatory note.

We see more evidence of conviviality, as the leaders laughingly pick up and gulp from beer and wine glasses, presumably from a table out of the picture. The newscaster talks of agreements signed, and rising share prices in Asia, Australia and New Zealand. Watching this, I silently thank Tom Wilkins. He's done what I asked. And then my eyes fill as I think of Tina and Sam. They're not here to see it. Kitty licks the back of my hand, her tongue like hot, wet sandpaper.

ASEAN meetings had hitherto been anodyne affairs, where little of consequence was decided. Before this particular gathering, though, there had been real friction, manifestations of which, unusually for ASEAN, had appeared in the media. There'd been conflict over a few dozen hectares of land straddling borders in south-east Asia, while competing claims over island specks off in the South China Sea, which had been simmering for years, appeared almost certain to boil over. There'd been threats not to attend and, on the first day, threats to pull out. China had talked about installing surface-to-air missile batteries being put up around Beijing, Shanghai and other major cities 'purely for defence'. There had been outbursts of hateful speech between the leaders of Indonesia, the Philippines, and Malaysia, over nothing of substance. Thankfully our Prime Minister, known for her ability to mediate and conciliate, had managed to get all the participants to turn up and sit in one room. It probably helped too that New Zealand – far away from everywhere – was hosting the meeting. And indeed, the universally acclaimed success of the meeting was attributed in part to our Prime Minister's genial personality and powers of persuasion, as well as New Zealand's role of honest broker.

186

And Zootherapy. Yes, the Heads of State dressed up as tuataras not only at the Summit's conclusion but also, and with no publicity, at the beginning of each daily session. In the warm afterglow of the summit meeting, the editorial in the *New Zealand Herald* is headed by a slogan that would be taken up by the media all over the globe:

WE ARE ALL TUATARAS NOW!

The favourable commentary keeps on coming. Logging into the *Economist* website a couple of days later I see this in one of their leader columns:

> *The 2011 ASEAN Summit might well be seen as a decisive turning point in international affairs. Certainly the fiery rhetoric characterising the territorial conflicts has evaporated. Whether this will translate into cooler heads prevailing on the ground remains to be seen.*

In a more in-depth article in its Asia section the journal gives Zootherapy a mention – its first ever in an international media outlet:

> *Much of the success of the meeting can be attributed to the host country's policy of remaining strictly neutral.... Another factor may have been a unique New Zealand form of interpersonal relationship management called Zootherapy. Essentially, this involves dressing up as animals and allowing your animal identity to dictate your behaviour.*

Along with Zootherapy, there was interest in tuataras, the animal I had suggested in my chat with Tom. They had to be something strongly evocative of New Zealand, to have a chance of flying with the PM. Now, a few days after the summit, I hear some pundit on National Radio opine that the choice of tuataras – the closest living relatives to dinosaurs - had something do with some Jungian wish of mine for the world to return to a prelapsarian past; to the time before our species left the Garden of Eden. Who knows? Who cares?

I just like the way tuataras are happy to sit around all day and take things easy.

THE RISE AND RISE OF ZOOTHERAPY, 2012-2017

And so Zootherapy became a presence on the world stage.

I won't write too much about the years since ASEAN. It's well documented and much of it you can't help but already know. As I write this, in 2017, the rise of Zootherapy after ASEAN looks as though it were inevitable and rapid. But, like life itself, or a plane journey that flies you from one side of the globe to the other in a day, you experience it as a slow-moving, protracted process. The popular mood in the western countries before ASEAN was already somewhat anti-establishment. Afterwards it become more so. The Summit kicked off interest in Zootherapy both in New Zealand and overseas.

Maybe anything truly original and innovative would have halted our species' disastrous piling up of weapons of mass killing, clashes of ideologies, our destruction of animals and their habitats. Perhaps it would have taken an impending asteroid collision, or a man-made catastrophe like a nuclear conflict begun by accident or design, to make us rethink our role on this planet. We'll never know because, as it happens, it was Zootherapy that came along.

ASEAN showed Zootherapy functioning effectively at the highest level of government. There was some trickle down. But, almost independently, the public – you know, ordinary people – got involved. It started in New Zealand with the referendum movement....

ZRI RALLY, 10 FEBRUARY 2017

...Which reaches its climax in Wellington today. The immediate flurry of interest sparked by ASEAN died down quickly, in a world of social media and short attention spans. Behind the scenes and absent from the mass media, though, the movement that led to today's events began: the movement calling for a referendum to ask New Zealand citizens whether Zootherapy should be mandatory for high-level international meetings held here.

The initiative, as far as I can make out, began with an alliance between various mostly charitable bodies, including the Lions, the Masons and Rotary, all with a genuine and non-political interest in doing good by the society that had helped them prosper. They convinced me to play a discreet, mostly advisory role. It was slow at first, but has been gathering pace. People joined marches that began a couple of weeks ago northwards from Invercargill, southwards from Cape Reinga, to converge today in Wellington. Kate's with me, as we look out of the window towards Parliament Buildings, watching the drama unfold while listening to commentary on the radio. It's a big crowd, a few tens of thousands apparently, and the weather's been relatively kind: it's breezy, but sunny. The city centre is seething and the crowd of marchers, swelled by a large local contingent, is spilling out onto the foreshore, with speakers from all parts of the country on podiums in the Civic Centre. There's to be a rally tonight at the 'Cake Tin' - the stadium close to the main railway station.

After taking no advice whatsoever, I've decided not to accept the invitation to appear on stage tonight. I don't want Zootherapy to be about me. I don't have much of a private life any more, but what little I have I want to keep that way. The New Zealand media are one thing; this is a country where you can still see ex-Prime Ministers shopping or swimming in the Freyberg public pool, unaccompanied by any security people. But international attention is something else: it would attract all sorts of would-be hangers-on and crazies. It's not like the old days; real air fares have fallen dramatically. Anyone with a grudge can afford to get here. After ASEAN I'd been seduced by the media, being asked my opinion on things about which I know nothing: wool exports, climate change, coral bleaching, the Oscars. No more. I opt for a quiet life.

And so I fade into the background, and the ZRI – the Zootherapy Referendum Initiative – remains a genuine people's movement. New Zealand legislation provides for a referendum on any topic if enough citizens sign a petition calling for one: it would have to be signed by ten percent of all registered voters within 12 months. The ZRI marchers have been gathering signatures along their routes to Wellington, and the ten percent threshold was quickly and easily surpassed. So, at some point in the first half of 2018 the people of New Zealand are going to be asked to give their answer to this question:

> *Do you think that, for meetings held in New Zealand of Heads of Government from more than two countries, said Heads of Government or their most senior representatives shall all simultaneously wear tuatara costumes for at least three consecutive hours between the formal beginning and end of the meeting, while the meeting is in session, or during one of the informal gatherings?*

How to make a simple proposition complicated. And even this question is festooned with superscripts directing readers to footnotes defining 'meetings', 'senior', 'costumes', 'tuatara', and 'gatherings'. I can live with that!

Tonight's rally, then, will be partly a celebration of success, partly a push for a 'Yes' vote. Naturally, the build-up to the referendum is attracting attention from overseas. Wellington hotels are full of TV anchors, camera operators, technical guys; there are journalists from all the media – I've seen Wellingtonians being interviewed in Lambton Quay, with the Beehive in the background. There are some fringe politicians, mostly from Europe, and mid-level civil servants from all over; there are quite a few alternative medicine practitioners too, and today I heard a radio interview with the owner of a private zoo in the US. Part of the international interest, it has to be said, is probably a result of the rally being held during our summer and the northern hemisphere winter.

DIALOGUE WITH JASON, JULY 2018

A cold, windy, wet winter's evening; it's already dark by the time Jason and I, having finished work, meet for beer and a pub meal at the Marble Bar on Lambton Quay. I'm now almost universally known around Wellington, and while I still get some of that lingering stares from people who have seen my image somewhere (on television, most likely) others know exactly who I am, and leave me in peace. This is New Zealand, and there's no fawning, thankfully, so I still have the option of chatting with Jason in a public place.

It's been several months since Jason and I last met, and a couple of weeks since the referendum.

'You did it, James; I've got to hand it to you.' We clink our pint glasses. 'Cheers; and here's to Zootherapy!'

There had been an overwhelming vote in favour of 'Yes' for participants at all high-level international meetings in New Zealand to wear a tuatara costume. This was no surprise, though the margin exceeded even the most optimistic of the opinion polls: 89 percent of voters on a turnout of about 75 percent.

Jason has followed Zootherapy as closely as I've followed rock music, which is to say, hardly at all. I'm glad about that; it means we can talk about other things, but tonight he brings up Zootherapy and the referendum result. He's quite ebullient about it: after a demonstration of Zootherapy at her school, his daughter has taken to wearing a tuatara outfit as often as she can. The media are full of questions as to how New Zealand, India, China and the other ASEAN countries will spend their 'peace dividend'. Jason's father, though, a retired military man, apparently has doubts.

'He sees it as a con. We let down our guard, and then what?'

'It's only the media that are talking about lowering our defence level. We might spend less, true, but we'll be like animals: we won't waste what we do spend.'

'What about all the personnel, what are they going to do?'

'The New Zealand army?'

'The military here and everywhere else: the generals, the squaddies, the navy, the pilots. And the spooks, the people who make uniforms, the tank manufacturers. I don't know: the people who paint warships and submarines. The whole lot of them. Once Zootherapy comes in and there's peace in the world? What will they all do?'

'Lump of labour fallacy, Jason. Market forces. Same as the buggy whip makers. They won't all go on the dole. They'll do something else. I don't know, clean up after floods, or go help with disasters in other countries, write poems, look after old people. They'll make a big thing of training exercises.'

'What for?'

'We're still going to need some of them.'

'All right, but they're going to get fed up of training for nothing.'

I recall a lesson from the history of esoteric organisations.

'Well, they can reinvent themselves. Like the freemasons. You know about the freemasons, right?'

'They do good works, and it's men only. And secret.'

'Something like that. But do you know how it all started?'

And I explain how, with the decline of cathedral building in Europe after the Middle Ages, some guilds of operative – that is actual, working - stonemasons began to accept honorary members to buttress their declining membership. These new members had nothing to do with carving stones; they were attracted by the rites, trappings and brotherhood of the lodges. So evolved modern speculative Freemasonry. The old stonemason guilds, without knowing where their adaptive membership drive would lead, changed into something profoundly different...

'...The guys in the military could do the same.'

'So squaddies will become altar boys? Interesting; swords into ploughshares. I get it.' He sips. 'Could happen', he says, sceptically. 'Somehow I don't think dad would be too thrilled.'

THE WORLD THAT ZOOTHERAPY MADE, 2020
As well as its bringing hopes of peace to a dangerously unstable part of the world, where conflict could have led to the slaughter of millions, the ascension of Zootherapy had two other benign effects.

One: it's been good for business. I do group sessions now in five-star hotels not only in Wellington and Auckland, but also in Sydney and Melbourne. In the quiet period between Christmas 2017 and New Year I move into a plush new office suite, close to The Terrace, at the parliament end, and now employ Kate for four full days a week to help with the burgeoning administrative requirements of my practice and the OSZ. I'm sometimes called on by the media to comment on things to do with Zootherapy and animals. I shun TV for the most part, but often give short radio interviews, which I can do without leaving my office.

Two: parallel to this interest in Zootherapy comes a blizzard of research showing just how intelligent, and in their way, wise, are animals of all species. The more we learn of the complexity and intricacy of animal life on land and sea, the more humble we become. All the findings show that animals, individually or collectively, are smarter than we ever thought. I'm no animal expert, but I see headlines like this far more frequently these days: *Monkeys could talk so why don't they?* And *Dogs deceive humans to get what they want.* And *Pigeons have a better understanding of probabilities than humans.* And *Animals are smart. Are humans holding them back?* I read about the stinging cell of a jellyfish that accelerates at 5 million times the acceleration due to gravity. We're becoming more considerate of the welfare of farm animals and pets: training methods are becoming less punitive; less about dominance, more reward-based and more respectful of animal intelligence. And instead of looking at human aggression through the prism of the twentieth century, with all its horrors, we look further back, beyond even the last ten thousand years of recorded history, over the two million years of the genus *homo;* all the evidence telling us that warfare was *not* a feature of human life, that the violence of the past few millennia was a mere blip in human history, that human nature is essentially peaceable, co-operative and even altruistic. We continue questioning our most cherished assumptions about what it means to be human. Zootherapy captures the imagination of these times.

You know what happens next: the citizens-initiated referenda in Italy and Switzerland. As in New Zealand these votes were partly a semi-serious attempt to change things for the better, and partly a thumbing of the nose at the existing power elite and its alienation from the people they were supposed to represent: an expression of people power, voiced by ordinary members of the public who'd had enough of politicians pandering to their wealthy backers: the bankers, pharmaceutical companies, landowners, warmongers and fraudsters – the only people, in fact, who could afford to pay people even to follow politics, let alone influence it.

Ordinary citizens in other countries began lobbying for animal costumes at leaders' meetings. They agitated for Zootherapy referenda, but didn't need them: politicians feared less the dressing up as animals than the prospect of consulting their citizens so, in public at least, embraced Zootherapy. Just as ideologues think belief rather than observance is what drives people, so the elites underestimated the power of their tongue-in-cheek performances. Served them right! It happened patchily at first; Sydney, western Europe, the American Midwest, Hong Kong, but the patches expanded largely, I think, because of the one feature common to the world's otherwise wildly differing political systems: the huge and hitherto widening gap between policymakers and people.

Zootherapy's cause was helped by the obvious malevolence and rancid self-interest of the people opposed to it: a smug, contemptuous, collection of ideologues, extremist clerics, billionaires, and the people they paid to understand and manipulate an increasingly arcane and corrupt political system The politicians thought that, compared with surrendering power to ordinary people, dressing up as animals was the lesser of the two evils. They couldn't have foreseen the effects such a concession would have on the global mood any more than I could have anticipated how my similarly reluctant agreement to sing my first, and only, Gorillagram all those decades ago would transform my own life.

My naïve optimism, a few years back, about swords into ploughshares or squaddies into acolytes wasn't completely misplaced. As the importance of the warfighting function of the military declined all over the world, so the different branches got involved in new activities, centred around rank and ritual, sure, but also sport and music. Some went the way of the freemasons, with an exaggerated, almost Ruritanian, significance attached to hierarchy and the customs formerly integral to military life: the emphases on tidiness, camaraderie, the raising of flags, the awarding of medals, and exemplary behaviour in adverse circumstances. I'm pleased to say that some of these repurposed military facilities offered Zootherapy courses, both for clients and for aspiring Zootherapists.

In counterpoint to the reduced threat of large-scale violence prefigured at ASEAN, there has been a rise in the readiness of ordinary people to stand up for themselves: to defend themselves against aggression, rather than surrender. That is having an effect that would surprise many: a net reduction in violence of all sorts, in all countries, in public spaces and behind closed doors. Psychologists explain that it's not only the fear of instant retribution that deters aggressors; there's also the greater respect the aggressors have toward people who are willing to defend themselves. This has incalculable effects especially in whole continents where the 'clash of civilisations' had threatened to end very, very bloodily.

There is still much conflict and cruelty in the world, but for the first time for decades, people expect things to get better. Sure, Zootherapy has something to do with that but, whatever people may say, or wish, I haven't created paradise on earth.

WHERE AM I IN ALL THIS? KITTY DIES, 2020
Where am I in all this? You might think that the success of Zootherapy has made me a happy man. It hasn't. What it has done is isolate me from people with a home, a family and people who understand what drives me. People are envious of the attention I receive, little knowing or caring that at the end of every day, I have only an empty house to go to. (And if they did care, what difference would it make?) It is as if Mr Zootherapy and Mr Sinclaire are at each end of a see-saw. My head is satisfied with Zootherapy, its impact on my clients and the world. My heart, like the house I live in, is empty.

'It's for the best', said the vet, and I know she's right. Several years ago, after an altercation with an unknown assailant, Kitty became an indoor cat. Then she developed kidney problems, necessitating a special diet. And now, inevitably, her disease has advanced and she's in constant pain. So we're putting her to sleep. She's done very well, for a cat, having lived, mostly happily, for just over twenty years, but that hardly assuages my grief. The last living link with my daughter and wife. I'm inconsolable.

For all I know it is Kitty's death that precipitated my crisis of faith. As people in their millions have taken to Zootherapy, I'm growing more detached from it. Zootherapy might work for the rest of the world, but it's stopped working for me. I have been so bereft that putting on a costume seems like an irrelevance or, worse, a mockery. And because I used to believe, because Zootherapy used to be my passion and source of light, that raises the stakes: now I deliberately refrain from practice, because I don't want to contaminate my first joyful experiences.

You hear of priests of all religions who lose their faith. But, after years or decades of leading their flock, they have come to rely utterly on the financial and moral support of their community. They can't leave it; some can't even speak the truth to their family. Their support network, their income, status, social life all depend on their keeping up the pretence. So every week they stand solemnly facing their congregation, intoning prayers to a God in whom they don't believe. They enact rituals mechanically. They publicly espouse values that they privately disavowed long ago. Their professional lives are hypocrisy. They have followers who trust them, confide in them, and *do* believe. What does that do to a man? I am finding out.

Outwardly, nobody would know. I still have clients and I can make Zootherapy work for them. But when I respond to their doubts, I hear myself being defensive. Same with the odd times I'm rung up by the New Zealand media and do a radio interview. I interpret perfectly innocuous questions as challenges rather than expressions of curiosity or genuine interest. Mostly, now, the media have got the message that I am not that interested, and they leave me alone. There are plenty of others who will speak, unofficially, for some offshoot or other of Zootherapy. (Some are so fanatical that I question their adherence to the teachings: their enthusiasm seems inversely proportional to their commitment to actual practice.) My business needs no advertising. I'm as busy as ever and earning or, more accurately, being paid more than I spend. I have a large office suite now in central Wellington, which comprises a studio for small group sessions, my consultation room for individuals, and an adjoining office for Kate, who now works five days a week, and even comes in at weekends sometimes. I've nicknamed her Cerberus ironically as, while she is as effective in screening my visitors, e-mails and phone calls as that three-headed dog of classical literature, guarding the exit from hell, she is as gentle as he was fierce. She edits and sends auto-responses to the many adulatory emails mostly coming from hundreds of ordinary people worldwide who have experienced the benefits of Zootherapy, either directly, or indirectly by the new hopes for peace that it offers a hitherto fractious world. She forwards the nicest ones to me.

It's all well-meant, but these days even the most grateful and laudatory messages leave me cold. I can't share their joy or enthusiasm any longer. I encourage them to keep up with their Zootherapy practice. But my heart isn't in it.

For all Kate's efforts, I can't avoid the low-level resentment that blights the life of anyone in the public eye. Zootherapy's success has made me a receptacle for people's envy, malice and hate. Even in New Zealand, this country of tolerance and peace, there is a pervasive, though not overtly malicious, 'tall poppy' syndrome. Hostile e-mails and the odd nasty letter or suspicious package from overseas are more serious: Kate forwards the most threatening of them to the Special Intelligence Service, New Zealand's security outfit, who have links to intelligence operations in the Anglophone world and beyond. I'm used to this and it doesn't really bother me. The worst that could possibly befall me has already happened.

So why the angst?

Gone are the days when I could relax in a café in Wellington, or have a beer with Jason or anyone from my past. The attention from others is too bothersome now. There's no-one at home to sympathise or laugh with me about it all. It's a small price to pay, I guess for having, let's say 'facilitated' world peace. I'm a public figure after all, though most New Zealanders have a sense of proportion grounded, I like to think, in their closeness to nature. I can still at least catch the bus into town, go to my office, and come home again without too much fuss. Even go shopping in the middle of the day, before having sandwiches at my desk. Until the day I pop into Parson's bookshop to buy a compact disc (Louis Armstrong), then double-back realising that I left a shopping bag by the counter.

'I saw him; it was really him', the young lady behind the counter is saying to her colleague, a guy in his twenties with a neatly-trimmed beard who's holding some CDs in his hand, with an expression of disbelief. 'Here? I don't believe you.' 'I'm telling you, it was him -'. She stops the instant she sees me. This is what it's come to? I can't even go shopping without attracting this mindless hero-worship? I retrieve my bag and scuttle back to the office. I've never really sympathised with celebrities and their complaints about – well – being celebrities. Until now.

It's not just that though. I've been disenchanted for a while. I'm still working with Zootherapy, but any of my accredited students could do as good a job. The acclaim that followed me after ASEAN has attracted people to Zootherapy for the wrong reasons. The problem is not the people who are drawn to it by its trendiness. I don't mind that. It's that some see it solely as a means to a pre-determined end, a vehicle for their worldly ambitions. There's not much I can do to stop that. I've kept a tight rein on official Zootherapy, but I can't stop the unofficial offshoots or syncretic variants, which seek to graft elements of Zootherapy onto existing belief systems. Some of them may do some good. Some don't. Worse, groups of cynics, necessarily beyond my purview, have dressed up their little power plays in Zootherapy-style rhetoric and ritual. The way in which Zootherapy has been corrupted by these charlatans worldwide bugs me. I could spend my entire life filing lawsuits. Or fending off the sharpies and shysters, many of whom, I fear will one day fly to New Zealand with the sole aim of battening onto my (admittedly tempting) fortune. I've lost control. I suppose it's inevitable. It's what passing the torch means.

And it's not all bad. There's been some interest in Zootherapy-type counselling, which diagnoses one particular animal trait that the client supposedly lacks and seeks to develop that. There's been some more committed role play: involving not only costumes, but also appropriate animal-like activities, reminiscent of Zootherapy's early days, with my individual clients and the group sessions with the pandas and elephants. This is instrumental Zootherapy: a means of fitting in better to a society whose parameters are a given, rather than a path to enlightenment. It's not to be disparaged, and I still teach it myself to especially needy clients.

There has been a helpful, but not entirely necessary, assist from technology. One instance: an application for computers or mobile devices that converts, in real time, the changing facial image of the user of the device as seen by its camera, into an image of a limited range of animals. So I could look into the camera and change my expression and see on the screen, as if in a mirror, the same expressions as worn by a dog, cat, cow or horse or, no doubt in months to come, almost any other animal. More ubiquitous are the ZED-glasses (ZEE-glasses in the US) and their imitators: ordinary-looking glasses with built-in software that transforms your vision into that of a cat or dog. You then, almost literally, see the world through the eyes of an animal. Combined with masks, which were cheaper and more practical than animal heads, they became the most common outward form of the Zootherapy practitioner. Children, especially, enjoy these masks: a fun complement to the Zootherapy lessons that, I'm delighted to see, have become part of the curriculum for many children all over the world right from the beginning of their school career.

I should be happy about those Zootherapy variations that worked, and that expanded on the original Zootherapy. And at some level I am. But because they're successful, I'm not needed. As to the more cynical or corrupt variations; they obviously disappoint me.

I can shrug off much of the opposition – a natural response to any sort of success enjoyed by a new idea. Zootherapy is mainstream now so there's always going to be a natural reaction against it. But, as I look on, humans are doing to Zootherapy what we do to anything borne of inspiration: imposing a rigid, hierarchical superstructure onto it. Okay, unlike some pundits of the age, I am respectful of the human need to gather together, share our hopes and aspirations in prayer and song, and collectively to acknowledge that, if things aren't that great, they could be a lot worse. To express gratitude for our lot, in short. It was, I can see now, the pervasive, contemptuous dismissal of such emotion that had pushed me away from the land of my birth. The mean-spirited denigration of sincerity. It validates inaction and smugness (which comes first, the indolence or the rationalisation?). So I look quite indulgently on the rites and rituals accreted around the Zootherapy philosophy. The core is the important thing and, while the music and ritual sometimes distract from it, they can't corrupt it. Besides, some people come to Zootherapy because they are first attracted by the rites. So overall, it's been a win for the world.

'Sex is like nuclear war', says an American bloke on Radio New Zealand, early one morning, trying to flog his new book. 'How do you price the infinite? Bill Clinton, for all his many faults, wasn't stupid.' I wasn't really listening but I can see what he might mean. Since Tina died, I've had no sex life despite the plenitude of commercial opportunities (this is a town of diplomats and conferences). I'd like to say it's because I'm loyal to her memory. Disciplined. In control. But no; it's more a matter of my lack of anonymity and Wellington's small size. How do you value, say, a nuclear catastrophe? By rights, we should be doing everything we can to avoid one. Zootherapy tells me that sex doesn't matter if it's not an option. But it matters more than anything else if all your basic needs have been met, and you're not in Zootherapy-mode, which, for whatever reason, is my default setting these days.

So yes, Zootherapy: a gain for everyone else, but it doesn't really compensate for a lack of a family life. And there's another thing that gets me down: I'm fed up of the subtle pressure to behave as people imagine I should behave: free of all problems, happy. Ecstatic even. As though I were one of those American TV preachers, with their perpetual grin showing off their dazzling orthodontics. Then there's the endless speculation about me and the questions I'm always asked: what do I eat or not eat? Do I drink? What's my star sign? Flattering at first, it gets tiresome after a while, believe me. I have to maintain a front. I can't joke about Zootherapy or about my experiences with it. Nor (please don't laugh) can I contemplate visiting any of New Zealand's numerous massage parlours: doing so could undermine the whole Zootherapy edifice.

But I don't need reasons to be miserable. I just am. And while the counterfactual might be valid, it wouldn't cut much ice with the ever-increasing numbers of people who have taken to Zootherapy or those who might join them. 'I'm a fragile defeated husk of a man, but thanks to Zootherapy I'm not suicidal.' Not a great marketing slogan. Well I guess animals have problems too.

Zootherapy's success has catapulted me out of New Zealand society. It's like the bright Maori schoolkids who do well at school. Success means being alienated from their family, tribe, support group. In exchange, and if they're lucky, they gain a middle-class lifestyle in a stable (read: boring) suburb. I guess that can be a net win. But it is a trade-off. Sure I could phone Jason and we could arrange for a drink after work next week some time, but he'll be in a hurry to get home and we'd have to choose somewhere private. The trains are sparse in the evening. There being nobody else to chat to, nobody who *understands*, I try to connect with a younger, wiser self:

> Younger Wiser James Sinclaire: Why are you so crushed?
>
> Older Lonely James Sinclaire: Wouldn't you be? I've lost my wife, my daughter. Even the cat's gone. I put the rest of my life into Zootherapy and that's failed me too.
>
> YWJS: There's no 'that'. You once said yourself that systems are never going to work. Any belief system or ideology is a distortion of the truth. I can quote you: you said that everybody wants a system that guarantees a reward of some sort. But it's that wish for a system that creates the problem.
>
> OLJS: I can't engage with this. It's too heavy. You're just intellectualising.
>
> YWJS: All I'm saying is practise Zootherapy or don't practise it. But if you do, do it with no expectation. There's no guarantee, there's no system. So think about it, there's nothing that can go wrong. It can't succeed or fail because there's no 'that'.

OLJS: Easy for you to say it.

YWJS: Remember Kitty? She had the right idea. Just ignore words and the narratives they generate, however alluring their poetry, or convincing their consistency. She didn't care, did she? And she had a good life.

The meaning of Younger James' theme and variations doesn't convince me, but they are self limiting. And when they stop the silence has a deep, potent energy. Zed-mode without the Zootherapy! It's always a surprise. Something independent of my will or motivation. Perhaps it's something I eat, or maybe it's hormonal. Or you just get tired of hauling the heavy iron of past hurts around. Whatever, I feel sure – once again – that there's nothing that a bit of Zootherapy practice won't solve. All this talk of Zootherapy. The lesson I seem to have to learn again and again and again is that talking about Zootherapy is a distraction and that Zootherapy itself is completely meaningless unless I'm doing it now. In that frame of mind, I can take anything on the chin!

But then come:

THE DEATH THREATS

```
Your a literel son of a bitch. God said we
hate dominion over animals.

We're coming to kill you pommy sheep s**gger

Eat s*** and die hipperkrit

Die you animal f**ker
```

I knew messages like this made their way to Kate's e-mail in-tray at the office. Along with the initial instinct to strike back somehow, I've felt ever so slightly sympathetic to my would-be tormentors on account of the poverty of their – foul – language. They haven't had the advantages I've had, I remind myself; in this case a cousin who'd spent time at a Red Sea diving resort where she learned how to swear in Arabic, and passed her pearls of wisdom on to me. 'May your private parts burst into flames!' (it sounds better in the original) was one of them and it's what comes to mind now. The messages are colourless and unimaginative, but disturbing in that they had somehow made their way onto my home computer and into my private e-mail inbox.

I pay a couple of forensic computer experts in deepest Upper Hutt to investigate. They can't find anything and are unwilling to make a home visit, saying they've done all they can. But for a few hundred dollars extra, they make the effort, arriving sometimef between dawn and sunrise, tired and grey after working all night. It doesn't take them long to confirm their diagnosis: the messages might have come from just one person's computer, or they might not. They might have originated overseas, or they might not. The miscreants who sent them to my home e-mail address might know where I live, or they might not. I'm not impressed but at least my crepuscular cyberconsultants fix me up with a Virtual Private Network, download something called the TOR browser, and get me to change some crucial passwords. Then the police say they'll put a discreet watch on my house (there are already electronic systems in my office block) and that 'we'll know about it', if my would-be executioners try to attack me at home. I am not greatly reassured. Perhaps it would be different if I consorted with other wealthy celebrities – for that is what I am now – to swap experiences and tactics, but I don't. There are many reasons for this, but the simplest is the most cogent: there just aren't any such celebrities who live in Wellington nor, come to think if it, in New Zealand. Anyway, no more death threats penetrate my cyber-defences and after a week or two I calm down. Until...

Exit Cerberus

It's a viciously windy, rainy, grey morning in September 2021. I'm late into the office and I'm surprised to see the normally cheerful Kate, sad and downcast. As I walk in, a large, thickset man, well barbered, in a heavy overcoat rises from the armchair. His face looks vaguely familiar. Their body language tells me something's wrong. Kate speaks:

'James: my husband, David.' Ah, that would explain it: he's an older version of the man in the silver-framed photo on her desk. Tall, with a strong grip as we shake hands. He has a commanding air. Is there a trace of superciliousness? I've seen it often on first contact, particularly with men, including new clients, as if they think Zootherapy is beneath their dignity, a bit of a con, and they want to give the impression that they're only in my office because of an insistent partner or a court order.

'How can I help?'

'I took a phone call last night, at home', David says, straight to the point. A faint trace of an Australian accent. 'An obscene call. He mentioned your name. He threatened Kate's life.'

I breathe out, sighing. Oh. It's getting worse. From e-mails in the office, to e-mails at home, and now a phone call to the home of my Personal Assistant.

We sit down. David continues: 'Kate tells me it happens a lot here', he gestures round the office. 'But we've had nothing like this at home, isn't that right?' Kate nods. He continues: 'I've told the police, of course.' He says nothing for a moment then, to Kate: 'Do you want to say it or shall I?'

In an uncharacteristically small voice, Kate turns to me: 'I don't think I can work here any more'.

They probably couldn't get my home phone number and my office building is secure enough. So perhaps it was inevitable they'd go after Kate.

Kate packs her personal things, mostly family photos, into a couple of carrier bags and a cardboard box. She shows me the notebook in which she's written all the computer passwords, and then she and David exit my life. I'm on my own now, in the office as well as at home.

I MOVE TO A HOTEL, 2021
With Kitty gone, there's only me in what the real estate agent unironically refers to in her listings as a 'family home'. Thankfully, it sells quickly, along with the furniture. There wasn't much else, my having gradually got rid of Tina and Samantha's belongings over the years. I put the things I can't bear to lose in translucent plastic 100-litre containers, which are then taken into storage in Petone. (These are things I can't part with, but also don't really want to see again, like the snake costume and some of Samantha's art. Reminders of what is lost.) Suburban life is for couples and families, not for single guys in their late fifties, especially those who don't drive.

Encouraged partly by the police, who would otherwise have to continue to watch my home, I move into the James Cook Hotel - on The Terrace again. I take a one-bedroom junior suite on the eighth floor, with a harbour view. Slightly enhanced hotel security will suffice, according to the police and, in the enclosed anonymity of the hotel, with all its comings and goings, I feel I have found my privileged (it's a four-star hotel) way of resolving the Hedgehog's Dilemma - how to trade off our need for intimacy against our need to avoid pain – as best I can.

I DECIDE TO RETIRE, 2022
During the long break, when New Zealand closes down for summer, Christmas and New Year, I have plenty of time to reflect. I'm coming

to the conclusion that I should retire from Zootherapy. Whoever rang Kate at home was technically adept. They encrypted the call and bounced it via anonymous internet servers. It could have originated anywhere. Crude, angry death threats from anonymous cybernauts sent via email are bad enough, though nowadays they seem to be an inescapable intrusion into the life of anyone in the public eye. But a voice call tormenting my employee at home crosses a line. Sure, her landline number is publicly listed, but they went to the effort of discovering her identity and composing a voice message with a creepy synthetic voice. It's serious. I've had enough.

Retire? Yes, I'm nearly sixty. It's not just the death threats. People know about Zootherapy and they know where to find out more about it if they're interested. My work's done. I want a complete break, without the baggage, the hangers-on, the invitations to endorse pet food, the adulation for the wrong reasons (or even the right reasons), and the interviews with clueless newspeople. I want the freedom to practise Zootherapy for myself, rather than as a means of fulfilling others' expectations, be they genuine or meretricious. I want the freedom *not* to practise it too. I want to be in nature, without beefy security guys lurking, however discreetly, in the background. There's nothing to keep me in Wellington – only some unhappy memories. My pals have moved on, some literally, up the coast or over the Rimutakas to a bucolic retirement; others, like Jason, have demanding jobs, homes and families and little time for anything else.

But is a decent retirement feasible? I have no financial worries, even were I to live to be 120. But won't my notoriety follow me, wherever I go? What about the cryonic option: disappear for a century or ten and come back when all the fuss has died down? Tina and I had discussed cryonics years ago. Well, why not? I used to think. We could afford it; put some money aside, and when the time came.... OK, the chances weren't high that we'd be successfully defrosted ('reanimated' in their words), cured of whatever killed us and go on to live another full, healthy life hundreds or thousands of years into the future. And preserving all our memories would tricky (though they'd done it with frogs and shrimp, I seem to remember), and there'd be more cell damage during the long years that you were immersed in liquid nitrogen. There were other risks too: earthquakes, lawsuits, power cuts.... No, the chances weren't high, though they were greater than the zero chance offered by burial or cremation. Then Sam came along, and we had other priorities. No, I really wouldn't want to come back to life alone, even if it were feasible. OK, not cryonics. But the otherwise unhelpful guys who'd tried to trace the emails sent to my home computer had presented me with another path toward the anonymity I crave. That evening I fire up the computer, open the TOR browser and, for the first time, search the Dark Web.

WHAKAREWAREWA THERMAL RESERVE, ROTORUA 2022
A sunny lunchtime, and two men: one tall, greying and solid; one compact with short blond hair, park their car outside the Whakarewarewa Thermal Reserve on the fringes of the town of Rotorua. It's a hot day; they're wearing sunglasses and tee-shirts. They pay in cash for admission to the area, site of hundreds of mud pools and around sixty geysers. Slowly they wander round the park. It's the middle of the week, but still fairly busy, with groups of tourists from Japan, China and Taiwan being shown around. There are a few elderly kiwi couples here too, and smaller groups of businessmen and women taking a break from conferences held in the hotels and motels nearby. Steam lingers over the hot pools in the still air. There's a pervasive, pungent, sulphurous, mouldy eggs aroma.

The tall man checks his watch, and the pair stroll around. 'There he is,' he says as they see a man in a beautifully tailored dark suit, standing at the back of a group businessmen, carrying a slim leather briefcase, falling back as the rest of the group moves off the viewing platform at the Pohutu geyser. 'He's seen us', says the compact man.

They meet. Perfunctory greetings. The geyser's quiet now and the trio walk slowly around the park, appending themselves to a group of Chinese visitors, pausing with them to watch the football-size gas bubbles bursting at the surface of the mud pools. 'You flew up today?' The man in the suit gives a short grunt that could mean 'yes' or 'no', and asks the pair:

'Any problems? Anything at all?'

'Nothing.'

The man opens his briefcase and hands a slim file to the tall man. 'A map, a plan of the auditorium, timings and everything else you need. It's all here.'

'OK.'

'And your insurance policy,' says the man in the suit, extracting a piece of paper from his briefcase. He'll have the original in his jacket pocket.'

'Signed?'

'Signed, authenticated, sealed and laminated. You're to get them to get it out of his jacket and read it out, once it's done. Right then and there. Insist. Repeat. Shout. Scream. Whatever it takes.'

The two men read the words on the paper and hand it back. 'Seems OK.'

'You know the score. Don't resist, and make a point of not resisting. There'll be some face-saving afterwards: you'll be out of action for a few weeks, as we discussed. We'll have your back the entire period. After that...' he opens the palm of his hand up to the sky.

The other two men nod. A brief goodbye and the man in the suit walks to the exit, and hails a taxi to take him to the airport. The pair take their time looking around the park, before getting into their car.

THE CHAT SHOW, 2022

It's 2022. Word has got round about my impending retirement, and I'm being interviewed for a retrospective of my life. I don't like being on TV, but it's almost my 60th birthday and it's a chance to get the story straight before I retire. The eponymous host is a lady called Pippa Scrimshaw. The first time I saw her programme, I thought her surname familiar. One of my clients? I checked my files the next morning, (there can't be many Scrimshaws around) and there had been an Ian Scrimshaw at one of my panda sessions for satyrs, back in 1999. Her father perhaps? Whatever, she's now a big fish in the small pond of New Zealand television talking heads, and she, or the pond she will next swim in, seems destined to grow bigger. The Pippa Scrimshaw Programme is a chat show, New Zealand-style, upbeat, with couches and glass tables on which rest bowls of fruit, and translucent blue and green plastic bottles of Fjordland water. It's being recorded before a live audience in Avalon, near Wellington. I'm used to speaking before large groups, though tonight's performance has an elegiac feel. Waiting in the wings, and hearing myself being announced, I narrow my eyes and imagine – for sentiment's sake – that I'm a gorilla. I intend this to be my last TV appearance, so I want to make a good fist of it.

There's a ripple of applause as I walk on to the stage: the couches have a forlorn look: Pippa sits in an armchair. There'll be just one other guest tonight: an academic from the US. And they've assured me there'd be no 'surprises', like old clients or friends or (God forbid!) relatives striding on to remind me of where I came from.

We skate quickly over the rise of Zootherapy from those early sessions with welfare beneficiaries to those first glimmerings of global peace, taking in the Kiwi Icon award, the ASEAN Summit, and the public enthusiasm that led to the referenda and the proliferation of Zootherapy in all its forms worldwide.

We reach the point at which advertisements will be shown when this show is broadcast. A monitor counts down the 150 seconds that the break will last. We make small talk for a minute, then fall silent until the end of the countdown, at which Pippa springs a surprise.

'And welcome back. Friedrich Nietzsche, George Santayana, Jean-Paul Sartre, Benedict de Spinoza, Arthur Schopenhauer, Henry David Thoreau, Voltaire, Ludwig Wittgenstein, Immanuel Kant,' she hesitates for a microsecond, 'Søren Kierkegaard, John Locke and David Hume: what do they all have in common?'

'They're all white males, all dead,' I say, 'And they're authors? Philosophers?'

'Correct', says Pippa. 'The leading lights in Western philosophy.' She goes on: 'Samuel Butler, Gustave Flaubert, Edward Gibbon, Franz Kafka, Charles Lamb, T.E. Lawrence, Henry James, Alexander Pope, Marcel Proust, Stendhal and Jonathan Swift.'

'Writers, historians.'

'Yes.' says Pippa, 'And poets. And what about these people?' She points to a monitor screen on which all the people named are scrolling upwards. New names appear at the bottom of the screen. I catch sight of Schubert, Brahms, Beethoven, van Gogh, and Michelangelo, but there were a dozen others.

'More white men', I say 'Great composers, painters.' I'm not sure what she's trying to prove.

'Correct; all white men, all dead. But what else do they have in common?' There's a long pause.

'They're not just men', says Pippa, 'They're single men: bachelors. None of them were married. And I want to ask you; I can't help wondering; you invented Zootherapy when you were single, before you met your late wife. And it was only after she died that, well, you began to apply it to the problems of the world.'

'Sorry?' I think I know what she's asking, but I'm not prepared for this.

'What I'm asking is; if your wife and daughter had lived, do you think Zootherapy would have followed the same path? Would you have had the time or the inclination to get involved in politics and try to end war? What I'm getting at is that all those great accomplishments of all those guys,' (she gestures to the monitor screen.) 'could only have happened because they were single and didn't have any distractions at home.'

I begin my answer as if I'm a detached observer, surprised by Pippa's or the TV company's research efforts and perceptiveness. It's a lot more highbrow than I'd expect from those evenings I spent binge-watching TV, those lonely times after Tina died.

'Yes, there could be something in that. If I'd had the choice. I suppose, if it hadn't been for the car accident....' I don't know what to say. She's probably right. I mean, who would choose to write symphonies or a history of the Roman Empire or develop a philosophy if the alternative were a decent family life? Do I say that and risk becoming emotional on TV? Pippa fills the silence:

'And I haven't yet mentioned Jesus Christ. You know, some people do think that you're the Messiah!'

213

Back on familiar territory, I can safely reel off my stock answer, to some scattered laughter from the audience: 'I am not, nor have I ever been, the Messiah.'

Pippa talks about how I – rather than Zootherapy – have brought peace to the world, ended the scourge of war, saved thousands of lives, millions of maimings and mutilations; and brought new hope to the billions on this fragile, solitary planet. It sounds impressive, but I've heard it all before, and my gestures and denials are automatic. Because what I'm really thinking about is that I hadn't really wanted to do any of that. I'd have given it all away for a few more years with Tina and Samantha.

LESTER B VENTURA

A few minutes more then, after the next break, it's time for the other guest on the programme. I see him waiting in the wings. First impression: he's obese. A rare sight in Wellington. Also, he's short and losing his hair. He wears a pea-green tweed jacket – surely too warm for sitting under the hot glare of the studio lights. He looks confident, but also as though he's going to seed. He looks like what he probably is: a tenured academic who's written a popular book, with or without integrity, and become moderately wealthy in the process. 'And now', announces Pippa, 'I want to welcome author and social commentator Doctor Lester Ventura.' A round of applause as he walks onto the stage, with a bit of a swagger, I think, and sits beside me on the sofa.

'Doctor Lester Ventura: welcome to New Zealand!'

'Very glad to be here, in your beautiful country.' He has difficulty pronouncing his R's.

'Doctor Ventura, you're a lecturer at the University of Nebraska-'

'That's Universe City College, Nebraska.'

'Right,' Pippa looks quickly at her notes and continues, 'You're also an award-winning writer, historian, journalist and speaker on a wide range of subjects, including the assassination of President Kennedy, the writings of', she looks down again, 'Immanuel Velikovsky, and the extraterrestrial origins of the Egyptian Pharoahs.' Ventura nods.

'And you're here to promote your recently published book on Zootherapy called *Zootherapy: Fooling All the People All the Time.*

'You got it.'

'Let's get straight to the point; you've said, and I quote, that Zootherapy is "mere self-indulgence", a placebo at best. And you say James Sinclaire is, quote, "a charlatan who uses cute, furry animals - and only cute furry animals - to suck people in to a feel-good moneymaking self-help new age suite of insubstantial ideas, dressed up in preposterous notions of transcendence and liberation." Pretty serious accusations?'

'I stand by everything I've written'.

'Is there anything you'd like to say to Mr Sinclaire?'

'I've got three main points. First: you want us to behave like animals. Now one of the things I've specialised in is cultural anthropology, and every civilisation has its own creation myth and in every creation myth there is some act like the eating of the Edenic apple that brings us knowledge and differentiates us from the animals. Now you are seeming to want to reverse that process. Second: aren't you just echoing what has been said for many years; ....'

And so he drones on, and so *it* goes on. These endless attempts to place Zootherapy within a familiar intellectual context. I could try to stop the flow right then. But I don't. Partly because he deserves a fair hearing, partly because I don't really think I have to defend Zootherapy (let the results speak for themselves) but more so – oh how much more so! – because offstage I see the camera crew, the prompters, the lighting boom guy, and the other technical personnel giggling and acting the goat, laughing at Ventura's seeming lack of self-awareness, his tendency to pronounce 'r' as 'w', and I don't trust myself not to join in if I open my mouth. Pippa is giving him a wind-up signal, but he ignores it, and it's when he says '...The German word for this is *Geschichtsmude*' that there's a brief explosion of mirth offstage, which I do my best to ignore, but I cannot help myself. Pippa's aware of it too but, professional that she is, she looks fixedly down at the table, biting her lower lip. I have to convert my muffled laughter into a coughing bout. I sip water, which does seem to calm me down, and at the same time Ventura's monologue ceases. The broadcasting crew quickly suppress their mirth but I take a bit longer, and emerge from my spluttering to see Ventura and Pippa looking expectantly in my direction. Suddenly, everything's quiet.

An old instinct comes into play; one that had served me well during those interminable meetings at the Ministry, when I would doze off then suddenly become aware of an extended silence and several pairs of eyes looking at me.

'There are arguments on both sides', I say, but the silence continues. I try again: 'I think this is one of those times when the old eighty/twenty rule applies.' Another long pause. That's not going to work either. 'Sorry,' I say to a point mid-way between Ventura and Pippa, 'Could you repeat that?'

'I was asking why,' says Ventura, 'if animals are so smart, why don't they get together and stop our taking over their land, destroying their habitat, or polluting the seas?'

'Professor Ventura, there are plenty of people who react peaceably to violence. It's just not in their nature to fight against a massively superior enemy. Are you implying that native Americans are unintelligent, that all indigenous folk everywhere are incapable of organising themselves to oppose the theft of their lands, or occupation?'

'Not at all. Technologically and numerically....'

He hesitates for a second and in that second a great swelling of sorrow for the man wells up from my heart. A deep, profound, overwhelming sorrow. He comes half-way round the world and we're mocking him and his speech impediment? Sure, I know he can take it; I know he makes a good living. And I know there are worse – far worse - tragedies. But still; the pathos! I want to hug his big sweaty body with his thinning hair, embrace the man and beg forgiveness and say to him and the world: I'm sorry! I'm sorry! I'm sorry! Instead:

'Ok, you're right of course. But can I say that intelligence: real intelligence, super intelligence, has an ethical component. If the choice is to wipe out or to be wiped out, what would the super intelligent do?'

No answer. I continue: 'It just might be that the very smartest - the animals and humans – that we try to kill off, don't want to live in a world where they're not wanted. Where does being smart get people? In the eighties all the talk was of nuclear war. I'm telling you, animals might not want to live in a world where brutality, indiscriminate pitiless brutality, is the order of the day. They might well be smart, in their own way. Even smarter than us. But *it would do them no good to be seen as such.*'

This is getting too heavy. I don't want to get into the persecution of intellectuals in Red China, the Soviet Union, Cambodia. Pippa turns to Ventura: 'You can't deny that there's been an astonishing fall in the numbers of wars all over the world since Zootherapy came on the scene.'

'Ah' says Ventura, 'but the numbers have been coming down anyway, for years. Well before Zootherapy came on the scene. Correlation is not causation. There's not the slightest bit of evidence to show that Zootherapy had anything to do with it.'

This was greeted by a few boos from the audience.

'Obviously,' Pippa says, 'some people would disagree with that, but let's move on. The subtitle of your book is "fooling all the people all the time".' Pippa turns to look at me, 'And the Professor calls Zootherapy's claims of transcendence and liberation "preposterous"'. Ventura nods. 'Do you have anything to say to these accusations?'

'Well, I'm sure the Professor knows of the testimonials to Zootherapy, the Zootherapy groups that have sprung up all over the world?'

'I'm just saying that your ideas are empty; Zootherapy is just another cult, or drug; just like cocaine, opioids, or cigarettes. You get people hooked and they feel good, but it's not actually doing them any good.'

A few more boos from the audience, but also a disconcerting ripple of applause that I like to think is generated by the volume, tempo and cadence of his delivery, rather than his words.

Encouraged, Ventura continues. In what he intends as a spectacular *coup de theatre*, he pulls out some papers from his jacket pocket:

'And what you teach is contradictory. This for example: in one of your lessons you explicitly say that anyone can practise Zootherapy at any time. But a couple of years ago' he waves his papers 'on June 12th 2020 to be precise, in a seminar to trainee Zootherapists here in New Zealand, you said that Zootherapy – and I quote – "cannot and should not be a substitute for religion". In other words, that it is not in fact a universally applicable tool. It's just another therapy. People either believe in it or don't.'

'I'm not sure there's a contradiction there, but let me just say that speaking to different audiences you emphasise different things. For an ordinary working guy to become a thief is a net loss to society. But if we can create thieves that's a net gain to society - if they were otherwise going to be murderers.' A mistake, I realise, as soon as I say it. Ventura, belying his shape and heft, smart as a whip talks over my last words:

'You're saying you're quite happy to use your techniques to create thieves?'

'I'm saying Zootherapy is about creating a better society, not a society of saints.' A small ripple of applause almost drowns my quietly spoken afterthought: 'That comes later.'

Ventura is ready with another riposte.

'How very public spirited of you! What about all the branding that you've done? The books, the courses: all the money you're raking in? Is it the money that motivates you, or is it that you created a movement – the only movement you could think of – where you would be top dog? I think you're just like any other cult: your ideas just happen to be those that create exactly the hierarchy that puts you at the top. I'm not saying you're a fraud: perhaps you genuinely believe in it, but I am saying you're deluded or motivated by self-interest.'

Only experience tells me it's futile to address his diatribe point by point. I still get more shocked into silence than capable of reasoned argument, when confronted by attacks like this. Pippa is just about to get things moving again when I say:

'You've never done it have you?'

'What's that?' he says.

'Zootherapy. You've never actually tried it.'

He shakes his head dismissively. 'I don't need to go to the North Pole to tell you it's cold there.'

'Do it now: pretend you're an animal. You're a cow or a dog – doesn't matter – looking at me now. Feel it.' I lean toward him. 'Look at me through animal eyes: look at me, Pippa, the audience, the cameras, the lamps, all of us. Look at us all through the eyes of an animal. Don't think about it; just do it. You don't need to say anything or judge anything or have an opinion. Just look and feel....'

I see it. I don't know whether the audience sees it; but it would be visible on the screen in close up. A tightening of Ventura's face. A very slight narrowing of the eyes. An alertness. I know immediately that he's experiencing Zootherapy.

It is one of those rare TV moments of total, unscripted spontaneity. There's a vibrant, energy-filled silence in the studio. A hint of a smile appears on Ventura's face. I sit back. Pippa looks from Ventura to me, then to Ventura. An almost inaudible murmur arises from the audience. The energy is almost palpable. After many seconds of this, someone claps. It's quickly taken up by the rest of the audience. Ventura shakes his head, bemused, smiling. Who'd have thought it? Add over-education to the myriad human pathologies that Zootherapy sweeps away.

It's a pattern I've seen over and over. God knows I have my own insecurities, which have made me prickly and defensive at times. But the kind of initial irritation or condescension or even rage that I have experienced from academics, or any number of high-status men and women, is very often a prelude to something dramatic: an intimation that Zootherapy is going to ignite exciting, disquieting insights they can't quite grasp just yet. Like the stars in a romantic comedy, when

220

one reverses into the car of the other in the shopping mall parking lot; the drivers then arguing and expostulating and thinking they hate each other. But we know what happens the next time they meet up. Ventura is standing in for the multitudes whose initial reaction to Zootherapy is similarly sceptical, cynical or downright enraged. Whatever else happens, I think, this show's going to make good television. His first, very public, Zootherapy experience could open the minds and hearts of millions.

The applause dies down. It falls to Pippa to continue the show and she opts for another commercial break. She gives a wind-up signal, and the monitor shows the digits counting down from 210 seconds.

Pippa makes small talk with Ventura, asking about his visit sightseeing in New Zealand. His time on the show is over, and he reclines comfortably to watch the rest of the proceedings. Pippa times it perfectly, and the chit-chat ends just as it's time for her to open the third and last part of the show.

'James Sinclaire, founder of Zootherapy, considered by many to be – OK, if not the Messiah, then the man who brought peace to the world. Your methods have helped thousands of people in New Zealand and around the world to live better lives. There are rumours that you're in line for the Nobel Peace Prize. You're approaching your sixtieth birthday. So... Mr Sinclaire, Mr Zootherapy; what next?'

'I don't think in terms of the future, Pippa', I say. 'It's one of the things that Zootherapy does: you just live in the active present.'

'Aren't you thinking of taking it a bit easier now? Whatever you think about it, people do see you as something of a messianic figure. Are you taking steps to secure your legacy?'

'That's for people with a past and a future, Pippa. Something that animals don't have; something I don't believe in. I try to stay alert and live in the present. That's what Zootherapy is all about. Staying alert; being on my mettle; as are all the animals.'

'You don't think about the future?'

'I don't let it worry me. I try to be always in the present mo-'

An ear-splitting spluttering explosion from somewhere at the back of the auditorium. I'm hit in the neck by something sharp and stinging. I slump back against the chair, aware of pandemonium all around, though I'm fading fast. Such a pity. Sure, before the show, I'd been yearning for a quick lapse into nothingness; an end to the turmoil and loneliness. But my demonstration of Zootherapy with this American guy had been electrifying: I still have something to offer! I still have a purpose! The Professor, the audience, I myself: we were living Zootherapy. I'm not seeing my life flashing before me. Could that mean I'm not dying? Such a pity if this is to be the end of it all. So tired. Dimly I hear shouting, screams, panic. Someone feels my neck for a pulse. The touch is familiar somehow. I recognise a faint scent. A woman's perfume. Vaguely, just before I drop off, I remember reading that nobody hears the sound of the shot that kills him. Bullets travel faster than sound, you see. But I heard the shot. So I can't be dead. Not yet. But I might be dying... It certainly feels like I am.

At this point Mr James Sinclaire's narrative ends. What follows is excerpted from a report three days later filed by news agencies after viewing a recording of the show.

RIFLE SHOTS

It happens in less than a second: the deafening sound of gunfire in a confined space. At the same time James Sinclaire slumps back on the sofa, a patch of bright red blood expanding through his shirt and jacket over his heart. Sinclaire was killed instantly, though the audience doesn't seem to know this. Pippa Scrimshaw, the host, is stunned. With mouth agape, she scurries round the back of the sofa. Lester Ventura recoils from Sinclaire, then also rushes to the back of the sofa. All this time, there's indistinct shouting from the back of the auditorium. With no further shots, Pippa Scrimshaw peeps over the back of the sofa. Seeing the stricken Sinclaire she shouts for a doctor, but even before she finishes, a female doctor in the audience dashes up to Sinclaire, a small slim handbag hanging off her elbow. After checking for a pulse, the doctor shakes her head, indicating that Sinclaire is dead. She takes her silk scarf off and covers Sinclaire's face with it.

It's clear to those on the stage that Sinclaire has been shot by at least one bullet in the chest.

TV viewers see only indistinct shots of the stage, the auditorium and then the ceiling, as the operator has abandoned his camera. After the clatter of a rifle being dropped to the floor, they hear shouts and scuffling. A couple of men are shouting in the back of the audience, loudly, urgently. They are standing at opposite sides, behind all the seats, right at the back of the auditorium. One's tall and heavyset. The other is pale and stocky. Both are shouting, their voices rough, powerful, strident. After a few seconds of confusion they roar in unison and their words become clear:

'I am not resisting arrest! I am giving myself up! I have dropped my weapon. I am not resisting. I am not resisting arrest! I am surrendering peacefully! I have dropped my weapon!'

There's the sound of more scuffling.

TV viewers now see into the audience. They see dim footage of the two shooters at the back of the auditorium opposite ends of the studio, with hands up, being restrained by security personnel and members of the audience. The camera now points at the stage, where it becomes obvious to viewers that Sinclaire is dead.

The two gunmen, now being restrained and manhandled, are shouting loudly:

'Search the body! Look for the letter! There's a letter there!'

The Doctor pulls out a clear plastic waterproof envelope from Sinclaire's inside jacket pocket. She wipes away the blood on its surface with a tissue and unseals it. There's a piece of paper inside, which she glances at and then hands to Scrimshaw, secreting the envelope into her handbag. Scrimshaw, looking pale, sits down and reads aloud the heading:

TO BE READ IN THE EVENT OF MY DEATH

All the time, we hear the two gunmen shouting: 'Break the seal! Break the seal and open it! Read the letter!'

The camera now is stable and focussed on Scrimshaw. The studio is confused but calmer. The sounds of scuffling cease, but a few members of the audience are restraining the two gunmen. Scrimshaw opens the envelope and silently skim-reads the letter inside. In the background we see studio officials put Sinclaire's body on a stretcher. At the edge of the frame we can just catch sight of Scrimshaw looking up from the letter and with raised palm, salutes the body, appearing to mouth the words 'Thank you', as it's carried off the stage.

Scrimshaw starts reading the letter, the contents of which would soon be known all over the world:

TO BE READ IN THE EVENT OF MY DEATH

This document is being dictated under my own free will before notarised witnesses named in a separate Annex, in Wellington, New Zealand on the fifteenth of August, 2022.

224

The people who killed me are innocent.
They are not murderers. I am paying them
to hunt me and kill me, as painlessly as
possible, like that of an animal in the wild,
at a time of their choosing, unknown to
me. I want to die-

Here Scrimshaw, apparently overcome by emotion, stops reading. She gestures to one of the men in the wings, who comes on stage, takes the letter from Pippa's hands, and continues reading aloud:

I want to die without anticipating death
and before physical deterioration makes
life unbearable. I put a contract out on my
own life. When you read this the contract
will have been fulfilled.

So please do not mourn for me. Alive,
playing the role of animals, I was already
at peace and free.

Free of guilt from the things I have done,
free from fear of the future.

And free also from the unwarranted and
unwanted adulation speculation that I find
overwhelming.

So, I repeat, please do not charge the
people who killed me with any serious
crime. James Sinclaire.

EPILOGUE

Mike Z and Brent P were held in custody in Wellington, New Zealand for a period of eight weeks following the killing of James Sinclaire. Crown charges of murder were contested by New Zealand's top criminal lawyers and were eventually dismissed. Mike and Brent each received a suspended sentence of six months, were each fined

$20 000 for importing a firearm into New Zealand without a licence and a further $10 000 for discharging an offensive weapon in a public place.

James Henry Sinclaire's will was made public several weeks after his death. After bequests to a former Personal Assistant and friends, the bulk of his estate was left to establish a Zootherapy Foundation to subsidise access to Zootherapy courses for disadvantaged people around the world.

Another bequest was made to establish and fund in perpetuity the Tina and Samantha Sinclaire Gorilla House and Primate Research Centre at Wellington Zoo, in Newtown, Wellington, New Zealand.

A SMALL TOWN IN NEW ZEALAND, 2022

> *And the wild regrets and the bloody sweats,*
>
> *None knew so well as I:*
>
> *For he who lives more lives than one*
>
> *More deaths than one must die.*
>
> Oscar Wilde, The Ballad of Reading Gaol

It's a few weeks after the TV show and I am reading a report of my death in one of the New Zealand glossy celebrity monthlies.

I'm in the cellar of a hotel (that is, a pub) in a small town somewhere in New Zealand. It's pleasantly cool and damp and, as well as several barrels and kegs of beer, a pair of dusty soda siphons, and a small generator, there's a camp-bed, a radio, a kettle, and other essential elements of makeshift, underground accommodation. The glossy's front cover promises 'new revelations' about my demise, and quotes from the famous letter found in my jacket:

> *So please do not mourn for me. Alive, playing the role of animals, I was already at peace and free.*
>
> *Free of guilt from the things I have done, free from fear of the future. And free also from the unwarranted and unwanted adulation speculation that I find overwhelming.*
>
> *So, I repeat, please do not charge the people who killed me with any serious crime.*

A bit portentous it sounds to me now, but I did write it myself and not under duress, contrary to various lurid conspiracy theories being aired on the radio and splashed over newspapers and the more popular journals, including the *New Zealand Truth*. From that learned publication I read that there's going to be a memorial service ('A Celebration of James Sinclaire's Life and Legacy') in a couple of months in Wellington Cathedral – God knows who's organising it - but I shan't be going. It's probably invitation-only anyway.

Larry opens the door at the top of the stepladder.

'Kai time, Tane!'

Larry comes down the stepladder bearing a tray with a couple of glass tankards, some sandwiches and a cold bottle of wine. He draws off some beer from one of the barrels and sits down. The lunchtime customers have gone; the doors locked. It's time for our final late afternoon drilling session.

'Now, who are you?'

'Tane Anderson, also known as Rob Anderson'. I'm still having trouble with 'Tane'.

'Tane, Tane, Taa Nee' says Larry drawing out the pure, long, sonorous vowels.

'And where's your whanau?'

'My whanau's in Gisborne and Aberdeenshire'.

'Welcome?'

'Haere mai'.

'Teeth?'

'Niho'.

'Hill?'

'Puke', the Maori word, pronounced as two syllables.

'Puke?' Larry says the English word.

'Huh?'

'Vomit. Chunder.'

'No idea'.

'It's ruaki, but you can get away without knowing that.'

Another half hour of this, at the end of which Larry opens the bottle of sparkling wine and pours it into the glasses.

It's my last day here.

'Whakahari', we say, touching our glasses.

I say the Maori goodbye: 'E noho rā'.

'E haere rā' replies Larry, 'Kia waimarie! Good luck!'

And so, a few weeks after my funeral, I emerge from the hotel, with a newly bald head and half-grown beard, blinking in the hard-edged New Zealand sun, to begin again; this time as Tane Anderson, a Kiwi of mixed Maori and Scottish descent, with a duly vague provenance: the 'east coasts' of both the United Kingdom and the North Island. Zootherapy isn't the only way of being reborn! My backstory has some features close enough to the facts: my wife died in one of New Zealand's innumerable car accidents and my two children (twins; one male, one female) are living in the US and the UK.

Sheep bleating in the distance; it's a warm, humid day, and the soft scented breeze, a contrast to the typical sharp Wellington wind, is noticeable as Larry leads me along the main street for a hundred metres to my new base and new life: one of the two corner shops -

'dairies' in kiwi parlance - in this small township somewhere in New Zealand. I'm to be the sole proprietor. Larry hands me the keys to the front door. The lock's well oiled and the door opens smoothly. A an old-style bell jingles as I enter.

HOW DID I GET HERE? TEAM OMEGA, 2022

It's a few months before my final TV appearance and subsequent... disappearance. I'm alone in the office, preparing for my last session of the day. A new client. There's a knock on the door.

A tall, well-built man, with broad shoulders and a slight suntan, he's wearing an exquisite dark suit. Automatically, I try assessing him. Emotionally secure but open-minded. I reckon he's a 'two-session guy': one who would need only that number of sessions before accepting that Zootherapy is valid and then responding positively to it. I'm often wrong in such assessments but, well, classifying is what humans do. (Proof, I guess, that I am indeed human, if proof were needed. And, given the reverential e-mails and fan letters I receive, along with the death threats, it seems it is.) He hands me a card. A diplomat wanting some discreet Zootherapy, perhaps, to deal with a drinking problem? Or maybe a visiting investment banker wanting to enquire about training sessions for his local employees? The man radiates stealth wealth. I glimpse on his wrist, emerging from immaculate French cuffs, a flash of gold: the slim case and off-white dial of a discreet dress watch. His card reads:

Earle Westfield

Nothing else. I turn it over and there's his name in (presumably) Chinese calligraphy.

I'm in no hurry to return home, so we sit down, and exchange pleasantries. I can't figure Westfield out. He speaks impeccable, Received Pronunciation, English. He hints that he's flown to New Zealand specifically to see me, but doesn't say from where. He implies it was a long journey but, this being New Zealand, that could mean he's come from just about anywhere. Not sure where this is going, I offer coffee, which he accepts, and it's then that my visitor hints at why he's here.

'I hear that you are contemplating retirement'. I wonder how he knows, and I raise my eyebrows. He waves his hand dismissively: 'A friend of one of your friends'. He continues: 'I represent a group of people who can make the whole process easier and more satisfactory.'

We get to discussing the approximate value of my investments. I have a rough idea from a conversation I'd had with my financial advisor a few months ago. Westfield then asks about my flat on The Terrace, the one I rent out. (How does he know about that? I don't ask, mesmerised by his smooth self-assurance.) He's well aware that the combination of my modest lifestyle and accumulated earnings from my private sessions and courses, from licensing, royalties, books, investments and the rental income from the flat have made me quite wealthy. He asks about my goals for retirement.

'I want to get away from all this. The sessions are fine, the courses, helping people; I can do all that, but I'm fed up of the admiration and the scorn – they go hand in hand! – the worshipful e-mails and the animal rights people wanting to me to do this or endorse that; the loss of my privacy. I can't go anywhere now. I have to watch everything I say. And the death threats, the publicity, the cameras. I've had enough. And the weird phone calls....'

'Understandable. That's what you don't want. And we can arrange that for you. But what *do* you want?'

'Privacy, peace, quiet; I want to be anonymous again. I want my life back. To walk around without having to tell the police. Without photographers. To be close to nature without bodyguards and drones overhead. Without having to plan it all in advance. That's all.' No, not quite: 'Oh, of course I want good health. Decent internet access. All the usual other things.' I'm having a protean opinion about Westfield. First a client, then a lawyer, then an auditor for the Inland Revenue (how else could he know so much about me?) or maybe a would-be manager of my investments. But now he throws me a curveball:

'Have you ever heard of the United States' Witness Protection Program?'

'Only what I've seen in the movies.'

'Close enough. They've got the basics right: in return for testifying against criminal masterminds, the US government gives you a new identity and sets you up in a new life, somewhere far away from everyone you ever knew. Including your family.'

I sigh, 'I wish....'

'You absolutely cannot contact anyone from your old life.' He pauses for just a second, gauging my reaction, which is neutral. Then:

'The people I represent can do this for you.'

He doesn't want to say any more this evening, citing his tiredness and being in an 'insecure environment'. We arrange to meet tomorrow.

Saturday. And, as usual, I have nothing planned for the afternoon and evening. I meet Westfield at 3pm in his suite in Wellington's InterContinental Hotel. Despite the fancy coffee machine in his lounge he orders coffee, sandwiches, and some petit fours from room service. It comes on a small trolley. When the door closes on the guy who delivered it, he waves a gadget about the size and shape of a pack of cards over the trolley. A couple of soft beeps and a green light: all's fine, it seems. (Is this guy for real?) It's safe to discuss my future.

Westfield's 'people I represent' appear to be a mix of permanent employees of, and trusted contractors for, a body that he can't or won't name. I'll call it Team Omega. Or maybe it's not really a body of any sort. Whatever, my connection with them began a few months ago, when I was surfing the Dark Web. If I remember rightly I put the words 'how to fake my own death', into the TOR search engine. I landed on a bare webpage which gave a phone number - and only a phone number. A couple of days later I'd had a brief, elliptical, phone conversation with a clear but faraway-sounding man with an American accent, who told me to buy a 'burner' cellphone, and gave me another phone number to ring once I'd done so. Which I did and, a month or so after that, when I'd almost forgotten about it, Westfield materialised in my office.

In his description, his team is a thorough, talented crew. In return for an eye-watering fraction of my assets, converted into US dollars and wired to several bank accounts ('I'll fill you in on that later'), Westfield promises a bespoke package comprising: simulated death, a new identity, a 'modest but secure place and role in a private, supportive environment'. He knows that, with Tina's parents gone, I don't have family any more. I have friends of course, but nobody who needs me, and nobody I really need. I'm maybe number ten on everybody's list of people to spend time with – and I mean everybody: in those fanciful surveys asking popular personalities – at least in the English-speaking world - whom they want to have dinner with, I'm right up there, below Jesus Christ and Winston Churchill, sure, but above Marilyn Monroe and John Lennon. People in Wellington seldom have dinner parties that big, and besides, Westfield assures me, once I have a new identity: 'You won't be in solitary; you'll make new friends.'

It sounds like a fantasy and many times in our conversations I want to ask 'Are you serious?' but mindful of how that question, when addressed to me, used to make me feel, I bite my tongue.

So this is how it happened

My death was staged. The shooters hadn't of course hunted me down over the years, as I'd implied in my farewell letter. And their rifles had been rigged to fire blank cartridges and tiny darts – flechettes, they're called in the trade - with transparent flights. The rifles made a lot of noise, temporarily deafening a few members of the audience. At least one of the darts hit and burst a heavy plastic blood-filled pouch that had been taped to my body. The shots, the blood: it was all very convincing, as was my slumping into the back of the sofa – much rehearsed with Westfield in his hotel suite.

'But can they keep it secret?' I'd asked Westfield at some point that Saturday afternoon or in one of our subsequent meetings over the next few evenings, 'I mean how many people are going to know the truth?'

'Most of us know only a small part of the truth. I'm not going to name names, but we've been doing this for years. Not one exposure yet. With a bit of help from us, you'll write a suicide note, and we'll create a diary of suggestive postings to be discovered on your computer at home. We'll sort out the details later; extreme depression maybe, or you suspect you have a terminal illness.'

'Not extreme depression, please. That would put people off Zootherapy.'

'Right. Not depression. Some mysterious untreatable illness?' I nod. 'We'll come up with something.' He takes a slim, silver fountain pen from his inside pocket and notes this down on the notepad provided by the hotel.

'People are still going to suspect something. There's going to be lots of people who know what really happened: the shooters, the doctors, for a start. Maybe the guys in the crematorium. Even the lawyers are going to suspect something fishy. Maybe someone will sell their story: I'm a public figure, as you know.' While I'm talking Westfield smiles gently. Nothing seems to faze him. I continue:

'Think about it. A conspiracy involving, let's say, a dozen people, minimum, who know something. Thousands, maybe millions who suspect something. You can't bump them all off.'

'No need. Think about it.'

'Pay them all to keep quiet? But there's no guarantee of that, is there?'

'We do look after our people, but we're more subtle than that.' I must have looked blank. 'It's quite simple really: even if someone does talk, or a bit of the truth somehow does leak out, we make sure it gets lost amongst the chaff.'

'Chaff?'

'False stories. Sightings of you: plausible, semi-plausible, right through to utterly outlandish. Doesn't matter. We have algorithms, heuristics *and* humans, generating false rumours, gossip, sightings, and planting them over all the media. Randomly, deliberately. Whenever necessary, or on pre-set occasions. You'll be seen drinking cocktails in Cuba or Rio, or leaving a suit at a dry cleaners in Fresno, or getting into a taxi in Lagos, living in a Mennonite community in Paraguay. Getting killed while training to be a stuntman in Equatorial Guinea. People get fed up with all this. Nobody takes them seriously after a while. If the real story ever comes out – and it won't – it would get lost amongst all the chaff. I mean, how interested are you in stories about Elvis being seen alive? Or Lord Lucan, or the Princess of Wales, Buddy Holly....'

'Clients of yours?' I chuckle and, for one tiny fraction of a second, I see Westfield look down with a hint of a smile.

'We've had all sorts of clients like yourself. All they have in common is that they need to leave everything, and everybody behind. That includes every single member of their family.'

'That won't be a problem', I murmur. (Who *are* their other customers? High-level crooks, embezzlers, corrupt politicians, third-world dictators...perhaps? I guess I'll never know.)

'We suspected that. In that respect, you're lucky. Some of our clients have to sacrifice contact with everybody – family, parents, even children – for their own benefit and to protect their loved ones. You understand? It's not to be taken lightly. Anyway, we've done our research. And we supply insurance, or should I say, reassurance. The slightest sign of trouble, you call a number we'll give you. Twenty-four seven. We pick up within a few seconds. We assess the risk, take you somewhere else if necessary, check it all out. If there's any truth to it, we start again. Somewhere entirely different; you get a different identity.'

'At an extra cost?'

Westfield gives me a look that makes me feel petty for posing the question.

'Look, I can tell you now, we do get calls like that, usually in the first few months, but not once have we had to relocate any of our clients. Not a single time. I assure you: we take care of everything.'

Including, it seems, security at the studio (how did they get their rifles in there?) and the Wellington police; there was an investigation into the shootings, and you will no doubt have been aware of the huge amount of fuss in the media but, after pleading guilty to relatively minor charges, and a few weeks in custody the two members of the hit team were quietly released. Some people reportedly saw them at Auckland Airport, boarding flights to Australia, but for all I know such rumours were planted by Team Omega's disinformation machine.

'What about my body?' I'd asked Westfield.

'Don't worry about that. We'll find a dead sheep or two.' He looked at me 'Seventy-two, seventy-four kilos?'

'Something like that.'

'Don't worry about it. We've got people in the funeral homes. We'll cremate. It's always best.'

Westfield stayed another three or four days in Wellington, during which time, as he anticipated, further questions occured to me. We spend most of Sunday together, and Monday and Tuesday evenings, in his suite.

'What about fingerprints?'

'We'll replace the water glass on the TV show with one with someone else's prints. We'll wipe down the prints in your office and hotel suite. We'll confuse everyone by planting multiple sources of DNA.'

'My assets? The flat?'

'You have the hard copy of your will?' He'd asked me the previous evening to bring it along. I nod. He leafs through it, and points to the simple list of bequests. 'You'll want to change these:' He pointed to several charities, accounting for much of my fortune. 'Put these names in instead. At this point he took a sheet of paper from the desk on which are typed half a dozen names and addresses: an eclectic mix: two men's names, four women's, and two companies; with addresses in the US, Singapore and Shanghai, and a PO Box in

Geneva. 'You'll have to call them,' (he named my lawyers), 'Go there with these details. They'll draw up a new will and you go back to get it signed and witnessed.'

I must have looked apprehensive. Westfield didn't say anything. We both knew that this was progressing beyond the point at which I could back out.

'Who are these guys?', I said, buying time and pointing to the names on the sheet of paper.

'Friends of ours. Remember we have costs; considerable costs.'

At some point we discussed how and where I want to live. Inevitably, there are trade-offs. I said I want to stay in New Zealand and, though I got the impression there were other options he would have preferred, being more distant from Wellington, he assured me that he could accommodate my request. 'You're one of our older clients', he said. He meant, I suppose, that forking out a bit more for my security in a slightly higher-risk environment would be offset by my relatively short life expectancy.

'What about a house?'

'We do that for you, out of the sum you transfer to us in your will. Tell us what you want.'

After some discussion, we both agreed a dairy would be a good idea. I have to have some occupation and human interaction for my own well-being. There were surprisingly few other things to be settled.

OUR LAST SESSION
Our last session, late in the evening.

I detect a familiar sulphurous whiff from Westfield's suit, as I enter his suite.

'You've been to Rotorua?'

'Just a flying visit. A bit of sightseeing while I'm in the country.'

'I've been to the lawyers, changed my will,' I say as I sat in my customary position on the sofa.

Westfield nods as if he already knows. This is the crucial session. I could still abandon the whole exercise. I am both thrilled and scared by the possibilities. It does seem pretty radical. I ask questions partly for information, partly to see if they will offer me a face-saving exit.

'How can I trust you? What if you just take the money and run? Who are you anyway?'

'Mr Sinclaire.' And in a rare gesture of intimacy, he pats me on the knee, 'I understand. It's a huge decision. But you know we can't supply references, and you know why. All I can say is that we've been in this business, in one form or another, for years. People you might have heard of, or read about; people who you think have died are living, a quiet, low-profile, satisfying life, under a new identity, thanks to our services. We can and will set you up in your new life, but we can't guarantee that you'll be happy with it. We give you the opportunity. After that, you'll be more or less on your own.'

'It's a lot of money', I say.

'You don't want a cut price service. Of which, I might warn you, there are usually one or two on offer.' He lowers his voice, 'They don't last long.' A brief pause, then in his normal tone: 'You'll just have to trust us. We've done our research. We don't know your exact state of mind, but we can see how you're living, and we can guess you're not exactly happy with it. Carry on like this and you're going to spend the rest of your life trying to evade publicity. Anyone you make friends with, or anyone who even visits you at home, is going to have their domestic circumstances scrutinised. *Your* private life is already almost gone. More and more of your income will be devoted to keeping the lunatics away. You know all this. What do you have to lose?'

My long pause speaks volumes. Then he clinches it:

'But think positive: think of all the things you'll be able to do.' In theory I'm already in that position. Right now I could fly first class to any city in the world and stay in top-class hotels. I could meet other famous people, intervene in politics, express my opinions about anything and have people take them seriously or, at least, pretend to. But Westfield knows me well: 'Walk in the countryside. Keep a cat, a dog. Go out for a beer. Without security people, stalkers, telephoto lenses following you all the time.' (He might have added 'Be who you are, instead of a vehicle for everyone else's expectations of what you should be.')

It's a balmy evening and I walk over to the window of the suite. People are sitting outside, having dinner, drinking, dressed up on the way to the cinema or theatre. Westfield, ever patient, comes to the window and for a moment we take in the streets below and the harbour in the background.

'What,' I ask 'if I meet someone and fall in love, enter into a relationship? Couldn't I tell her?' He continues to look outside, then turns to face me:

'If she lives locally, then I guess you can.' I don't see why her location would make a difference, but I let that pass. It's an unlikely scenario anyway.

Tina, years ago, had told me how hospital patients sometimes regress into infanthood. Confined to their beds, and with an exaggerated respect for the medical profession, they lapse into passivity. That's how I feel now, with Westfield's soothing talk, his suave reassurances and calm manner.

THE DIE IS CAST

Yes, he was persuasive, no doubt about it. Out of habit, I tried to bargain the price down a bit, but he was adamant. Perversely, this reassured me, just as buying a souvenir or second-hand book from a dealer who won't budge on price tells me he's offering something he values highly. I had little leverage, and I suspect Westfield knew that. I was tired of the life I was leading, and Westfield knew that too.

Of course, if my trust were misplaced and nobody shot me during the TV recording, Team Omega would have siphoned away almost all my assets. That actually wouldn't be so bad. I'd still be able to practise Zootherapy and could quickly rebuild by fortune, if I felt the need, by giving talks, selling my riches-to-rags story, or advertising dog-food. And if the worst really did happen, and they fired real bullets … It wouldn't be a bad way to go: a touch of martyrdom wouldn't do me any harm. Look at it this way: my work's done. Zootherapy's out there for everybody. The gist of it is freely downloadable from the internet. And my life recently hasn't exactly been a box of birds. But, hang on: why would they want to get rid of me? They'd be prosecuted for murder and, with a couple of hundred eye-witnesses and a live recording, even the New Zealand justice system would feel bound to lock them up for some meaningful spell. And so, at the end of that final session with Westfield, when he asks whether I need more time to think about it, I say I don't. We seal the deal with a handshake and, in the doorway to his suite we say goodbye. We are never to meet again. From now on I'll be in the hands of Team Omega and its innumerable unidentifiable 'assets'. I walk home from the InterContinental, both apprehensive and elated.

HOW THEY DID IT

Team Omega were thorough. The day of the recording they subtly altered my appearance. 'Better to do this beforehand, rather than spend the rest of your life doing it afterwards', Westfield had explained. They sent one of their people, posing as my last ever client, to my office to do some strange things to my face. 'Just call me Doris', she said, though to me she looked less like a Doris and more like a Märta or Karla: tall, blonde, long limbed, with a healthy, fair complexion. She mentioned 'facial recognition software', and thereafter we studiously talked only about the minutiae of her visit. With an array of tiny syringes, and vials of fluids and pastes, she filled out my nose and lips, and primped my cheeks. She added some flesh to my earlobes and altered the line of my eyebrows. Then, she explained, were some injections of 'dermal filler' into my gums, which were to remove temporarily the black triangles between my teeth. Finally, she inserted some tinted contact lenses, to lighten the colour of my eyes. 'They're 90 percent water and will dissolve in a couple of days. You don't have to do anything.' It would help, she said, that I'd shunned television for some years before the chat show but, especially with the advent of ubiquitous digital cameras, there were numerous images of me in circulation. 'We'll see to your hair afterwards', she said. Finally, in her presence, I swap my jacket for another, with slightly padded shoulders, lined with pouches of blood ('Not human,' Westfield had assured me). As soon as she'd gone, the fear set in. No going back now.

I left everything behind. Personal things in my hotel room at the James Cook. My clothes and laptop, wiped, except for some brief, suggestive diary entries and search enquiries (supplied by Team Omega), hinting at my impending demise from some rare pancreatic ailment. When I locked up my office for the last time, I left everything including my desktop computer there, its entire hard drive encrypted. (I'd torn up the pages of the notebook with the passwords and flushed the scraps down the toilet.) Carrying nothing, I caught a taxi from the rank on Lambton Quay to take me the twelve miles to the Avalon studios where the Pippa Scrimshaw Show is to be recorded. I sit in the back. Picking up on my mood, the taxi driver is silent. There's only the road noise and the occasional digital squawks and squelches from the taxi's radio set. It's after the evening rush hour, so traffic on State Highway 2 is thin. Cars are turning their headlights on, and my anxiety level is as high as it's ever been. This is how exactly how I felt when I migrated to New Zealand, and I'm asking exactly the same question: what the hell have I let myself in for? I'm suspended between two lives, again. I look beneath me and there's only emptiness. No safety net, no ground. The future's unknown, the past is somewhere to which I can never return. All my pals and memories; I'm leaving it all behind with no possibility of return. We pass close to the T-junction where the truck crashed into Tina's runabout and extinguished my family. I look away, half hoping we'll swerve over the median strip into an oncoming vehicle and end my life too. Or maybe we'll go just a bit further over the rocky margins and into the Stygian blackness of Wellington Harbour. I shiver. For all I know the taciturn taxi driver, whose face I haven't seen, will turn around and I'll be staring into a skull; the Face of Death. All right! Enough melodrama: after all these years, I've learned a bit of objectivity and remind myself that these glimpses of despair, though horrific, are fleeting.

So it proves, and twenty minutes later I'm met at the entrance to the studio and my reminiscences cease the second I'm ushered into a dressing room, where a young make-up artist hands me a hot moist towel. I wipe my face, which she then briskly brushes with powder 'to stop the glare'.

The worry about whether Team Omega will do what I'd paid them to do recedes as the show gets going, but does not quite disappear. Even as I heard the rifle shots, felt the sting of the flechettes and slumped into the sofa, I half-suspected they'd taken the easy way out, and shot to kill. Before the chat show, there had been times when that wouldn't have bothered me. When I'd have welcomed it. But I've been energised by the interview, the on-air enlightenment of the Professor, the electrifying emotional charge in the auditorium. Everything's changed. I want to live!

And Team Omega did the decent thing. Who says the Dark Web is all child porn, drug stores, and scammers? The 'doctor' in the audience who was so handily close to the stage and pronounced me dead? I am pretty certain now that she was Doris, who had prepped me for my death scene in my office. I surmise this from her voice and touch and the faint familiar scent from her scarf that I breathed in while playing dead on the sofa. The driver and 'paramedics' on the ambulance that spirited me away from the studio must also have been on contract to Team Omega. (In retrospect I suspect one of the flechettes contained a tranquiliser, or perhaps Doris surreptitiously injected me. Either way, there'd been a sting in my neck, and I hadn't been faking the faintness I'd felt after the shots were fired.)

My ethical bodysnatchers, mindful I suppose of video cameras, took me quietly in their ambulance to Wellington Hospital. I was barely conscious; I think they took me into the morgue, put me on a gurney. They must have replaced Doris's scarf with a cloth or shroud of some sort. Then they transferred me into the back of a van. I suspect there was a decoy car, or pickup truck or whatever, that preceded me out of the hospital. And so, in due course, and in the middle of that night or early the next morning (my memory's hazy) I arrived in this town and was secreted into the basement of the hotel.

Larry oversaw most of my induction, including my rudimentary Maori lessons and briefing on my new identity. I think he was on contract to Team Omega, as he was there temporarily, filling in for the husband and wife team who managed the place, Janice and JJ who were visiting relatives in Brisbane. In retrospect, I realise he was surprisingly unconcerned about my background or what brought me to his basement. At such close quarters, despite Doris's ministrations, he would surely have recognised me as Mr Z. He certainly didn't give the impression that he thought I was one of the more dodgy guys seeking to change his identity like, maybe, an ex-assassin who'd ratted out on his Mafiosi friends. (And it was a few weeks later, after he'd left the township, that I realised why Larry had looked familiar to me: he had played a cameo role, having been called into the room at my lawyer's office to witness the signing of my new will. He'd been introduced as a 'visiting intern from Fiji'.)

I am to run the local dairy, and live in modest quarters at the back of the shop. It might not sound much, but to me it means the luxury of privacy. The dairy's my sole asset now. It's quite enough. It brings in a small income, and I am close to the hills and trees.

In the dairy, 2030

And after eight years, I'm still at the dairy. It's the middle of the afternoon, a quiet time, before the after-school rush. I'm preparing a pot of tea in my living room. There are country sounds: a distant dog barking, sheep bleating, and the far-off sighing of a tractor negotiating the gentle slopes. The water in the jug's boiled and it's time for me to relax, before the doorbell jingles and the primary school boys and girls come out of school to spend their pocket money on lollies and ice cream. This is about as hectic as it gets these days, except on Saturdays when I'm busy selling tickets for the evening lottery draw. As well as running the dairy, I help a bit with Meals-on-Wheels (though I never did learn to drive on New Zealand's roads) and do the odd bit of unpaid labour for the old folks round here: stacking firewood, walking their dogs if they're not well, and feeding their cats if they're stuck in bed.

Courtesy of Team Omega, Tane Anderson had a thin but plausible internet history: a few social media postings backing up my fictional geographical provenance. My mythical social media relatives, being mostly in the UK, were conveniently distant and diminishing in number anyway. My physical friends, clients and former colleagues in Wellington no doubt regretted my death, but none were close enough to be devastated, and after a brief frisson, they would have got on with their lives. After Tina, I'd become a bit of a social recluse anyway. I'd always fantasised about the best way to die: what air crash investigators call 'controlled flight into terrain' (that is, flying into a mountain) seemed an ideal option. Sipping wine, watching a movie one minute; gone the next. The big pluses: you get international headlines and your folks get to share their grief with others at prayer meetings and counselling groups. My own death was even better: it achieved all that, plus I got to live.

ZOOTHERAPY AFTER THE CHAT SHOW, 2030: HISTORY AS A RELATIONAL DATABASE OR: IT WOULD HAVE HAPPENED ANYWAY

You can't do multivariate analysis on history. Too many variables. Nobody knows what would have happened if Zootherapy hadn't come along. My death granted me instant martyrdom; I'd already been touted as a messiah; dying with such drama on live-to-tape television served to spread that meme amongst all too many. Doesn't bother me here and now, of course, but is there any truth to it? Did I bring peace to the world? Short answer: yes. Slightly longer answer: yes and no.

Much longer answer: the world was in a strange place at the time of my valedictory chat show appearance: there were huge masses of people who could not or would not buy into their country's political system; systems that were taking on a feudal character, with a privileged caste at the very top: corrupt, predatory and exploitative and, below that, a well-paid class of mercenaries: hacks, apologists, flunkies, careerists and lawyers, who worked to protect their oligarch overlords from exposure. And at the bottom, the almost entirely disenfranchised. But they were informed: they could see very clearly what was going on. There was a sullen reluctance to buy into the system, but nobody wanted to blow it up. Partly because of the apathy that caste systems engender, partly because history tells us that revolutions are likely to be hijacked by even worse leaders; and partly because everyone had some stake, however nugatory, in the status quo.

Zootherapy happened to come along at just the right time. It worked on many levels to give us humility and hope.

The dramatic easing of tensions at the highest political level that began with ASEAN continued after my death. One commentator compared the effects of political Zootherapy to compulsory drinking of slightly too much alcohol at high-level meetings: tongues would loosen, inhibitions would disappear. Another said that when politicians put animal costumes on – as they were mandated to – it was as if they were taking all their clothes off: it's a bonding ritual!

When Zootherapy, through public pressure, became compulsory the large-scale violence that were the baleful outcome of bad feeling between international leaders - the same conflicts that the ancient Greeks had thought an inevitable part of human destiny - came to an end. They just fizzled out. The referenda over the years after ASEAN, whether they were the tip of the iceberg of a powerful, pro-human movement, or the iceberg itself, did their job. Large-scale war within and between countries has become unthinkable. Those political leaders who won't publicly and at least symbolically practise Zootherapy have no credibility anymore; still less any chance of being elected or otherwise retaining power. Zootherapy in politics is now as ubiquitous as everywhere else: education, government, big business, smaller enterprises; even in what remains of the military.

Zootherapy also works for our leaders when they practise alone, the same as for everyone else. Rather than try to shape the world to deal with their insecurities, politicians confront them. Then one of three things happens: they see them as the harmless phantoms they are; or they oppose them effectively now, without delay; or they live with them. Much more helpful than what they used to do: infecting others with their fears, echoing and amplifying them, magnifying them in their own minds, putting off addressing them, never being able to focus completely on anything else and then imposing their anxiety, anger and fear on their own or other countries' citizens. Zootherapy works on many levels. How seriously can politicians take themselves when they know that at the end of every cabinet meeting, or meeting with overseas counterparts, they will compulsorily (that's what the referenda decided!) have to step into the costume of a cow, or bunny rabbit, or tortoise? It has a trickle-down effect: There are plenty of people without a trace of empathy or humility: being obliged to practise Zootherapy publicly, or even just to pay lip service to it, effectively deters them from going into politics.

Zootherapy proliferated explosively once I'd died. Some say it's *because* I died. But I prefer to think morphic resonance had something to do with it: as when rats in one country find their way through a maze, and suddenly rats all over the world get the idea. The world's bristling with connectivity now. I don't think it's some hippy-dippy New Age theory, or an erroneous extrapolation of quantum entanglement to the macro level: it's the result of seeing in ourselves a common core that is animal. No doubt there's some cynicism behind the now universal gestures our politicians make toward Zootherapy but, even so, the willingness to perform that gesture indicates some humility. Not a bad trait for those who lead us.

Zootherapy helped end victimhood and blame-narratives and their venomous offspring: identity politics. It emphasises the things we have in common. More subtly, it means politicians don't try to justify their current actions by what they've said in the past. It's bashed the bricks out of ideological walls and so given the people in power free rein to act according to what's actually going on, rather than some dead ideology.

New Zealand was one of the first beneficiaries; not only because that's where Zootherapy began but, perhaps more, because of the country's comparative youth: the tensions hadn't become institutionalised. Conflicts overseas took longer. Max Planck is supposed to have said that science advances one funeral at a time. As with science, so with Zootherapy. Young people have no time for the ethnic, religious and ideological conflicts of their parents. Zootherapy makes us inescapably aware, at a visceral level, of our common ancestry. I'm gratified to see that Zootherapy today continues relatively uncorrupted compared to other therapeutic belief systems. Sure, there have been the unofficial variants of Zootherapy that followed the conventional trajectory of inspired teachings: enthusiastic uptake, then capture and codification by intellectuals and established elites. The corporates move in too; and the chancers, charlatans and shysters attracted to it because their real aim is to lord it in any kind of power structure; commodification and ossification follow. But despite their best efforts Zootherapy itself didn't and won't surrender to organisational Zootherapy. The core practice keeps winning. Zootherapy has a built-in defence that comes not in the form of words warning against corruption - which can be, and usually are - themselves made into an object of worship, but in its practice: seeing the world through the eyes of an animal. It's the only essential feature of Zootherapy, and it means you just do not take strings of words, seriously - however elegant and beguiling they may be.

They tried – my God how they tried! – to market Zootherapy in the same way as everything else. They tried to hold me up as a martyr, the titular head of a power structure which they themselves would build and dominate. But it didn't work this time: our real teachers are the animals, and we don't need insecure, power-mad intermediaries to understand them.

And youngsters. They take to Zootherapy with much less self-consciousness than us oldies. It's a joy to behold. The first cohort of those who practised Zootherapy as children is now in their twenties: it's when I see their combination of non-doctrinal idealism and pragmatism, and their willingness to work together to reform this still-blighted world that I am inspired. I shan't live to see the full impact of it, but I can die happy. I might have gone through less agonising myself, if Zootherapy had been around when I was young. It's an irony (I think): the guy venerated as the founder (I'd say 'discoverer') of Zootherapy is less suffused with its spirit than any child brought up with it, as many are now at home and school. Maybe all my agonising during the dark days, maybe even my obsession with my Zootherapy career; maybe all that could have been avoided if I'd practised Zootherapy at an early age.

And yes, the world is still blighted. There are still millions of people suffering from the warped instincts of other humans. The weak are still beaten and exploited by the strong. Many will die without having a chance to enjoy a moment of happiness. But Zootherapy has replaced despair with hope and, another happy consequence, we treat animals better too.

My early fears, sparked by the unleashing of Karl's violence and Peter's anger, that Zootherapy would give licence for uninhibited aggression were never realised. Some of my fans say it's because Zootherapy makes it clear that violence is unnecessary now as a way of securing food for ourselves and our genes. Entire chorus lines of philosophers debate issues like this. Makes me glad I've found my true vocation: selling lollies and downmarket magazines.

Mr Zootherapy today, 2030

James Sinclaire had to die. So too did Mr Z. You can become a New Zealand celebrity and stay grounded. And being *born* a world celebrity might be enviable in some ways. But *becoming* a world celebrity is quite different; a trial by ordeal, and that's what I began to experience after the ASEAN summit. At first I almost welcomed it: Zootherapy would find a global audience and I'd never have any money worries. But then the negatives started to pile up and it became clear that, while nothing could contaminate Zootherapy's core teachings, my celebrity status was harming me. I couldn't walk in the bush without notifying the police. I had to pay people to screen my emails and phone calls - and even then one of the crazies got too close to Kate. And then there was that familiar story: I became so distracted and stressed by the worldly success of Zootherapy that I almost forgot Zootherapy itself.

But this time I could see it coming. I knew deep down that the hyperinflated, hyperprojected image of me was a distraction that would emphasise my self; my self as a separate individual, with all the problems inherent in having a distinct, human identity; of living in an overlay that obscured and over-rode my animal insight and intuition. Zootherapy was improving the quality of life for millions around the globe. It had brought about world peace, for heaven's sake. And there I was at its pinnacle; a glorified object of awe. I was beginning to take myself seriously. But Zootherapy was already out there; there was nothing left to accomplish. TOR and Team Omega came in to my life at just the right time.

The endlessly replayed TV show with Lester Ventura's dramatic enlightenment and my melodramatic death, filmed in front of a live audience, did Zootherapy no harm. It also did wonders for Pippa Scrimshaw's career: she now hosts her own breakfast show in the UK. I see her appealing face frequently on the front page of the celebrity gossip magazines in my rotating display rack. I'm pleased

251

too that the TV show benefited Lester Ventura almost as much as Pippa. He quickly appended a postlude to his book and he (or his publishers) changed its title to read: *Zootherapy - Fooling All the People All the Time? You decide.* Sales shot up.

The glossies and newspapers that I stock are my main source of information about the wider world. While I occasionally connect to the internet, to protect my new identity and on Team Omega's 'strong recommendation' I do so through the TOR browser, my tracks further obfuscated by one or two other tricks, all of which slow down the connection to a trickle. No loss really, when there's nature all around, beaming its myriad messages to me day and night.

In New Zealand Zootherapy is as strong as ever. The animal costume in the living room is now as ubiquitous as portraits of Michael Joseph Savage used to be. More cheering still, Zootherapy has percolated down into primary schools: it has an obvious appeal to the kiddies. It seems like a long journey; from my putting on a gorilla costume to world peace and Zootherapy classes for schoolchildren. But it's not: in Zootherapy the first step is the last step. Zootherapy is the antithesis of accumulation of knowledge and experience. Stepping into that MAF cafeteria in my gorilla outfit, I was no different from the person writing all this down several decades later, and no different from the kiddies in the local primary acting the goat (or the tuatara, or the kiwi) when they have their first Zootherapy lesson.

The appealingly cinematic arc of my life and death hasn't been ignored. The unimaginatively titled but commercially successful *Life and Death of Mr Z* is the most well-known dramatisation, but there have been others, and documentaries too, invariably featuring the last minutes of my interview with Pippa. (Though nowhere on TV or the internet is there *close-up* footage or still pictures of my being killed and wheeled away. An uncharacteristic outbreak of good taste amongst broadcasters and uploaders? More likely Team Omega somehow got hold of possibly incriminating evidence and destroyed it. As I say: they were thorough.) And, according to the *New Zealand Women's Weekly*, there's another Hollywood movie in the making, being timed to come out in a couple of years: the tenth anniversary of my on-screen demise.

It all makes for good entertainment, and the inevitable commercialisation and liberties taken are not wholly negative. One commentator, forgetting that I'd been cremated, sniffed that 'Sinclaire must be turning in his grave at the panoply of products purporting to have something to do with Zootherapy: Zootherapy diets, Zootherapy workouts, Zootherapy virtual reality theme parks, and yes, on many porn sites, a Zootherapy category.' (No explanation required....) But I don't mind: Zootherapy works even for people who take it up for the wrong reasons. Some commentators, not convinced by my fabricated terminal illness, thought there must be something weird about Zootherapy if its founder takes out a contract on himself and gets himself shot dead at the age of 60, but they were a minority. Most people respected my wish to die with all my faculties, bright, lucid, alert. I'm less sanguine about the memorials established in my name, and I'm not too keen on some of the wackier theories (James Sinclaire was: an emissary of God/from a distant galaxy/a hologram etc). Or the one that says Zootherapy as I taught it conceals some occult gnostic meaning that I'd made available only to some super-elite group of wealthy initiates. But I'm philosophical about all this. When people practise Zootherapy, they see the nonsense for what it is. And, if they don't practise, nonsense about Zootherapy is no more useless than nonsense about anything else.

Running a dairy in rural New Zealand a guy gets plenty of time to ruminate: was I someone who saw a gap in the market and filled it?

253

Would something like Zootherapy have come along even if I'd not been around? If I'd been more sociable as a child and teen, would I have settled down, done something more conventional with my life? Was it really my celebrity status, or just growing old, that disillusioned me in my previous incarnation?

I'd often questioned whether Zootherapy depended on me for its viability. I always suspected that the beliefs underlying religion, or homeopathy, crystals, tarot or alien abduction hypnotherapy (yes, that was a thing back then) might not be valid, but they work even so, as framing devices for the intuition of the practitioner. The appurtenances – ritual, music, crystals, the hypnotic swirls – are there to relax the client and deepen practitioner-client empathy. The goal is understanding, not truth. You have to have some unreason about you. You have to bypass the reasoning faculties. There've always been the odd ones doing it, mystics, hermits, shamans and jesters. But Zootherapy is for everybody. It strips us of our narratives, cultural and personal. And it makes me glad now, in retrospect, that people kept asking me, right to the end, whether I were serious about Zootherapy. If too many people hadn't thought that Zootherapy was taking the Mickey, then it would have been something they could approach through reasoning. It would have been something else: pantomiming, play-acting or mere role-play. Which is what Mr Z himself thought he was doing at the beginning.

THE TANKER DRIVER, 2030

I rarely leave our little township. There's no occasion to and I feel safe here. The characters here might have their suspicions about me – my voice at least would be fairly well known – but they don't say anything. I never got the sidelong glances that had been an everyday occurrence since the Kiwi Icon award. Sometimes I suspect there's a tacit agreement round here not to talk or ask about our pasts. Sounds unlikely, right? But think about all the important things people in smaller places just don't talk about: our pornography consumption, our intimate bodily functions, our ecstatic experiences, not only with other people, but with music, religion, nature. A few days ago, one of the regular milk tanker drivers had a funny turn in my shop. He'd finished collecting the morning milk and called in for some cigarettes. Suddenly he turned pale and short of breath. He insisted he just needed to sit down. I took him into my living room at the back, and put the kettle on. It took him a few minutes to recover. He gratefully accepted a mug of tea and we chatted a bit then, seeing my gorilla costume hung up on the back of the door, he asked about Zootherapy; quite innocently, I think. He gestured toward the costume.

'I've got a tuatara. I Zed-up,' (current argot for wearing a Zootherapy costume) 'at least once a week.'

'Sometimes it works, sometimes it doesn't.' I say, with minimum profundity but maximum evasion.

'There's a Zed group at the plant.' He means the milk processing factory that employs him. 'We have Zed sessions at our team meetings; I do it at home with the missus at the weekend too. And when the grandkids come round, Sundays. Not sure I believe in it all, but it's fun for the kids.'

This is what I like best about Zootherapy. You don't have to take it seriously. Its outward form brings people together even if it's something that they think is a bit hokey. They do it 'for the kids', or because others are doing it, because it's expected of them, or (as the decades pass) because their parents or grandparents did it. Belief in Zootherapy is like belief in Santa Claus used to be, except that Zootherapy comes unmoored to a particular culture or belief system. It's not only an unserious outward show in which everyone can participate, but it can work at that level and that's fine.

My guest pauses to sip his tea. 'A rum do, that. Getting himself shot on television.'

Eight years after the fact, and it's still a conversation topic. But is he fishing? Early on in my retailing career I would have contacted Team Omega after a comment like that. They'd have promised to look into it and calmed me down. Now I'm less bothered. I'm older now, so the stakes are lower, for one thing. But also I meant what I said in my final TV interview: I do like to live like an animal, constantly on guard. And I am still on my guard here. As Westfield said to me, all those years ago, shaking hands for the last time at the door to his suite at the InterContinental, 'Don't worry about it. Stay vigilant and you'll never have anything to be anxious about.' A statement worthy of a Master Zootherapist.

From an article in the *New Zealand Listener* I see that they are thinking of making my birthday an annual public holiday. I can't support that with any enthusiasm; if they must commemorate something then it should be Zootherapy itself. They could choose the anniversary of that first Gorillagram. It was a summer's day, I recall, and I am sure a diligent researcher, armed with my address at that time, could unearth it from some ancient database or other - the taxi company's maybe? The same article, better written and more thoughtful than the ones I would see in the *New Zealand Women's Weekly* or some of the glossy New Zealand monthlies, sums up the 40 years since Zootherapy first appeared in the public arena:

Sinclaire discovered a technique for bringing about that meditative state then known only to mystics, often celibate, often solitary, and always, whether through history or by intention, seen as exotic and unattainable by westerners. Through a simple imaginative act that anybody of any age who has interacted with any animal can do, we learned to circumvent the constraints of the intellect and see life free of anxiety about both an uncertain future and a traumatic past.

There's a brief overview of the growing use of Zootherapy along with support animals in the treatment of trauma patients, the anxiety-prone and, most heart-warming of all, to the young in the teeming cities of the world's poorer countries. This was a movement that began in New Zealand, as the *Listener* takes great satisfaction in reminding us.

In stripping the mystic state of a specialised language and religious dogma, Sinclaire made it available to all humanity. Though he always denied the slightest notion of divinity in himself this, and in particular Zootherapy's unifying influence on previously squabbling tribes and nations, was and is seen as a messianic achievement. Truly a New Zealand hero.

Any more of this, and my head would swell to such a diameter that I'd not be able to negotiate the narrow passage between the shop and my living room.

GOODBYE, 2030

Somehow I don't think I'm the only one. The people in this small town are interesting. Some have accents that I find difficult to place, and all are quite incurious as to my origins. It's almost as if there were an unspoken pact not to discuss the past.

I wonder sometimes just how influential is Team Omega, or its competitors in the creative disappearance industry. In the cemetery there's the grave of a chap who died a few years ago, aged 87. The headstone is marked: *Neil Kenneth Thomson, 1937-2014, The 'Best' Elvis Impersonator.* Pedant that I am, I wonder whether the quotes around 'Best' are an ungrammatical (but common in these parts) attempt at emphasis - I doubt stonemasons employ copy-editors. Irony in this context? Possibly. But more likely, so I believe, the quote marks were supposed to go round *Impersonator.* Then there's Cathy, the strikingly tall and slender lady, around seventy, with large almond eyes, a wistful expression a refined English accent, who organises the Meals-on-Wheels service in this area. Her hair's greying now, but you can see that it would have been blonde in her past. She and Sandy (her housemate or partner, whatever; she's a down-to-earth kiwi ex-herdswoman on a dairy farm) make a winning, high-energy couple. After Meals-on-Wheels we often have tea together at their place or mine. We've chatted about Zootherapy but only when it's been an item in the news. She does have an aristocratic bearing and I pick up hints of a painful past. I have an idea about who she might have been in a life before she came here. And then there's the swarthy-looking chap who runs a guest house up in the hills and coaches at the local lads in soccer. Wasn't there a time when unlucky footballers from certain countries used to get death threats? My imagination, probably, and anyway it does no good to speculate. There had been a time when I tried to link everyone in our little township to somebody that might have had reasons to use Team Omega's services. But then I realised that I didn't really need to know, and I certainly don't want people doing that with me. Sensing a tacit agreement never to voice such thoughts, I've complied willingly.

AFTERNOON TEA WITH CATHY

Early afternoon, on a hot February day, and Cathy and I have just finished our Meals-on-Wheels duty, and we're having tea in my lounge. All this talk of being the Messiah; I didn't really take it seriously, except insofar as it gave me an out: I'm single because I'm special! These tropes, that I'd somehow absorbed, that permeate society still, about how you can't be creative unless you have some mood disorder and how you can't save the world unless you forswear having a monogamous relationship with a human being. What comes first? Either way I had a reason or an excuse not to look for a partner, not to risk rejection. But it's been many years since Tina. And - don't believe all that publicity - I didn't exactly save the world, whatever the media say. Not 100 percent anyway. In between sips of tea, Cathy catches sight of the gorilla costume hung on my door, she points to its well-defined plastic stomach muscles:

'That's some six-pack!'

'Actually it's an eight-pack', I say, pedantic as ever.

'Is that what you've got?', she says, pointing to my (fairly) slim torso. She's mentioned my figure before, in an envious tone though in truth, and especially given her height, she's probably underweight.

'I wish,' I say, 'More like a one-pack.' I quickly lift up the front of my shirt, so she can see, and let it drop again.

She laughs. And it's only a few hours later, in those moments before I go to sleep, that I realise what I should have done, and what I now think and hope she wanted me to do: I should have stood up, and walked just that couple of strides over to her, and then let her look, and ...just possibly, if she were at all inclined, feel. Where might that have led?

Well, there'll be another opportunity, I'm sure. And I'm learning: it took Zootherapy and two or three decades before I could look back on similar incidents, even before Tina, and realise that, yes, there had been times when a lady showed interest in me. I'd just never believed it possible. Now, progress: less than half a day.

I think back to a few weeks ago. Same setting: tea in my back room after Meals-on-Wheels and we'd fallen into talking about our pasts. I'd mentioned my fictitious upbringing in Aberdeenshire and then, to deflect the conversation, asked Cathy about her life back in England. As I got up to boil some more water for the teapot, I really wanted to ask what made her come to New Zealand, but I said instead:

'It's easy enough to live and operate here, isn't it coming from Britain. I mean, same language, similar culture, despite being so far away.'

I'm in the kitchen now. Hearing no response, I glance back at Cathy and see, to my surprise, that she's quietly weeping. I take my time, making up a plate with biscuits, so that she's composed when I return to my lounge. I say nothing; but she gives me the briefest expression of gratitude as I witter on about the weather, set the tray with the teapot and biscuits down, and then gently squeeze her shoulder before sitting.

My dogs are normally fed around this time, and I can hear them whimpering outside and scratching at the back door. But I want Cathy to leave in her own time.

'They're missing you?'

'They've probably just seen a rabbit or something', I say. 'You've got dogs haven't you?'

'No; when I lived in England, yes, lots. And a horse.'

And then, quite without thinking about it, I slip into Zootherapist mode.

'What I find is the dogs clear my head. If I get resentful or anxious about something, I just imagine what it's like to be a dog. When I had problems – which you don't want to hear about – I did a bit of Zootherapy. It's quite simple really.'

'I don't know....'

'Look, say you've got some problem: family, relationship, bad health, whatever.' She nods. 'And say, ok, imagine you're back in England, with your horse, right? And he?...' she nods again 'is looking right at you. Now listen carefully. What's his name?'

'Brandy.'

'OK, I want you to see yourself through Brandy's eyes. You're in the stable, looking at each other. Now you're Brandy, seeing yourself, your hands as you stroke down his head. The stable...what's it like.'

'Warm, smells of straw and you know...'

'Right. And you and Brandy, you're feeling the warmth...And what else? What's Brandy feeling?'

'I've just thrown a blanket over him; he's tired, in a happy way, and he loves me stroking him.'

'Imagine how he feels; with you stroking him, nice and comfortable in his stable. He's looking into your eyes, and you're looking into his. You feel his warmth and comfort. You see yourself through Brandy's eyes..' Long pause. 'Are you there, are you imagining how Brandy felt? Now you see your past through Brandy's eyes. He's not interested. All he knows and sees is the warmth of the stable, and your stroking his long face, the feel of your hand as it soothes him. Nothing else. The two of you, as one unit. You experience everything he experiences; all your senses feeling everything he's feeling. Alive in the moment. That's all.'

I say no more. The combination of my words, my tone of voice, and her imagination is enough. We can't eliminate her troubled past; not this afternoon anyway. But I've shown her that it can shrink to nothing, even if just for a moment. The insight might not remain, but the memory of that insight can remind us that there is a chink of light in the pervasive gloom. This is the core of the Zootherapy teaching. It doesn't stay with you all the time. But it doesn't need to.

Cathy's phone beeps. Sandy wanting to know if she's on her way home.

We haven't mentioned Zootherapy since, but I do sense a closeness with her. It's never too late....

But at the moment my household still comprises me, and my dog and three-and-a-half cats (one of them's feral, and never comes in the house). Most of the time, they tolerate each other. When they do have a spat, it's quickly forgotten.

THE FINAL LESSON

Will this tome never finish? A bit more patience, please. We're nearly at the end.

There's Zootherapy in the short term, where we instantly see the world differently. Then, with repeated practice, comes a seeping in of merging with our environment. Our faults and awful behaviours are the pathology of atomisation. In the stage play that is our society, outliers – psychopaths, sociopaths and saints – and everyone in between, all play essential parts, while having our rough edges knocked off. But when we're atomised, the extreme aspects of their natures become destructive and cruel. We strive for separation and then seek ways of merging again. Zootherapy helps lower those barriers put in place by our economic system, which creates prosperity and alienation in equal measure. Zootherapy makes clear to us that we're meant to live in society and on our Earth. Then you look back, you see how people who hurt you lived in their separate little cells, and you can only forgive. You even forgive yourself.

Zootherapy is not about leading you down a certain path. It's about removing the obstacles to your finding your own path. You can't know, before putting on an animal costume, the direction you will take. You've read about the life it has given me; and even now, in what will probably be my final year, I put on the tuatara head and shoulders almost every evening, and I let Zootherapy do its work. I did something good didn't I? Sure, there's still nastiness in the world. Still there are cruelties and sadness. But I like to think Zootherapy moved the sum total of human and animal suffering down a notch or two. Not a lot, and not as much as I'm given credit for, but enough to give humanity hope when it needed it most, changing our direction, reversing our headlong dash over the cliff of hyper-individualism.

Actually Zootherapy wasn't especially original: for centuries sages and mystics wiser than me have suffered agonies seeking and finding enlightenment. All I did was find another way; one that, most of the time, happened to work for me and, because it worked for me, could work for everybody. Just as a poem or metaphor delights us more than detailed description, so imagining our world anew comes more easily to us than the endless accumulation of dead facts about our ever-changing world. So, instead of learning some political or philosophical theory, or chanting, or following a guru, or physical torment, or rational enquiry, Zootherapy begins and ends with imagination. Something we can all do, instantly. We simply imagine ourselves as we actually are: animals with a human overlay that is sometimes, but not always, problematic. We become animals whose human faculties are an optional extra, to be deployed only when needed.

There's too much hagiography about me, as if people need their heroes to be perfect. So let me finally get a few things straight:

- I blundered into Zootherapy. There was no great intellectual insight.

- I did it for selfish reasons: yes, it was a selfish desire to live in a better world, and that would be best achieved by making things better for all humans and animals.

- It's very simple. The courses on offer, the support groups, the websites, the ever-proliferating merchandise, the costumes, might attract you to the concept and keep you engaged, but they're not necessary.

- I left out all the boring bits. Ah yes, the boring bits: the writing of case notes, the legal hurdles you have to jump over to set up a small business, the tax assessments, the travelling to give speeches... OK, you get the picture.

If anything differentiates humans from animals it's not (*pace* Beaumarchais) drinking when not thirsty and making love in all seasons (chimps do that too) but the urge to create routines, systems, algorithms, formulas. Rather than deal with things as they arise, we want the illusory security of a system or ideology that will handle it for us. I'm not so different; there was always a part of me that had the urge to create a system. And so:

- Where Zootherapy succeeded was precisely in its failure to be what I started out wanting it to be.

Even the costume is unnecessary. After that session with Karl, I had thought the costume was the crucial thing, the one essential element. Later, it became dispensable in an emergency, then a prop, a reminder, and an aid to the practice of Zootherapy. And then it became a distraction from Zootherapy; an excuse not to bother with Zootherapy because it wasn't the right time to put a costume on. So it became something incompatible with Zootherapy – an impediment, taking you away from the immediacy of the experience. And now; well, the gorilla costume is just there, hung up behind the door. Sometimes I put it on; sometimes I don't. It just is. It's there if I want it. I can see it simply as another part of the environment. Just as my cats and dogs see it.

I used to go on the internet and see how some of my friends and schoolmates did in life. And, while it's me who gets the posthumous praise and encomia, they are the ones I envy. They have wives, children, grandchildren, homes and families. Real homes, I mean, with warmth, mess, arguments, hugs, silliness. Why did I have to become a world-saviour? I didn't really want it. I guess at some level, I was scared of family life, and it took a Zootherapy-inspired level of confidence and an exceptional person, Tina, to change that. Everybody needs some transcendent organising principle: for a few, mostly happy, years in the middle of my life, my family was mine. Before and after that, I had Zootherapy. And because Zootherapy happened to fill a need, I now get called the Messianic figure *de nos jours*. Me, in my rooms at the back of my shop in an obscure corner of an obscure country; me with my kettle, a random assortment of mismatched crockery and a couple of beat-up armchairs. Well, there are worse fates. Ladies, gentlemen, I didn't choose this one, and I wouldn't choose it now. I say this not so much as an appeal for sympathy - I shall, after all, be really dead when you read this. Nor because I feel resentment over the path that I was destined to take. No, I say it so that you will value Zootherapy more highly. It was dearly bought.

GONE

I have hopes for myself and Cathy but, pending our next post-Meals-on-Wheels tea and, except for my cats and dogs, I still live by myself. It would be sad in a way except, forgive my sentimentality, for that other important word in the Maori language: *Aroha*, with its rich, pure vowel sounds open at the beginning and end; so much more expressive than its English equivalent *love*. Our little community here is a (mostly) happy mix of lifestyle block owners, small-time farmers, labourers, mechanics, with a fair sprinkling of outsiders, like me. I like to think that Zootherapy played a role in fomenting social harmony here, as it has in other parts of the world. Or maybe a society like this doesn't need Zootherapy, but Zootherapy makes it more likely that societies like this can be created and sustained. Whatever, we never talk about these things but there is a strong sense, merging into *Aroha*, that we all have something in common, even if it's simply our lack of need for the attractions of city life and our unstated delight in the land and its plants and animals.

You won't find this little town on the map nor – Team Omega's reach extends far – see it on satellite pictures. I've been deliberately obscure on its topography and not only because my descriptive powers are lacking. Besides, by the time you read this, I'll be gone as also, no doubt, will some of my companions here. And, I suspect too, that Team Omega has other enclaves in New Zealand and elsewhere into which their newer clients can be reborn.

As with space, so with time; In the years to come, my life, before and after Zootherapy, will be just as untraceable and just as mythical. Shrouded in the mists of time, my past life or lives will lose their rough edges and merge with mystery, rather like the ancient lineages of kings and emperors throughout history that trace themselves back to celestial beginnings. I hear in the distance the sound of the school bell. The kiddoes are coming out of school and will be here in a few minutes, clamouring for ice cream and lollies. I finish my coffee, and put this week's copies of *New Zealand Truth* (INSIDE: MISSING TYCOON NOW A WOMAN!) on the rotating stand by the till. Once the kiddies have their sweets I'll close the shop for an hour and walk the dogs. And if you skipped the rest of this book for whatever reason you haven't really missed anything: just do what I do. You don't need an animal costume or an animal head, or even a pair of Zed-glasses. Just find an animal; doesn't matter whether it's yours or somebody else's, or nobody's; whether it's dog, cat, cow, bird or fish. Look into its eyes and see yourself as it sees you. Now go ahead, and see the entire world through its eyes. There.

Printed in Great Britain
by Amazon

29097798R00152